HOT
AND
COLD

TREVOR DOUGLAS

vinci
BOOKS

Chapter One

Bridgette Cash shifted her '66 Mustang Fastback down into second gear and eased the car to a halt in the Vancouver police department parking lot. Her grip tightened on the steering wheel as she gazed up through the misting rain at the four-story glass and brick building in front of her. It had been almost four weeks since she had last stepped inside police headquarters. She glanced down at the angry red line than ran across the back of her hand and thumb and sighed. The knife wound was another permanent reminder of how dangerous her work could be.

After fifteen months in the job she couldn't imagine doing anything else. But she found it almost impossible to switch off, even during her latest recuperation leave.

She gazed up at the building again and frowned as she thought about the meeting she was due to have with her boss in a few minutes. Chief Inspector Felix Delray was a veteran cop and he wouldn't simply take the word of a police psychologist that she was ready to return to work. Bridgette knew he would grill her about her mental state before he made his decision. She nodded once as a concession that she would do the same thing in his position.

She thought over the questions he was likely to ask her. He would probe using all his skills as a police detective to satisfy himself that she was ready to return to the rigors of work and murder investigations. She had seen him interview dozens of suspects. Delray had a conversational tone that was subtle. He would engage her in casual conversation and then slip in a probing question. She wouldn't lie—that wasn't her style—but she would need to choose her words carefully. Although she had stopped taking medication, she still had trouble sleeping and would regularly wakes up in sweats. Bridgette gently tugged at what remained of her left earlobe, a habit she had developed during periods of intense concentration. Unlike her right ear, the bottom of her left lobe was uncharacteristically flat—the legacy of a bullet that had almost ended her life during a shootout in her first murder case. The shootout haunted her for months but she rarely thought about it now.

Bridgette checked her watch—it was closing in on nine AM. Just time for her to make it up to the second floor for her meeting. She sighed as she switched off the engine. Delray only had her best interests at heart, but her worst fear was that she would be assigned desk work until he was satisfied she was ready to return to her role as an investigator. She found desk work soul-destroying. Despite her IQ of one hundred and fifty one, she had never pictured herself as an analyst sitting behind a desk.

After getting out of her car, she buttoned her coat to keep out the rain and then walked across the parking lot. She decided she would head directly to Delray's office rather than her desk in the common area where all the detectives sat. They were all aware of her most recent ordeal and another brush with death. Her peers were all well-meaning, but she wasn't ready to answer questions about her recovery or what she would be doing next. She disliked being the center of attention and figured it would be easier to steer the conversation away from anything personal and onto what she was doing next after she had met with her boss.

The ride up in the elevator gave her a final moment to rehearse her answers before the meeting. She murmured, "Let's get this over with," as the elevator door opened. Bridgette walked down the short corridor to Delray's office and paused in the open doorway. She studied her boss for a moment before knocking. Delray was in his early fifties and had the build of an aging wrestler. His short, dark curly hair was now graying at the temples, giving him an almost distinguished look. He was street-smart and had a loud voice that some of the junior detectives found intimidating. Bridgette smiled to herself. His thick dark-rimmed glasses were perched on the end of his nose, almost defying gravity as he read an open file on his desk.

She knocked once. "Hi, Chief."

Delray looked up and smiled. "Well, well, look who's back. Come in and take a load off, Bridgette."

Delray's office was twelve-by-fourteen and barely large enough to accommodate his desk, two filing cabinets, and three visitors' chairs. Almost every square inch of his desk was covered with paper files. To an outsider, it looked chaotic, but Bridgette knew better. Delray was highly organized and had a sharp mind. Like most Vancouver police officers, he had started in uniform before his promotion to detective. He had risen through the ranks and had developed a reputation as an honest, hard-working police officer who got the job done. Never one for police politics, Delray had been promoted to chief inspector of homicide in his early forties and refused any further promotions, citing he wanted to stay with 'real police work.'

Bridgette knew this was code for he couldn't stand the politics, a sentiment she shared and respected.

They made small talk for a few minutes, with Delray bringing her up to date on the team's murder cases. The office fell silent briefly as Delray leaned forward and clasped his hands together. Nodding towards a file on his desk, he said, "I've read the file from the police psychologist. She seems satisfied that you're ready to return to work."

Delray raised an eyebrow and added, "But I want you to tell me how you're feeling. Are you ready to come back to all this chaos?"

"I am, Chief," said Bridgette with a nod. "I'm bored at home and there's only so much time I can spend at the gym."

"I've been in your position once myself," said Delray as he leaned back in his chair. "You've had a pretty rough couple of months…"

Bridgette nodded again, but said nothing in response. *Here it comes*, she thought.

"Solving murder cases generally doesn't mean risking your life…" Delray paused and held Bridgette's gaze. "But of course, we know that the Alex Hellyer case was different."

Bridgette sighed as she relived the shootout on the roof of a Vancouver hospital several months ago, as she and her partner had tried to arrest Hellyer for murder. They had both come under intense fire from Hellyer as he tried to escape. Hellyer was subsequently arrested, but not before Bridgette had shot him in the chest. The man had almost died on the operating table as the surgeons had removed the bullet. Diagnosed as a psychopath, Hellyer then spent weeks in the hospital under armed guard while he recovered. The night before he was due to be transported back to a normal prison, he had escaped. Despite a state-wide manhunt, Hellyer had evaded capture and had come after Bridgette who was holidaying in a cabin on the Fraser River.

"It's not every day you're hunted down by a psychopath," added Delray. "What you went through would haunt most people for the rest of their lives."

The nightmare had culminated with Hellyer breaking into a house where she was hiding. Bridgette glanced down at the knife wound on her hand as she thought about their final battle. She grimaced as she relived the moment Hellyer had fallen down the staircase and broken his neck as he tried to stab her. "I take a lot of solace knowing he can't hurt me or anyone else ever again."

"You must dream about it?"

"I dream about a lot of things, Chief. But I am sleeping and I'm off all medication."

Delray nodded. Bridgette could see he wasn't convinced and added, "What happened with Hellyer is going to stay with me for a long time. I know that, but I'm not letting it define me. My psychologist thinks I'm ready to return to work and I agree with her."

"Well… that's good to hear," said Delray as he picked up the psychologist's report. "Ultimately, the decision on your return to work is up to me. I've got to decide whether you're up to the rigors of normal detective work, or if I assign you something else to do."

"You mean desk work?"

Delray nodded. "Being chained to a desk isn't your style or mine for that matter… I have something else in mind."

Bridgette let out a sigh of relief. "Thanks, Chief."

"Don't thank me just yet," said Delray as he placed her psychologist's report on the top of a pile of files. "You ever hear of the term 'Hot and Cold'?"

"As in the legal tactic?"

Delray nodded.

"I studied a couple of them during my criminology degree," said Bridgette with a nod. "It's a tactic prosecutors sometimes use when a suspect is charged with multiple murders, but you only try one case at a time."

"You got it. The murder trial for the first victim is known as the hot case, while the trials for any subsequent victims are kept on ice, just in case they don't get a conviction the first time around."

Delray picked up a file from his desk and handed it to Bridgette. "This is one of those cases. We failed to get a conviction on the first murder charge, but we now think we've got enough to go ahead with the trial for the second murder victim."

As Bridgette opened the file, Delray asked, "You ever hear about the murder of Fiona and Tessa Halloran?"

Bridgette shook her head. "Not that I recall."

"It happened about thirteen years ago—long before your time here—so I'm not surprised."

As Bridgette scanned the case summary, Delray continued, "Fiona and Tessa were sixteen-year-old twins. They were murdered in a remote wooded area, just back from the Gulf Beach in north Vancouver. One of them died from blunt trauma wounds to the head and the other was strangled."

Delray continued as Bridgette flipped through the pages in the file. "A guy called Remmy Chilton was charged with their murder two days after the incident. He was a loner and a drifter, and we have eyewitnesses who placed him near the murder scene, close to the time of the twins' death. There was a baseball cap found near the murder scene that was matched by DNA to Chilton."

"Sounds like a fairly straightforward case," said Bridgette as she closed the file.

"You would think so," said Delray with a grimace, "But he got off on a technicality."

Bridgette raised her eyebrows. "So what happened?"

"They lost crucial evidence between the arrest and the trial."

"What kind of evidence?"

"The baseball cap. It was sent to the lab for DNA testing—so far, so good. They found a hair in the cap which was a match for Chilton. But when it came time to return the cap along with other DNA evidence from the crime scene, the cap was missing."

"How does that happen?" said Bridgette with a frown.

Delray massaged his temples for a moment. "Back in the day, Vancouver Police were directed to use a government-appointed facility called VGL for all its DNA and forensic testing. VGL stands for Vancouver Government Laboratory in case you're wondering. It doesn't exist anymore because they were incompetent."

"In what way."

Delray shifted in his seat. "Evidence occasionally went missing, and DNA tests were often thrown out of court because they weren't accurate. Long story short, the place had an incompetent director. It took three years and a government inquiry before he could be fired and the place overhauled. In the meantime, a lot of cases, including this one, suffered."

"But why would you proceed with a court case when your prime piece of evidence goes missing?"

"Richard Temple is the reason."

Bridgette nodded knowingly. Dr. Richard Temple was the senior crown prosecutor for British Columbia. She had heard mixed reviews about his capability, but she'd had little to do with him and didn't offer an opinion.

Delray continued, "You can imagine the media coverage the murder of twin girls generated. There was a lot of pressure on Temple to proceed to trial. But that was a mistake. The missing cap made the jury doubt the chain of evidence."

"Even though they had a DNA match on the hair?"

Delray nodded. "Temple got one thing right, at least. Not trying both murder cases concurrently at least gives us a second shot."

"What a mess."

"It was an embarrassment for the police department and the beginning of the end for VGL."

"So why now? Why wait thirteen years to retry the case?"

"Chilton has been missing. Shortly after he was acquitted, he moved to the USA and everyone lost track of him. Vancouver Police weren't ready to charge him for the second murder so he was free to leave. He worked on boats out of Maine and basically lived off the grid."

"So what changed?"

"He got picked at the border three days ago."

Bridgette frowned. "Trying to re-enter Canada?"

"Apparently, Chilton isn't very bright," said Delray with a shrug. "He claims he didn't know there was a warrant out for his arrest. I've set up a preliminary interview for you with Chilton for two o'clock this afternoon. No one from here has spoken to him yet, and he hasn't been officially charged. I just want to know if he's going to change anything in his story before we formally charge him with the second murder. The murder file has all the background. Let me know if you need more time, and we can postpone the Chilton interview."

Thinking the meeting was over, Bridgette went to rise from her chair, but Delray motioned her to sit again. "We need to discuss one more thing about this case."

"Okay."

"There's a second reason why I chose you for this. This could all get very ugly if it's not handled correctly. Temple has already called the Commissioner. He wants Chilton charged immediately and no mistakes like last time."

"But if the cap is still missing?"

Delray grimaced. "We go without the cap. Temple thinks focusing on the hair found at the crime scene and the eyewitness accounts can lead to a conviction."

"And you agree?"

"I've had a quick look at the case. If nothing else has changed, then yeah, I think we can get a conviction. Temple will have to be upfront with the jury about the missing cap, but the hair is the main piece of evidence, anyway. That's what ties him to the crime scene. And we have photos of the cap at the crime scene and Chilton never denied he owned a cap like the one we found."

As she got up to leave, Delray added, "Temple is leaving the prosecution service to enter politics. The media are going to go nuts again over this case and he will manipulate it any way he can to get positive exposure. I don't expect any problems, but with the politics involved, you never know…"

Chapter Two

After meeting with Delray, Bridgette returned to her desk in the common area. As she suspected, she was the focus of their attention, with her colleagues welcoming her back and wanting to know how she was feeling. Bridgette told them she was better, which was mostly true, and looking forward to getting on with her next case. She discussed the Halloran case with several senior detectives, who warned her to be careful. From their experience, Prosecutor Temple played dirty and wasn't afraid to double-cross people, even those who worked on the same side as him.

Bridgette thanked her colleagues for the warning, reassuring them that Delray had said something similar. After switching on her computer and spending a few minutes sorting through a backlog of emails, Bridgette pulled out the case file for the Halloran' murders and read the summary. They had found the twin girls about forty yards from Gulf Beach in the hinterland. Bridgette wasn't overly familiar with the area. She remembered visiting the beach once as a small child when her mother and father were still alive. Her memories were sketchy, but she recalled the hinterland was dense with trees and undergrowth. She decided to scout the entire area the next day to get a better understanding of the murder scene as she recalled the suburb beyond the hinterland was affluent: big houses, large blocks, and well spread out.

After reading the summary, she opted to review the photos of the crime scene before she read any of the reports. She knew from experience that photos told their own story—without bias or assumptions—and she hoped this would help her determine if anything had been missed in the initial investigation.

The photographs were sorted into two folders, one for each sister. She opened the folder for Tessa Halloran. Tessa was found strangled and partly covered with leaves in a thicket. She flipped through the photos, which appeared to be in chronological order. The first images showed Tessa's body in the thicket. There was little to see in the pictures apart from the victim's lower legs. The next series of images showed Tessa after they had removed her body and placed it on a nearby trail. Despite the trauma of death, Tessa's beauty and athleticism were evident to Bridgette.

She flipped through some other notes in the file that revealed Tessa and her sister were both five-feet-ten and played in the state volleyball team. Bridgette pulled a legal pad out of a drawer in her desk and noted their height. Even though she had a photographic memory and would forget nothing she read, the visual stimuli of a note on a page helped her think.

Switching her focus back to the photos, she studied the pictures from the morgue. There were clear strangulation marks around Tessa's neck. The coroner's report detailed the bruising and concluded Tessa's attacker was probably right-handed. She made a note about this and kept flipping through the photos. A photo of the back of Tessa's head intrigued her. It showed bruising and a gash that was about an inch long. Bridgette read the coroner's notes. Dirt and small rock fragments were extracted from the victim's wound and analyzed. Forensics matched rocks in the area to the victim and the coroner concluded the wound was consistent with Tessa hitting her head on a rock in the area shortly before her death.

Bridgette frowned and wrote 'Head wound - Tessa' on her legal pad. Had she been trying to escape her attacker? Had she slipped and hit her head when she had fallen? She would read the investigator's notes later. But it seemed plausible that the killer had overpowered her, strangling her before hiding her body in the undergrowth.

Bridgette checked the time of death before she continued. The coroner had estimated it to be somewhere between three and six p.m. Bridgette leaned back in her chair, her mind abuzz with questions. She wrote several more notes and then turned her attention to the crime scene photographs of Fiona Halloran.

Bridgette studied the face of Fiona. She, too, shared Tessa's beauty, which wasn't surprising. They had found Fiona lying face down on a pathway further up in the woods. Temple had decided to try Fiona's murder case first because of the proximity of the cap and DNA evidence to her body. Bridgette flipped forward in the case file to a hand-drawn map, which showed the location of both bodies in relation to the beach. Fiona was discovered about thirty yards from her sister on a path away that lead from the beach to a nearby suburb. She lay face down in the photos. The coroner's report showed Fiona had a cracked skull from two blunt force blows to the back of the head. Death would have been almost instantaneous. Forensic evidence suggested the murder weapon was a tree branch or similar, though it was never recovered.

Bridgette flicked through the other photos from the crime scene. The wooded area seemed to have lots of undergrowth. She saw potential in a fallen tree branch being used as an improvised weapon. She made a note to check her hypothesis when she visited the murder scene tomorrow.

Bridgette pushed back from her desk again and stroked her left earlobe as she asked herself, *'Why does he strangle one girl and then beat the other to death?'*

Bridgette scratched a few more notes on her pad. The summary report didn't explain why the girls were in the hinterland. They had been holidaying in a house nearby with their family, but the family hadn't realized they were missing. Had they come for a meet-up? Had they been returning from the beach when their killer confronted them? Bridgette checked the coroner's report for Fiona's time of death. It showed the same time range as her sister: between three and six p.m. The coroner couldn't determine the order of the murders or if one person was responsible for both deaths.

Bridgette picked up several closeup photos taken of Fiona's skull in the morgue. The coroner noted the location of the trauma wounds as just behind her left ear and concluded the attacker was likely right-handed if she had been hit from behind while running away. Bridgette made more notes on her pad and then sat back again. She thought it was strange that the coroner was open to the possibility that the same man didn't kill both girls. Had there been more than one killer?

Bridgette doodled on her pad as she considered different

scenarios. There appeared to be no motive for the murders. Were they thrill kills? Just some random opportunity that presented itself? She thought about Remmy Chilton. Had he been following the girls? Was he looking for an opportunity to rape one or both of them? She scanned through the final summary of the investigator's notes. This was the conclusion of the lead detective, Cliff Robertson. She knew little about Robertson other than he had retired six years ago. She made a mental note to ask Delray if she could contact him. It would be worth getting his point of view once she had sifted through all the evidence and interviewed Chilton for herself.

Bridgette then read the coroner's report for each murder victim in detail. Both girls had been wearing T-shirts and white shorts. Their clothing was intact and there were no signs of sexual assault. She checked back over both reports —Chilton's DNA was not found on either body. Bridgette frowned as she wrote the words, 'Was he interrupted?' on her pad. She wondered if someone discovered him and he had fled the crime scene before he could act on his real motive.

Bridgette continued to scan through the photographs and paused when she came to the images of a teal baseball cap. The notes showed the cap had been found just off the trail, eight feet from Fiona's body. She studied each image of the cap in detail. The lab had enhanced two of the photographs to reveal a human hair caught in the inner lining. The baseball cap was an NBA cap for the Charlotte Hornets. She didn't follow the NBA but recognized the cap had the original team logo.

Bridgette swiveled around to her computer and keyed in the words 'VGL laboratory scandal', and pressed enter. The search engine mainly returned news articles covering the crisis period for the organization. Bridgette checked the date stamp for the top articles—most were at least ten years old. She scanned the headlines for each piece. The majority focused on the government's announcement that the Royal Canadian Mounted Police would lead a new facility to replace VGL which was being closed down.

One article caught Bridgette's attention. She opened it up and read the report. It detailed a pattern of behavior within VGL. DNA tests were regularly botched, and forensic evidence had been lost in multiple cases. The article also hinted at the presence of thieves within the organization. VGL lost several weapons, cameras, and phones while they had been in their custody.

Bridgette picked up a photo of the cap again. It looked almost new, and she wondered if it had value as a collector's item, which was why it had gone missing. She started making a few more notes as a voice called from behind her, "Hi, Bridgette."

Her heart skipped a beat as she turned to see her partner, Levi Frost, leaning over the partition that separated their two cubicles. She admonished herself to hold it together as she responded, "Hi, Levi."

Chapter Three

Levi Frost had been Bridgette's partner for just a few months. The grind of his former job in undercover ops and a messy divorce had taken its toll on him. He had needed a fresh start and Delray was happy to give him a role in his team working with Bridgette as a detective.

Frost was almost thirty-five when he joined the team. Despite being six years her senior, Delray made Bridgette the senior partner as she had more experience in Homicide. They had gotten off to a rocky start, but eventually figured out how to work together and had already solved two murder cases.

At six foot three, Frost could lean the elbows of his angular frame on the petition that separated their work areas in the Homicide room. He smiled and said, "I heard you were back. How are you feeling?"

It had been almost a month since Hellyer had come after her while she was on vacation. Cut off from all outside communication because of a weather event, she did not know that Hellyer had escaped. Frost drove three hours to warn her after he realized the escapee might be coming after her. He had found Bridgette collapsed in the woods near the Fraser River after an almost fatal encounter with Hellyer. Frost got her to an abandoned house to get her warm and dry again. They both assumed Hellyer had drowned, only to discover they had made a mistake when he reappeared in a psychotic state. The final confrontation had left them both emotionally and physically exhausted.

Bridgette zoned out as she relived the moment Frost had picked her up and carried her in his arms down the stairs and past the body of Alex Hellyer after their final encounter. Despite the horror of what had just occurred, it was a moment she wouldn't forget. She felt a closeness to him she had never felt with anyone else when he reassured her she was safe. Bridgette had thought about that moment every day since. In the days that followed their return to Vancouver, Frost had visited her every day in the hospital during the early part of her recovery. But once she left the hospital, her psychologist had wanted her to have a full break from work to heal emotionally, even though Frost was a friend.

Frost seemed to understand and had no contact with her since, apart from a few text messages to check in on her recovery.

By the time she was ready to return to work, Bridgette thought she had her feelings about Frost under control. She was confident they could resume work as partners, but now, as she stared up into the face of a man who had saved her life, she wasn't so sure.

She saw his lips moving and realized she had zoned out. She held up a hand. "Sorry, Levi. I zoned out for a moment."

"Are you sure you should be here?" inquired Frost gently.

Bridgette flushed. "I'm fine… I was going stir-crazy at home. So I'm glad to be back."

"I hear you've picked up the Halloran case?"

"Yes. I met with the chief earlier. It seems straightforward, but who knows?"

"I hear Prosecutor Temple is all over it?"

"Apparently," said Bridgette with a frown. "The commissioner is already being pressured by him. It could get political. How about you? What are you working on?"

"I'm helping Watson and Holbrook with the Stenlake case. You hear about that one?"

"The guy they found floating in the river?"

"It looks like an accident," said Frost with a nod. "But we're not certain yet." Frost looked at his watch. "It's nearly lunchtime. You fancy a bite to eat in the canteen?"

Bridgette looked at her desk. "I can't. I've got an interview with the prime murder suspect in the Halloran case in two hours. I've still got a lot of prep to do."

"What about tonight?"

"Tonight?"

Frost ran a hand through his short, dark hair that now had a fine grey fleck. It was a habit Bridgette noticed he did often when he was thinking. "We could get a drink or even a bite to eat?" he said. "It's been weeks since I've seen you and we've got tons to catch up on."

Bridgette wasn't sure what to say. Their previous dinner dates had been more like meetings when they were working late on cases. Frost's invitation was casual, but it felt different as alarm bells went off in her head. She had told her psychologist about her feelings for her partner during a therapy session. Bridgette had been advised not to start any relationship during her recovery, and especially not with someone she worked with.

To her surprise, Bridgette found herself saying, "I should be done around six. Where did you have in mind?"

As Frost went to answer, his phone buzzed. He glanced at the screen and then mumbled, "Sorry, this is forensics, I gotta take this..."

Bridgette sat staring at her desk, wondering what she had just done while Frost talked on his phone. After a brief conversation, Frost disconnected.

"Good news?" asked Bridgette.

"Maybe," said Frost, as he reached for his coat. "Forensics want to show me some tests that they've just run on Stenlake. I need to hustle over there now. Can I call you later?"

Bridgette managed half a smile. "Sure..."

As Frost picked up his car keys, he said, "I'm thinking maybe Black and Blue—that new steakhouse. Do you know it? I haven't eaten a good steak in a while and the guys I'm working with say Black and Blue is pretty good."

Bridgette tried to keep it casual as she responded, "That sounds great."

She let out a sigh as she watched Frost turn and walk to the elevator. Shaking her head, she murmured, "What have you done?"

Bridgette's short meeting with Frost left her flustered and she found it hard to concentrate on her preparation for the interview with Remmy Chilton. Why had she accepted the dinner invitation? She could have easily made an excuse; *'It's my first day back,'* or *'I might have to work late,'* would both have worked. Anything would have been better than saying *'Yes.'* The words of her psychologist had echoed in her mind.

She had debated texting Frost back several times to cancel. But every time she picked up her phone, she got cold feet. She finally admitted she really wanted to see Frost and left it at that. Eventually, she got back into her groove as she prepared for the Chilton interview. The two hours flew as she memorized his original statement and a few key questions.

She arrived at the interview room a few minutes early to setup. Delray had offered to join her, but she declined the offer, saying she thought Chilton would be more likely to open up if she was on her own. After checking the recording equipment was working, she sat down to wait. She had opted for one of the standard size interview rooms. It was a twelve-by-sixteen room with one table and four chairs. It was a room she often favored when she was trying to get a suspect to confess. She found smaller rooms had a more intimate feel and were more conducive to getting a suspect to open up.

She didn't foresee a confession happening today. Her aim was to determine if Chilton planned to alter his testimony significantly from the one he had provided thirteen years ago at the first trial. Bridgette frowned. Richard Temple was expecting the second murder charge to be laid before the end of the week. But she knew it was never that simple. Chilton had thirteen years to revise his testimony to further distance himself from the crime. She knew if his story differed significantly, or he said he couldn't remember, the case could get very messy.

A knock at the door interrupted her thoughts.

Bridgette stood and said, "Come in."

Two uniformed police officers escorted Remmy Chilton into the interview room. He was in handcuffs as she expected, but everything else about the man was a surprise to her. Chilton barely stood five foot three and had a slim build and short, wiry hair. She knew from the file that he was thirty-four, but he looked ten years older. His craggy, tanned skin and bleached hair was a telltale sign of a life spent outdoors. He didn't make eye contact, and shifted his weight between his feet as he stared at the floor.

Bridgette raised an eyebrow as she looked at the police officers. "Where's his lawyer?"

The officer on Chilton's left shrugged. "He said he didn't need one."

Bridgette motioned Chilton to sit.

"Detective, would you like us to stay?" inquired the other officer.

Bridgette said, "No, thanks," as she started the recording equipment. She waited for the officers to leave before sitting across from Chilton. Chilton continued to look down without making eye contact.

Bridgette introduced herself and then added, "You know you have the right to have an attorney present for this?"

Without looking up, he mumbled in a high voice reminiscent of a jockey, "I don't need a lawyer. I ain't done nothing wrong."

Bridgette shrugged and read Chilton his rights. She stared at him for a few seconds, but Chilton still refused to make eye contact.

"Look at me, Remmy. Do you know why you're here?"

Chilton looked up. "They say I'm being charged with murder. But I don't understand. They let me to go free last time."

"You were only tried for the murder of Fiona Halloran last time. This time it will be for the murder of Tessa Halloran."

Chilton's eyes widened for a moment. "I don't understand. I thought the court case was for both?"

Bridgette studied him for a moment. She wasn't sure if he was a talented actor or not very bright. She decided to take a different approach. "You left Canada straight after your acquittal. Why was that?"

Chilton shrugged. "The reporters wouldn't leave me alone. My mom had been very sick and died while I was in prison. When I got out, I went to visit her grave. But they were all there filming me and watching me."

"You mean the media?"

Chilton nodded. "I couldn't stand it. So I decided to get out of Canada."

"You have American citizenship?"

"Yeah. My mom was Canadian, but my dad was American."

"Why did you hide out?"

"I didn't really hide out," said Chilton with a shrug. "I didn't have much money, so I decided to hitchhike across to the east coast. Got as far as Maine before I ran out of money. I fix boats and got a job at a marina."

"You're a marine mechanic?"

"Sort of," said Chilton. "I'm not qualified, but it's all I've done ever since I left school at fifteen."

"Did you know that there was a warrant out for your arrest?"

"Only when I got back to Canada. While I was in Maine, I had no idea. I don't read the papers much and no cops ever came looking for me... at least not that I know."

"So where did you go after Maine?"

"I didn't go anywhere. I stayed in Maine until two months ago."

Bridgette raised an eyebrow again. "You stayed in Maine... for thirteen years?"

"I only meant to stay a couple of weeks to save some cash before I got on the road again. But the owner liked me. I didn't have anywhere to live, so he let me sleep in a back room at the marina. He was happy to give me the room for free if I did night-time security for him as well as my day job."

Chilton explained that he liked the job and living on the marina so much that he stayed.

"So what changed after thirteen years?"

Chilton's face dropped. "The owner sold the business, and I was out of a job. He was real sorry about it and tried to get me a job with the new owner, but they were bringing in their own team. He gave me a nice bonus, and we both left the marina on the same day. Kinda sad really..."

"Where is the former owner now?"

"He's retired but he still lives in Maine. His name is Hector Thorne. I got his number in my phone, but the cops took it. If you can find it, you can call him. He'll definitely vouch for me."

"So why did you decide to return to Canada?"

Chilton shrugged as he stared down at the desk again. "I wanted to come back and visit my mom's grave. I figured now that I was at a loose end, it was the right thing to do."

Bridgette made a couple of notes on her pad and then leaned forward. "So what happened when you got back to the border?"

"They dragged me into a room and put handcuffs on me. They made me wait for six hours. Said I was being held because the computer said I was a criminal and wanted for murder. I said they'd made a mistake but nobody was listening. Next thing I know, I'm being loaded into a police van to be brought here." Chilton held Bridgette's gaze. "And that's the God's honest truth, ma'am. You call my old boss and he'll vouch for me. That's all I can tell you."

Bridgette got up from her chair. "This is going to take a while, Remmy. Do you want a coffee? We've also got Sprite and Coke."

"A Coke? But not the diet stuff, if that's okay?"

Bridgette said, "I'll see what I can do," as she knocked on the door.

One of the uniformed police officers appeared a moment later. Bridgette said, "I'll be back in a few minutes. Can you please come and sit with Mr. Chilton?"

Chapter Four

Bridgette returned a few minutes later with two Cokes. She rarely drank sugary drinks, but today she was prepared to make an exception. She had done enough interviews in her career to know when people were lying. There were always telltale signs; the way they shifted in their chairs, fidgeted, avoided eye contact or had a subtle change of pitch when they answered questions. Chilton showed none of those signs. He was going to be a harder nut to crack. Bridgette thought sharing a Coke with him would put him at ease. People who were relaxed were more likely to drop their guard and make mistakes.

She would be subtle—writing things on her pad that were of no consequence while storing up the holes in his story in her mind. When he had laid out his story, she would use his own words against him. Bridgette didn't expect to get a confession, but hopefully enough to press ahead with a charge of murder. After handing Chilton his Coke and turning on the recording equipment again, Bridgette sat back down opposite. They were quiet for a moment while they drank from their bottles.

Finally, Bridgette said, "I want to go back thirteen years now, Remmy. To the day when Tessa and Fiona were murdered."

Chilton's eyes widened slightly, but that was the only response he made. Bridgette continued, "I've read your statement, but I want you to tell me, in your own words, as much as you can remember about that day."

Chilton was silent for a moment and then let out a long breath. "It was a long time ago. I'm not sure I remember everything…"

"Just tell me as much as you can. It doesn't have to be in order."

Chilton shifted in his seat while he thought. "Well… my mom was sick. I was working in Winnipeg when I got the call. I caught a bus over here to see her. We hadn't talked much in two years…" Tears welled in Chilton's eyes. "She was dying," he murmured. "Breast cancer… I didn't realize how bad it was until I got here. They had her in one of those places where they take care of the dying."

"You mean a hospice?"

"Yeah," said Chilton with a nod. "It was plain she didn't have much time left, and I wanted to spend every day I could with her. But I was low on money and I needed a job…"

Bridgette made a note on her pad. So far, Chilton's story was almost identical to his testimony thirteen years earlier. "Go on, Remmy, you're doing well."

"Someone, I can't remember who, told me the marina was looking for a mechanic. So after visiting my mom, I caught a bus up there to check it out."

"And by the marina, you mean the one at Eagle Harbor Park in West Vancouver?"

Chilton nodded. Bridgette kept a close eye on his body language. "So what happened next?"

"I got there about three in the afternoon. There was a boat shop and a place that sold burgers. I asked to see the boat shop owner about the job, but the man said he was out on an errand and wouldn't be back until around five. I had a couple of hours to kill and I didn't have much money for food or anything, so I just went and sat down at the park to wait."

Bridgette knew which park Chilton had put in his testimony, but asked him to clarify. "Which park was that?"

"The one just next to the marina. I'm not sure what it's called."

"And what did you do while you were there?"

"I don't remember," said Chilton with a shrug. "I was in shock about my mom. I hadn't seen her in so long and I was feeling guilty.

"Do you remember seeing anyone while you were there?"

Chilton shook his head. "I don't remember."

"Okay, so what did you do when you left the beach?"

"I waited till five PM, just like the man told me to, and then I went back. The man from the burger shop was just shutting up and said the boat shop had closed early and the owner wouldn't be back until tomorrow. "

"So, what did you do?"

"I don't remember exactly... but I was starving. I hadn't eaten all day, and I asked the burger man if he could give me something to eat. He had a couple of burgers leftover that he hadn't sold and gave them to me for free. I said thanks and decided to go for a walk."

"While you ate your burgers? Wouldn't you just want to sit to eat them?"

"The man from the burger shop said there were no more buses heading back into the city for at least an hour. He told me I would have to walk down to Marine Drive to get a bus. He said the quickest way to get there was to head down to Gulf Beach Park and then cut across through the woods."

Bridgette made a couple of notes on her scratch pad. It was just up from Gulf Beach where the murdered girls had been located.

"Okay. So then what happened?"

Chilton shrugged. "I walked down to Gulf Beach while I ate my burgers."

Bridgette had studied a map of the area. She knew Gulf Beach was close to a mile from the marina and would take about twenty minutes to reach at normal walking pace, but she asked anyway. "How long did it take you?"

"I… I don't remember. Maybe twenty minutes?"

"So that would mean you arrived there about five-thirty PM?"

"I guess…"

"So then what happened?"

"I was looking for a rubbish bin to put my burger wrappers in when I thought I heard a cry."

"What kind of cry?"

Chilton frowned. "I wasn't sure. At first I thought it might be a gull because we were at the beach. I remember looking out across the water—you know, maybe someone was in trouble swimming or something, but I couldn't see anyone. Then I heard it again. It sounded like someone crying out for help, only it sounded like it was coming from the woods."

"You mean a human calling out for help?"

"Yeah... like a woman's voice, but muffled."

"What was she saying?"

"It sounded like *help*, but I can't be sure."

"So what did you do?"

Chilton coughed and took a sip of his coke. After wiping his mouth, he said, "I sprinted up this track into the woods. But I couldn't see or hear anything, so I called out."

"What did you call out?"

Chilton frowned. "Umm... I don't remember exactly. Probably something like, *where are you?*"

"So then what happened?"

The color drained from Chilton's face as he stared into space. He murmured, "The path split in two. I went up the right side, but I couldn't find her. I came back and then went up the left side... She was just lying there. She wasn't moving or making a sound. I was pretty sure even before I got to her that she was dead."

Chapter Five

Bridgette glanced at her watch as she sat alone in Delray's office. It was now close to six PM and her boss was late for their meeting. After the marathon interview with Remmy Chilton, she was happy for the extra time it gave her to compose her thoughts. She sat with her eyes closed, breathing deeply as she replayed the interview over in her mind. It was not what she expected. She was unsure about the next steps. She would convey what she had learned to Delray—it would be his call. But she figured whatever path was chosen, the case was about to get messy.

Her thoughts were interrupted by the booming sound of her boss's voice as he entered his office. "Sorry I'm late. I got caught up on level four with the commissioner. You'll never guess what he wanted to talk about?"

"Remmy Chilton?"

"You got it," said Delray as he sat down. "Okay, tell me —how did it go?"

Bridgette looked at her boss for a moment, unsure where to start. Delray raised an eyebrow and said, "I've seen that look before. It sounds like it could've gone better?"

"You could say that. I'm not sure where to start."

"Walk me through it from the beginning. And don't leave anything out."

Bridgette let out a long breath. "It took just over three hours. And, to cut a long story short, Remmy Chilton's testimony was pretty much identical to the one he gave thirteen years ago."

"Well, that sounds like a good start…"

"I'm not so sure," said Bridgette with a grimace.

"If his testimony is the same as thirteen years ago, what's the problem? Surely we can just process the murder charge and hand it over to Temple?"

"I don't think it's going to be that easy."

"Why?"

Bridgette started by giving Delray a rundown of the interview. She explained that Chilton's recollection of events in the lead up to the murder was almost a word-for-word match with his original testimony. She got as far as describing how Chilton found Fiona Halloran's body in the woods and then paused.

Delray waited a moment and then asked, "What are you thinking, Bridgette?"

"When he described how he found Fiona, he choked up," said Bridgette with a frown. "His voice wavered, and he was close to tears. Reliving the moment clearly upset him."

"But we know that happens with a lot of murders," said Delray, interrupting. "Remorse is a very natural reaction. Revisiting past events can bring back feelings of regret even if you're the murderer. If you want a second opinion on the video, I'm happy to take a look?"

"I'd appreciate that, Chief. I didn't see any signs he was lying during the interview. There was no change in the pitch of his voice at critical points. He maintained eye contact after we established a rapport and his body language looked normal."

Bridgette explained how she had approached the questions from various angles, but had failed to trip up Chilton with any of his answers.

"Okay. So what about the cap? Did he try to deny it was his?"

"No. He freely admitted it was his cap. He said he didn't realize he'd lost it at the murder scene until the police arrested him."

Delray chewed on his bottom lip for a moment. "Okay. So what about the rest of his story?"

"He realized straight away that Fiona was dead and sprinted back to the marina to call it in from a public phone—"

Delray held up his hand again. "Hang on—in his original statement, he didn't mention the phone call. We caught him out on that because we record all incoming calls and got a voice match."

"When I put that question to him, he said he didn't want to get involved because he knew he would be a suspect. When the original investigating detective made the connection to him, to his credit, he admitted to it straight away. In the original investigation, that appears to be the only lie he told."

Delray leaned back in his chair. "So what's your take on this guy? Is it possible he's extremely intelligent, and this is all a ruse?"

"Anything's possible," admitted Bridgette. "But his story makes sense. Finding a young woman who has just been murdered is going to be stressful. I tend to believe him when he says he wasn't thinking straight. Also, if he was the killer, why would he call it in, anyway? Surely you would want to get as far away as possible and hope the bodies weren't discovered right away?"

Delray drummed his fingers on his desk for a moment. "Okay, let's move on. How does his testimony fit with the timeline?"

"It appears consistent, but I'm going to check it out myself tomorrow. We have an eyewitness from the original trial that says he was at the marina until shortly after five PM."

"That's the guy from the burger place?"

"Correct," said Bridgette with a nod.

"And, if memory serves, it was his evidence that helped us track down Chilton so quickly."

"Yes. Chilton got to talking to him and opened up about his mother being in a hospice."

"I remember now. There aren't too many hospices in Vancouver, and it only took them a few hours the following day to track him down. They arrested him while he was visiting his mother, as I recall."

Bridgette nodded, but said nothing. She thought it insensitive of the detectives to handcuff Chilton in front of his dying mother and then haul him away without giving him a chance to say goodbye.

Delray added, "So let's back up a moment. Walking to Gulf Beach takes approximately twenty minutes, right?"

"Yes."

"Which puts him at the murder scene at about five-thirty?"

"Correct," said Bridgette with a nod.

"What time did he make the call from the marina?"

"Just before six PM."

"So assuming he sprints back, that gives him roughly twenty minutes to commit the murders? We have his DNA at the crime scene, and he admits he was there... so what's the problem?"

"Apart from calling it in, which I think is unlikely if he was the murderer, there are a lot of things about it that bother me."

"Like what?"

"For starters, he's barely five foot three. The two Halloran girls are almost my height—around five-ten. And they played representative level volleyball. How does a guy the size of a jockey get the better of two athletes that are so much taller?"

"You sneak up behind them with the branch of a tree," said Delray with a shrug.

Bridgette frowned. "It just doesn't fit. How does he stalk and murder two girls and then return to the marina in less than thirty minutes?"

"Anything's possible..."

Bridgette got up and walked across to Delray's window. As she stared down at the parking lot, she said, "But it's highly unlikely, and that's what bothers me." She turned to face Delray and added, "The timing fits with discovering a body. But for me, it's too tight to stalk two girls, strangle one and then beat the other to death."

They were silent for a moment before Bridgette returned to her chair.

"Perhaps he had a brain snap?" mused Delray. "Maybe he saw them heading into the woods just as he arrived?"

"Maybe..."

"So, what do you want to do?"

"I'd like to go to the marina and then follow Chilton's

path to the beach, the crime scene and then back again. I'll get a better feel for his story and the timings once I've seen it for myself."

Delray scratched at his chin. "So, what are you telling me? Do you think he's innocent?"

"I want justice for Fiona and Tessa Halloran. But right now, I'm not sure the guy we've arrested had anything to do with their murders."

"That begs the question then…"

"What question?"

"If Chilton didn't do it, then who did?"

Chapter Six

Bridgette was ten minutes late arriving at the steakhouse for her dinner date with Levi Frost. She had texted him earlier to let him know the Chilton interview and her meeting with Delray had run overtime, but she still felt guilty. She hated keeping people waiting.

After pushing through the heavy brass and glass front doors of the Black and Blue restaurant, Bridgette barely noticed the upmarket interior as she scanned the room for any sign of her partner. The main bar was in the middle of the lower level and featured a twelve feet high glass cabinet for displaying the vast array of spirits and liqueurs it sold. The wrap around bar area was packed, which surprised her for a Monday night. She didn't expect Frost to be waiting at the bar and looked up to the mezzanine level where she spotted him sitting at one of the tables. She mouthed the word *'sorry,'* as Frost waved down at her.

A moment later she joined him and reiterated her apology has she sat down at a small table covered with a starched white tablecloth. "Sorry I'm late. Today has been crazy—I just couldn't get away. I hope you haven't been waiting too long."

Frost half-smiled. "I expected your first day back would be busy. How did it go with the Chilton interview?"

Bridgette noticed he had changed out of his work clothes and was now wearing a cream sweater over a pair of navy blue slacks. "It wasn't what I expected."

"How so?"

Bridgette explained how the interview had taken close to three hours and then gave him a summary of her conversation with Delray.

When she had finished, Frost said, "That's one heck of a day. So, what are you going to do tomorrow?"

"I'm heading up to West Vancouver to retrace Chilton's footsteps. I want to confirm that all the timings he gave in his testimony are valid."

"Do you think he's on the level?"

"I'm starting to have serious doubts that he had time to murder those two girls."

"That's gonna make things difficult for the chief," said Frost with a grimace.

Bridgette nodded. "Yes. I know he's getting heat from the commissioner. Anyway, enough about me. How was your day? How did you go with the forensics on the Stenlake case?"

"We've upgraded the case from an accidental drowning to suspicious. They found traces of chlorine in victim's lungs. We're still working with the theory that he drowned in a swimming pool and someone later threw his body in the river. Maybe it was to cover up an accident, but maybe it was murder—we just don't know yet."

Bridgette raised an eyebrow. "Well, that's going to keep you busy."

"Yeah. I figure Delray's going to put a team on it now that it's a potential murder. I was thinking maybe you'd be on the team soon enough if the Chilton thing was straightforward."

"This one is just heating up," said Bridgette with a sigh. "I can't see that happening just yet."

The conversation stalled for several minutes while the server came and took their orders.

When they were alone again, Frost said, "Hopefully, this place was a good choice. I know you don't eat red meat, but the seafood here is pretty good."

Bridgette half-smiled. "Thanks, Levi. I appreciate it. I'm looking forward to my scallops."

Frost took a sip of his beer. "How are you holding up after your first day back?"

"I think I'm going okay. Today really flew. I'm sure I'll sleep well tonight."

"Sleep's important," murmured Frost, as he sipped on his beer again. "My recovery didn't really begin until I started getting a decent night's sleep."

Bridgette was aware of Frost's backstory. He had worked undercover for years but took nine months off after a boy died during a police chase he was part of. She knew that Frost, more than most, understood how long a recovery took.

She cocked her head and said, "And what about you? You've been with homicide, what... six months now? Are you happy you made the change?"

Frost put his beer down. "Yeah, real happy." He shook his head. "It's gone so quick. And it's nice to feel like a cop again."

"You didn't feel like a cop when you worked undercover?" said Bridgette with a frown.

Frost's features darkened as he shook his head. "It was out of control. I wouldn't still be a cop if I hadn't asked for a transfer."

"Sorry, I didn't mean to pry."

Frost held up a hand. "You're not prying. And you of all people don't need to apologize…"

Frost leaned back in his chair. "I know I told you a bit about the last case and why I was so messed up… but I never really told you about the job itself, did I?"

"No."

Frost glanced to his left and right. Only five other couples were dining on the mezzanine level, and none of them were seated close by. "Undercover work is not what most people think."

"I've heard stories, of course. But you don't know how much to believe."

"We had a different creed to the rest of the force…"

"I guess that's part of the job?"

"I was twenty-two when I joined Narcotics. It was my first job out of uniform. They were looking for volunteers… so I signed up."

"You mean to do undercover work?"

Frost nodded. "They never really explained what we would be doing… at least not at first."

Frost took a few minutes to elaborate on his initial three months in the covert squad. He told Bridgette how he had to grow his hair long and got a completely new wardrobe before adding, "During that period, I just observed. Sometimes I tagged along with one of the more senior cops who'd been working undercover for a while. Sometimes I just stayed in the van and listened in on the drug deals as they took place."

Frost's train of thought was interrupted by the server

returning with their meals. The size of Frost's steak left Bridgette impressed. When they were alone again, she joked it could feed most men for a week.

Frost grinned and said, "I'm not most men!"

They were quiet for a few moments as they ate their meals. Frost put his fork down after eating half his steak. "I need a breather while I get a second wind. How are your scallops?"

"Some of the best I've ever had. Black and Blue was a good choice."

Frost nodded and as he looked around. "Monday night's the perfect night to come here. It's quiet enough that we can talk without shouting." His grin faded as he added, "Are you up for hearing my story? It's not pretty, but I feel you should know my… background. We've been through a lot, and you've told me all about your family and what you did before you became a cop. But I haven't been as open…"

Bridgette put down her fork. "I don't want to pry, Levi. Just share what you feel comfortable with."

Frost looked down at his plate. "I did things while I was in Undercover that I'm not proud of. I figure you'll find out eventually, so it's best you hear it from me."

"We've all done things we're not proud of."

"True enough. But you're my partner and a friend, and I don't want anything to jeopardize that. So you need to hear this."

"Okay…"

Frost ran a hand through his hair and then fidgeted with his napkin. "I got addicted to cocaine while working undercover. I'm not proud of it, but there it is." He stared up at her intently, the weight of his words ringing in her ears. "I'm clean now—have been for over two years," he added solemnly. "I thought you should know."

Bridgette nodded once as she regained her composure. "Have you told the chief?"

"Yes. He's the only one who knows outside of the Narcotics team. I actually told him before he hired me."

"How did he react?"

"He wasn't surprised. He's been around long enough to know that's a common fate for guys working undercover. He said after what I'd been through, I deserved a second chance."

"I didn't think undercover work was that bad."

Frost grimaced. "The regular force turns a blind eye. They don't want to know as long as we get results. I'd only been working undercover for a couple of months before I had to start smoking joints."

"Wow… I'd heard stories, but…"

Frost shrugged. "You have to start at the bottom dealing with street criminals and slowly work your way up to the real players. It takes time and the only way you gain their trust is by hanging out with them, and that means doing drugs."

"Is that how you got addicted to cocaine?"

Frost grimaced. "Partially. But if I'm honest, it was as much the job as anything else. We had access to all kinds of drugs and sometimes the rush it gave me helped when I was on the job. When you're working with criminals who have put associates in the morgue for only slight indiscretions, it focuses your mind. You knew every night could be your last as you try to build a case. The cocaine helped… I don't mean to be melodramatic, but that's the truth."

"You did well to get out of there."

Frost nodded. "I consider myself one of the lucky ones. One of my colleagues has been missing for over twelve months. I'm sure he's dead, but no one has ever discovered his body and probably never will. And there are others…"

"Others?"

Frost sighed. "Another cop who started at the same time as I did ended up a junkie and was discharged. And a third guy had post-traumatic stress. I'm not sure what happened to him…"

"I had no idea," said Bridgette with a shake of her head.

"Most cops don't. For obvious reasons, the undercover guys don't say much and the brass turns a blind eye. If they don't know, there's nothing to report."

"I guess if you want to get close to the real criminals, that's what you have to do."

"And that's the problem," said Frost with a nod. "You have to live this life for months at a time. You play the part of a low, or medium level drug dealer, and hopefully get introductions to members higher in the organization before you make the real bust."

"And all the while, you're living a double life. Part cop and part drug dealer."

"No," said Frost shaking his head. "The life consumes you. It's not as if you do your eight or ten hours and then go home to your family. This is all-consuming. You can't afford to have contact with family, or regular guys in the police force. You never know who's watching. If they see you for who you really are, you're as good as dead."

They were silent for a moment while Bridgette processed everything Levi had told her. Finally, she said, "Thanks for being honest with me. I… I know that couldn't have been easy."

"Thanks for listening." Frost frowned and added, "Are we still good?"

Bridgette held Frost's gaze as she nodded. "We have a lot in common… the job has burned us both. Perhaps in different ways, but…"

Frost held her gaze, deep and intense. "And yet we're both still here," he murmured, his voice full of emotion as he slowly raised his fork to continue eating.

Chapter Seven

The dinner with Levi Frost hadn't gone as Bridgette had expected. She had hoped to use the evening to explore their friendship or whatever it was they were trying to navigate their way through. But Frost's confession that he was a recovering drug addict had rocked her. After returning home later in the evening, she had gone to bed with Frost's confession still weighing heavily on her mind.

She had found his openness and honesty reassuring. And she couldn't deny it—she still had feelings for him. She tossed and turned until around four-thirty AM, before finally giving up on sleep. It was too early to head to West Vancouver, and even too early for the gym, so she went for a run instead, then showered and ate breakfast. She was on the road and driving north just after seven.

Bridgette had only gone a few blocks before her best friend, Renee Filipucci, called. Bridgette pressed answer on her car's hands-free system and said, "Hi, Renee."

"Hey BC. How did your first day back go?

"It went great. I even got a new case."

"Well, that is good news."

"I agree."

"So have they got you pulling big hours again? I called you about eight o'clock last night and when you didn't pick up, I got a little anxious. I know your psych wants you to take it easy for a while."

"Sorry, I was kind of… busy. But I left the office before seven. That's good for me."

"I agree. By your standards that is pretty good. Did you hit the gym? I needed a night off. My body is a little wrecked at present."

"Not really." Bridgette cringed, expecting more questions.

"Not really? You didn't just go home?"

"Not exactly. Levi's on a new case. And we couldn't find time to talk at work. So, we got together last night for a meal to catch up."

"Nice. Where did you go?"

"Black and Blue."

"As in the restaurant?"

"Yeah, the steakhouse."

"I went to Black and Blue three weeks ago. That doesn't sound like a catch up meeting after work, BC. That sounds like a date."

"We had a meal together—and we talked about work. That's all," said Bridgette.

She instantly regretted how quickly she had delivered her response as Filipucci shot back, "Are you hearing yourself, BC? A work meeting? At Black and Blue? Who picked the restaurant?"

"He did."

"And you don't think that's a date?"

Bridgette rolled her eyes. "Okay, *maybe* it was a date."

"I remember you told me you had a moment with him on the Fraser river after your escape from that nut job. But I thought that was the painkillers talking. This sounds… different."

"Maybe…"

"So, how'd it go?"

"Well… it wasn't what I expected."

"Bridgette, I'm your best friend. I'm gonna need more than *it wasn't what I expected*."

Bridgette wasn't sure how much she should share. "I was hoping we would get the opportunity to talk about our friendship… and where it may be headed. But we never got the chance."

"You never got the chance? You have the guy all to yourself for two or three hours, and it doesn't come up in conversation?"

Bridgette pulled up at a set of traffic lights. "No… It wasn't like that. We talked… mainly about Him.. It was—"

"Yeah, I've been out with lots of guys like that. Run as fast as you can. Trust me, BC, if they only want to talk about themselves, they're not worth the effort."

"No, it wasn't like that. He…" Bridgette paused for a moment to gather her thoughts as she accelerated away on a green light. She wasn't about to betray Frost's confidence, even to her best friend.

She chose her words carefully. "We talked mainly about his work—what he did before he joined Homicide. His work in Undercover was a lot more challenging than I could have ever imagined."

"So where does that leave you? Do you need another date to work this out?

"Maybe. We're not working together at present, which is kind of a relief. I'm taking it day by day and we'll see what happens."

"You need a strategy, BC. You shouldn't let this drift."

"I don't want to force anything, Renée. That's not my style. I think I'll just play it by ear."

"Okay. It's your life."

"Thanks for understanding."

"No problem. Say, I'm in the city all day today. You wanna catch up later for coffee or lunch."

"Sorry, I'm out all day. Why don't you come over tonight and I'll cook us a stir-fry? I should be home by seven."

"Sounds good, BC. I'll see you then."

Filipucci disconnected, leaving Bridgette alone with her thoughts. She checked the navigation app on her phone—she would be in West Vancouver in twenty minutes. She thought of Fiona and Tessa Halloran and pushed her thoughts about Levi Frost and her conversation with Renee Filipucci to the back of her mind. She wanted the twins to get the justice they deserved, and would do everything she could to make sure nothing was overlooked.

She murmured, "Time to focus, Bridgette," as she changed gears and pulled onto the freeway.

Bridgette pulled into the parking lot at the West Vancouver Yacht Club just before seven-thirty AM. She sat for a moment and surveyed the scene in front of her. The marina was much bigger than she expected and home to hundreds of boats of various sizes. Cruisers and sailboats dominated the slips, but there were various forms of smaller watercraft as well. Bridgette shook her head in amazement as she did the math in her head. Millions of dollars worth of luxurious vessels bobbed in the marina; an impressive fleet of gleaming boats by anyone's measure. She murmured, "The lives of the rich and famous…" as she got out of her car.

She stood for a moment to get her bearings. On her left, there was a path to the docks. On her right, steps led up to the marina's boat shop. Bridgette turned right and walked up the steps. She stood for a moment in front of the shop. She could see several employees through the front glass windows busy inside, getting ready for the day. The boat shop didn't overly interest her, and she turned her attention to the cafe next door. The signage said 'Eagle Cafe' but that was a stretch, she thought. The building was small, about the size of a shipping container. It had a window like most diners in the city for serving customers. She noted the menu, which was painted on an aging sheet of plywood. It boasted burgers as one of its specialties. She assumed this was the burger place Remmy Chilton had mentioned in his statement as she stared at the opening hours. The menu indicated that the cafe opened at eight AM daily. Bridgette needed to speak to the owner but didn't want to hang around for half an hour waiting. She glanced at her watch to mark the current time as she turned to her left. Now was the perfect opportunity to time Chilton's journey down through Eagle Harbor Park and then to Gulf Beach.

Bridgette set off at a reasonable walking pace. She could have walked quicker but kept the pace easy as she tried to emulate the speed of someone walking while they ate. She noticed the woods were thick in this part of Vancouver, and in places, stretched down to the water's edge.

The walk took her on a path through to a small strip of beach sand. The beach was only about thirty yards long and ended in a rocky backdrop that separated the ocean from the wooded area beyond. She had been walking for ten minutes and knew from the map that this was called Kew Beach—about halfway along her journey.

A walking trail to her left beckoned her forward, drawing her into the woods. She followed its winding path, enjoying the solitude and the calming presence of birds chirping in the trees. Bridgette had no idea where it would take her, but she guessed this was the path Chilton talked about that led to Gulf Beach. She could hear the gentle washing sound of the ocean lapping against the rocks and caught glimpses of the brilliant blue water through the trees. The path only ever seemed to detour inland by about twenty yards at most. It seemed to Bridgette as if the path had been created by people as a convenient shortcut. Even though the up-market houses in the nearby suburb were only yards away, she felt disconnected. This was like walking through a forest and it was difficult for her to see more than a few yards in any direction. She understood how easy it would be to murder someone in the area without being seen.

Bridgette kept up a steady pace, trying to put herself in the shoes of Remmy Chilton as she walked. If he had wanted to kill, it would have been hard to find a target unless he had followed them into the woods. She winced as she realized there was so much more to learn about this case. The case file was lacking information about the girls' activities before the murder. Had they been relaxing down at Gulf Beach before heading home? Had they been up at the marina and were then followed by Chilton as they walked home along the path she was now on? She didn't know, and this would mean interviewing the girls parents. Which would mean opening up old wounds.

A moment later, Bridgette stepped from the woods and onto a sandy beach. She checked her watch. The walk from the marina to Gulf Beach had taken nineteen minutes. She grimaced and said, "Well, Remmy, it looks like you were telling the truth in this part of your story."

Chapter Eight

Remmy Chilton's breath came in short, ragged gasps as he sat at the cold metal table, the same one as yesterday when the detective with eyes as sharp as ice picks had drilled him with questions. The air was stale and heavy, pressing down on him like the weight of her accusations.

"What the hell?" he murmured. His voice was a hoarse whisper, barely carrying across the lifeless room. *'How could they charge me with murder all over again?'*

The walls seemed about four feet apart, suffocating him with their sterile indifference. He glanced up at the mirror window, knowing they would be watching. Internally, he screamed, *'Should've stayed in the US!'* as he thought about how it had all gone so horribly wrong when he had reached the Canadian border. All he wanted to do was visit his mom's grave. He put his head down so they couldn't see and murmured, "Is that too much to ask?" The words tumbled out, each one etched with regret and longing. Coming back to Canada to pay his respects and find closure had become another cruel, twisted joke at his expense.

The dampness of fear coated his hands. He breathed in deeply to control his panic as he wiped his palms across the coarse fabric of his jumpsuit. As he recalled his conversation with the guard minutes earlier, the room felt smaller again.

"Who's your lawyer?" the guard had inquired.

"Got some court-appointed guy called Guy Fenton," he had replied, his voice brittle and threatening to crack.

The guard's harsh laughter as he quipped, "I hope you like prison food," had left him rattled. He was trapped with no way out.

Remmy swallowed down the lump that formed in his throat. He tugged at the metal cuffs that bound him to the floor, a grim reminder of the gravity of his situation. They clinked mockingly, the sound a cold whisper promising captivity. To pace would be a luxury, a small semblance of control in a world where he had none. "You might assault your lawyer," they had warned him when they had shackled him to the spot.

Remmy shook his head. *'Assault a lawyer?'* The idea was ludicrous. He could barely swat a fly, let alone lift a hand to anyone, even in self-defense.

Suddenly, he was tired and wanted it all to end. He rocked slightly, the chains giving a soft chorus to accompany the motion. Let them watch. Let them laugh. Let them stare. It was nothing new to him.

"Always the joke, aren't I?" he muttered under his breath, the words barely audible. It was a truth he'd come to accept at a young age, one that had chased him through school and across borders from childhood to this moment. They could laugh all they wanted, but inside, where it counted, he knew who he was.

A knock on the door interrupted his thoughts. He lifted his head as the door creaked open. A young man stepped through—the lawyer, he figured, if the dark blue suit and the leather briefcase were anything to go by. Guy Fenton was younger than he was. His goatee was more an apologetic suggestion of facial hair than a statement, and the acne scars told tales of recent adolescent battles.

"Mr. Chilton, I presume?" The lawyer's voice cracked slightly under the weight of professionalism it tried to project.

"Yeah, that's me," responded Remmy, without any attempt to hide his disappointment.

Remmy's gaze settled on the man who was supposed to be his lifeline in a sea of accusations. With a cheap, synthetic click, the lawyer's briefcase popped open. Fenton withdrew a yellow legal pad, his hands betraying a subtle tremor as he settled into a chair opposite. He smoothed back a lock of hair, revealing a sheen of perspiration on his brow.

"It's nice to meet you," Fenton said, offering a smile that didn't quite reach his eyes.

"Likewise," Remmy replied, although nothing could be further from the truth.

As Fenton launched into a monologue about the charges Remmy faced and the dates for court appearances, Remmy felt the weight of the world pressing down on him. The words 'murder' and 'second-degree' circled like vultures in the stale air.

Fenton's voice faded into background noise against the pounding in Remmy's head. *If he's already this defeated, what chance do I have?* he wondered, the walls inching closer with every syllable that suggested guilt.

He was brought back to the moment when Fenton asked, "Any questions, Mr. Chilton?"

"Yeah. How can they charge me for murder a second

time?" Remmy's voice was steady, surprisingly calm, given the tempest raging in his gut. "Isn't there that thing about double jeopardy?"

Fenton sighed. "Double jeopardy doesn't apply here." His pen hovered over the page as if reluctant to mar it with bad news. "The last trial was for Fiona Halloran. This time… it's for her sister."

Remmy's hands clenched beneath the table, his knuckles whitening. Memories cascaded behind his eyes — images of Fiona lying dead on the trail. "But I'm innocent! I had nothing to do with any murder," he pleaded. He leaned forward, blurting out his original statement in under two minutes. "I told the cops everything—where I was, what I saw. I've been straight with them since the beginning."

Fenton's nod was mechanical, his pen scratching as he jotted down notes that seemed more like an excuse to avoid eye contact rather than noting down anything meaningful.

Remmy noticed the sheen of sweat on Fenton's brow, which now threatened to bead, as the lawyer responded, "Your cap and DNA were found at the crime scene… And there are no witnesses to corroborate what you were doing before the discovery…"

Fenton raised his eyes and met Remmy's gaze. "How do you explain being there in the first place? And why would a jury believe you?"

Remmy's heart hammered against his chest. "Because it's the truth!" The words spilled out, bouncing off the walls and returning to him as a reminder of his predicament.

Fenton scribbled more notes on his pad, the sound of his labored breathing the only thing breaking the thick silence that had settled between them.

Remmy clenched and unclenched his fists beneath the

table. When he finally felt in control, he said, "I never said I wasn't there. And I called it in. But I didn't murder anyone." His voice was steady, but it echoed hollowly against the sterile walls of the interview room.

Remmy's eyes narrowed as he studied the lawyer, searching for some sign of competence or confidence. All he found was a furrowed brow and a set jaw that did little to hide his inexperience. School had been a relentless grind for Remmy, where every report card served as a reminder that he was never smart enough, never good enough. Yet, in this moment, staring into Fenton's flustered expression, Remmy wondered how intelligence was measured. Grades and degrees seemed meaningless as he pondered the hopelessness of his situation.

Finally, Fenton cleared his throat and looked up. As their eyes locked, Fenton's voice finally cut through, barely louder than the air conditioner's hum. "I've reviewed the evidence, and I think we need to go with a plea bargain."

Remmy frowned. "What's that?"

Fenton launched into legal jargon, most of which was lost on him. But he understood enough to know that plea bargains weren't for the innocent. They were the last resort of the guilty, a white flag in the battleground of the court. But here they were, laid out before him like a grotesque feast he had no appetite for.

When he finally finished, Remmy said, "I didn't do it. Don't you understand? All I did was look for a girl I thought was crying out for help…"

"Look, Remmy," Fenton started, pausing as though each word was an effort. "It's… it's a compromise. We—you— acknowledge some responsibility. It's not saying you did it, just that you played a part."

"Played a part?" Remmy shook his head as he clenched and unclenched his fists again. "You want me to lie?"

"No, not lie." Fenton's head shook slightly, his eyes dodging Remmy's piercing stare. "It's about reducing risks, managing the outcome. Sometimes... sometimes the system doesn't work the way it should."

"Shouldn't we be trying to make it work, then? Isn't that your job?"

"Look," Fenton murmured, his voice barely audible. "We try for a reduced sentence. Hopefully, you might only have to serve... ten years."

The words hung in the air, heavy with finality. Remmy's breath caught in his throat as he responded, "Ten years? For something I didn't do?"

Fenton cleared his throat, a feeble attempt to reclaim some semblance of authority. "It's the best option on the table, Remmy. It's about minimizing damage now."

"Damage?" Remmy's laugh was hollow, devoid of any humor. "You call losing ten years of your life 'damage'? Can't we just fight for the truth?"

Fenton's eyes shifted to the side, unable to hold the raw honesty in Remmy's plea. "Sometimes, the truth isn't enough," he admitted, his voice low. "The story is back in the papers again. Twin girls murdered in the prime of their lives. Everybody in Vancouver is talking about it. The jury will be under pressure to put someone behind bars."

"And that someone is me..." lamented Remmy.

Remmy felt a throbbing pain in his head as he tried to absorb Fenton's words. Suddenly, he felt desperately tired and cradled his head in his hands. Lost in the shock of his predicament, he didn't hear the lawyer stow away his legal pad, nor his instruction to think about a plea bargain overnight.

Hot and Cold

The door opened and closed, and Fenton was gone. Remmy lifted his head and looked around the room—he had never felt more alone in his life.

Chapter Nine

Bridgette stood and surveyed the scene in front of her. Gulf Beach was a stretch of rocky shoreline approximately two hundred yards long and fifty yards wide, separating the woods from the ocean. It was not what Bridgette had expected. The local government had created an elevated viewing platform about sixty feet back from the water's edge. It was made of sand, concrete and rocks and featured a bench seat and a garbage can.

Bridgette followed a well-worn path down to the structure. She stared at the garbage bin, wondering if this was where Remmy Chilton had disposed of his burger wrappers. She glanced out at the ocean, momentarily mesmerized by the morning sun glimmering off its surface. The distant sound of a truck shifting gears brought her back to the present as she turned towards the woods. She felt a sense of unease settling on her as she took in the horrifying reality that someone had murdered two girls within its depths.

After walking back off the rocks, she noticed a well-worn path leading up into the woods. She figured this was the path the locals took to cut through the woods to the surrounding suburbs.

Bridgette followed the path into the woods, her feet crunching over dry leaves and twigs as she walked. The filtered sunlight cast eerie shadows around her. She ventured forward, her photographic memory sifting through the photographs from the crime scene for a match for what was in front of her. After rounding a bend in the path, something caught her eye that made her stop. It was the bough of a tree branch hanging across the trail. Anyone taller than six feet would need to hunch down slightly to carry on. Her heart rate increased as she remembered an almost identical photo in the case file to the scene in front of her. Fiona Halloran's body had been discovered a few feet ahead, just beyond this tree.

Bridgette crept forward. Even though she was a cop and used to seeing dead bodies, the thought that a young woman's life had ended here in violence was unsettling. She paused when she got to the place where Fiona's body had been found. She crouched down and looked at the ground in front of her. After thirteen years, she wasn't expecting to find any clues. But being so close to where the girl had breathed her last breath brought back all the reasons why she was here.

She murmured, "What happened here, Fiona? Were you running away? Or did he sneak up behind you?"

She stood and looked further up the path which curved out of sight about thirty feet ahead of her. She then turned and looked back. The trail was relatively straight as it descended towards the beach. It seemed unlikely that someone had simply snuck up behind her without her noticing.

Bridgette closed her eyes and tried to imagine what might have happened. She assumed Fiona had been aware of her attacker and was trying to escape. Had she tripped? Or was her attacker simply faster than she was? She remembered the autopsy report determined Fiona had died from two blows to the back of her head. Perhaps she had been attacked elsewhere, and this was where she finally fell?

She absentmindedly tugged on her left earlobe as she pondered her questions. She realized how vulnerable a young woman would have been here on her own. She frowned and murmured, "But you weren't alone."

Bridgette quietly backtracked, her gaze taking in the woods around her as she walked. When she reached a fork in the trail, she took a right turn and counted off fifteen steps before coming to a halt. According to the case file, Tessa's body had been discovered just off the path on her left. An eerie stillness settled around her, as if death itself were reminding her that it had taken another life here.

Bridgette crouched down and pushed aside some branches. The area beyond was dark and ominous, with the undergrowth tugging at her clothing as she tried to keep it out of the way. She pictured the photo of Tessa's body lying face down in this spot. Her mood soured even further as she pondered the tragedy of another life cut short in its prime. She stood up and checked her watch. There was little more to see here. She would use the next hour to explore each of the trails thoroughly before returning to the marina to interview the owner of the Eagle Cafe.

It was just after ten AM when Bridgette returned to the burger shop. The establishment had three customers now; a young man eating a burger while leaning against a lamp-post, and an older couple sipping coffee at one of the small tables.

Bridgette noticed a man in his sixties cleaning down a bench inside the diner with a bright green rag. As she approached the serving window, the man smiled warmly and said, "Good morning. Can I help you?"

Bridgette decided to order a drink to break the ice. She figured if she engaged the man in casual conversation first, she would probably learn more. She normally drank peppermint tea but didn't think the cafe's beverage menu extended that far and went with a black coffee instead. After ordering her beverage, she stood next to the window while the man busied himself with her order.

The man had a slim build and thinning gray hair. He was wearing a North Face jacket over the top of blue denim jeans. She figured this was his standard uniform, except perhaps in warmer months.

The man spoke first. "I haven't seen you around here before. Are you just visiting?"

"Kind of. I actually work for the Vancouver Police."

The man raised an eyebrow. "The police. Are you a cop?"

"A detective," said Bridgette as she flashed her badge.

The man chuckled. "I don't mean to offend, but either I'm getting old, or you police officers are getting younger by the day!"

Bridgette smiled. She was twenty-eight, but didn't think her age was relevant as she replied, "Well, sir, I'm the youngest detective in our squad, so maybe you're right."

The man placed her coffee on the ledge and stuck a hand out through the window. "The name's Mac. Pleased to meet you, detective."

"Likewise," said Bridgette as she shook the man's hand.

"So, what're you doing here? We haven't had any burglaries recently."

Bridgette took a sip of her coffee before replying, "Do you remember the Halloran sisters?"

The man's features darkened. "You mean the girls who were murdered down at the beach?"

Bridgette nodded.

"That was thirteen years ago," said the man with a shake of his head. "Awful business. I remember the young guy they arrested for it. He was here at my shop the day of the murder, as a matter of fact."

"Are you John? As in John Mackenzie?"

"I am, but most people just call me Mac. I'm the owner here. I had a partner back then, but it's just been me for the last six years."

Bridgette explained how Remmy Chilton had been re-arrested and was likely to face a trial again for the second murder

Mackenzie listened intently and then said, "I didn't think they could do that. Trying one case rather than two seems almost unfair." The man's face dropped as he added, "But I knew those two girls. It would be nice to see the bastard who did that to them finally locked up."

"I couldn't agree more, Mac. That's why I'm here. I was hoping you might tell me what you remember about the day."

Mac scratched his head. "Well… that's not a day I'm gonna forget in a hurry… I don't remember seeing the girls on that day, but the boy—the one they arrested—I remember him. He came around mid-afternoon looking for the boat shop owner. Said he was looking for a job, and the way he was dressed, boy, did he need one."

Hot and Cold

"What did he look like?"

"Well, he was short. Much shorter than you, and he had on an old pair of jeans and... maybe a black windbreaker. And a baseball cap. And he was skinny—looked almost like he was homeless, actually. I went to tell him to clear out, because we get a few unsavory types around here looking to steal things. But then he told me his mother was sick, and he was looking for a job at the marina to tide him over... I actually felt sorry for him."

"So what happened next?"

Mac scratched his head again. "The owner of the marina was out for the afternoon as I recall. I remember telling him to come back around five and catch him as he was closing up for the night."

Bridgette didn't want to lead Mackenzie and simply asked, "So, did you see him after that?"

"Yeah," said the man with a nod. "He came back at five. He told me the assistant at the boat shop said the owner wouldn't be back until the morning."

"Do you remember anything else?"

"I remember he told me he hadn't eaten all day, but didn't have much money. Wanted to know if I had any food I was throwing out."

"And what did you say?"

"I gave him two burgers. A guy ordered them at about four, but never came back for them. They were cold by the time I was closing up, but the young man didn't seem to mind. He was grateful for the food and thanked me several times."

"So then what happened?"

"I never saw him after that. He wanted to get a bus back into the city, but I told him there wouldn't be another stopping near the marina for at least an hour. I told him his best bet was to walk down to Gulf Beach Park and cut through the woods to Marine Drive. He thanked me for the burgers again and then started walking down towards the park."

Bridgette nodded. "And that was the last you saw of him?"

"Yep," said Mackenzie with a shake of his head. "The following day, I heard about the murder of the two girls on the radio, and then two detectives came by to interview me. I couldn't believe it when they said the young man was their prime suspect."

"And why was that?"

Mackenzie frowned. "He didn't look like the kind who would kill an ant, let alone murder two girls."

Chapter Ten

Bridgette stepped out of the elevator and walked towards Delray's office. Exhausted from the lengthy investigation in West Vancouver, she pushed her weariness to the back of her mind as she paused at the open doorway of Delray's office.

Delray was sitting in front of his computer, his glasses perched on the end of his nose. Without her needing to knock, he mumbled, "Come in, Bridgette." She detected a somber tone to his voice as he added, "You should close the door too…"

Bridgette sensed something was off when Delray requested the office door be closed. She was sure she hadn't done anything wrong, and asked, "What's wrong, Chief?"

"I've been upstairs, with Cunningham," growled her boss as he removed his glasses.

Assistant Commissioner Leo Cunningham was Delray's superior. Delray couldn't stand him, and his contempt was clear. "The news outlets know that we've arrested Chilton and have connected it to the murders from thirteen years ago."

"That's going to make the investigation difficult," said Bridgette with a grimace.

"It's a lot more complicated than that."

"Why?"

"Cunningham has sold us out," fumed Delray. "He's held a joint press conference with senior prosecutor Richard Temple. It will be on the six o'clock news in a few minutes."

"Is he allowed to do that? Did he get clearance from the commissioner?"

Delray nodded. "The commissioner backed it. Said we needed to be proactive. He doesn't want a repeat of what happened thirteen years ago."

Bridgette hesitated before asking, "So, where does that leave us?"

She watched as her boss's face darkened. Delray took a deep breath to compose himself before speaking. "They're drawing up the paperwork to formally charge Chilton with murder…"

Bridgette raised her eyebrows. "Did you tell them that we're not certain Chilton is guilty?"

"I did. They weren't interested. The media is expecting a charge, and that's what they're going to get."

They were silent for a moment before Delray said, "So, how did the trip to the marina go?"

"Chilton's story checks out," she said. "I timed his walk—it matched up with what he said." She then went on to explain how she had interviewed John Mackenzie and how he had also confirmed Chilton's testimony.

Silence lingered in the office for close to a minute before Bridgette broke the silence. "I don't believe Chilton had enough time or motive to commit those murders. We could be sending an innocent man to prison."

"There's only one thing for it then."

"And what's that?"

Delray held her gaze. "We need to keep you on the case. If Chilton didn't commit those murders, then someone else did... and we have to find them before this thing gets to trial."

After her meeting with Delray, Bridgette couldn't wait to leave the office. The weight of his words, pleading for her to find the true culprit in the Halloran case, weighed heavily on her as she straightened a pile of files on her desk.

As she reached for her jacket, her phone buzzed. She debated letting it go to voicemail, but saw the number and quickly answered. "Detective Bridgette Cash speaking."

The line crackled with the echo of a long-distance call. A weary voice filled with years of experience and caution said, "I received a message telling me to call this number. Is this the Vancouver Police?"

Bridgette had left a message for Hector Thorne in Maine. She was pleasantly surprised that he had returned her call.

"Yes, this is the VPD. Is this Mr. Thorne?"

"I'm Hector. What's going on?" asked Thorne, with concern lacing his voice.

"Do you know Remmy Chilton?"

"Well... yes. He used to work for me. Is everything okay?"

Bridgette tapped her pen against the notepad, each click a muted echo in the room now shrouded by shadows as the evening crept closer. She saw no reason to hide any of the details and told Thorne how Remmy Chilton had been arrested for murder when he had tried to re-enter Canada.

On the other end of the line, there was a sharp intake of breath, followed by a gasp, faint but clear. "It can't be true. Remmy's not a murderer," Thorne murmured, disbelief etched into his words.

"I'm sorry, sir. But… he's currently in custody and charges are due to be formally laid in the next day or two."

"I can't believe it…"

"Sir, I understand this is difficult to hear. But, can you tell me how long you've known him?"

"Long enough to know Remmy isn't capable of what you're saying," snapped Thorne. "I've seen him help more strays—both animals and people—than I can count."

"He says he worked for you for about thirteen years. Is that correct?"

"He came to my marina looking for odd jobs to earn some extra cash. He ended up staying on until I sold the business a month ago. He was my marine mechanic by day and my security guard at night."

"So he lived at the marina?"

"Yeah, had himself a little spot there. It wasn't much, but it was his and I never had a moment's trouble with him. What murder has he supposed to have committed?"

Bridgette started giving Thorne a brief overview of the Halloran case, but he interrupted. "You mean the twins near the beach?"

"Yes. You knew about that?"

"Yeah… He told me about it, after he had been with me a couple of months. He said he'd been found not guilty and hoped they would eventually find the real killer. How can he be charged a second time?"

Bridgette briefly explained how Chilton had only been initially charged with Fiona's murder, but not her sisters. There was silence on the call for a moment before Thorne responded, "I can't believe it…" his voice tremored with the shock of what he was learning.

"You clearly don't think he's capable of murder?"

"Remmy couldn't even clean down spider webs, for fear he might hurt one of them. To think he had anything to do with the murder of another human being is ridiculous. I know him as well as anyone, and he's simply not capable."

Bridgette sighed as the silence enveloped them. She felt the weight of the case beginning to weigh her down as Thorne confirmed Chilton's testimony, lending further doubt to the charge that he was a murderer.

"Thanks for you time, Mr. Thorne. I really appreciate it."

"If there's anything else I can do to help, you let me know, okay?"

After promising to follow up tomorrow for a more formal version of his testimony, Bridgette ended the call.

As she leaned back in her chair, her mind was racing. She stared up at the ceiling with a furrowed brow. Thorne's testimony only added to the weight of evidence proving Remmy's innocence, but Bridgette knew it wouldn't be enough to convince Richard Temple. She would need to find another suspect to prosecute if she wanted any chance of clearing his name. The thought made her shake her head in frustration and guilt; the possibility of ruining an innocent person's life weighed heavily on her mind. With a heavy sigh, she murmured "No pressure," but deep down, she knew this was the most pressure she had ever faced in her career.

Chapter Eleven

Levi Frost stepped out into the chilled night air and soon was on a bustling street in downtown Vancouver. He soon found his destination—a dimly lit bar he hadn't been in since his days in undercover. He scanned the room for Tony, but he wasn't there.. Thinking his contact would arrive soon enough, Frost got a soda water and sat in a booth at the back, where he could easily see the front door.

He sank into the fraying upholstery, its darkened fabric stiffened with some unknown substance. His gaze shifted from one figure to another in the room as he waited. It was a habit from his days in undercover that he couldn't break. He glanced at his watch as he took a sip of his drink—it was just after six PM. It was normal for Tony to be late.

Frost's thoughts drifted to his partner. He remembered she would be working on the Chilton case in West Vancouver today. It wasn't surprising he hadn't heard from her. Once she was on a case, she became methodical, focused and *'in the zone,'* as he called it.

He leaned back on the sofa, sipping on his water as he thought about their date the previous evening. He hadn't expected to unload on her like he did. All that anxiety and fear he was used to compartmentalizing had suddenly spilled out. He shook his head. Where had that come from? He felt a surge of guilt at having taken up so much of their time together. It was not what he had planned for the evening.

The sight of a man entering the bar broke his thoughts. The man paused just inside the door while he scanned the room. He hadn't seen Tony in a year, but it felt like just yesterday they were discussing drug deals and all manner of illegal activity in Vancouver.

Tony Staples was a reformed gangster, but he was still well-connected. He did nothing for free and Frost knew today would cost him. Tony's gaze settled on him and he gave a subtle nod as he walked in his direction. Tony's hair was cut short and neat, emphasizing his medium height and build. He wore a charcoal sports jacket over navy blue slacks and looked more like an accountant than a reformed criminal.

He slid into the booth opposite Frost and said, "Levi, it's been quite a while."

"That is has, Tony. Can I get you a drink?"

Tony smiled. "I'm not planning on staying long. No offense, but I can't afford to take the risk of being seen with you."

Frost grinned. "Without my beard and hair, who's going to recognize me?"

"Probably no one, but I haven't stayed alive this long without being cautious. Now, what did you want to see me about?"

Frost looked up at a flat-screen TV in the opposite corner. The six o'clock news had just started and the Chilton girl's murders were one of the lead stories. He pointed at the screen as images of Fiona and Tessa Chilton flashed up and said, "Remember the twins who were murdered at Gulf Beach?"

Tony twisted his head and studied the screen for a moment. "Yeah, I remember. Damn shame—they were so young. They nabbed some guy for it as I recall, but he got off on a technicality."

"He's been rearrested."

"How does that work? Doesn't double jeopardy apply?"

"They only tried him for one of the two murders. They're going to try him for the other murder this time."

Tony looked back at Frost. "Is this what you wanted to see me about?"

Frost reached into his pocket and withdrew a neatly folded roll of bills. He slid them under the table to Staples who pocketed them with a practiced hand.

"Keep your ears open," said Frost, giving him an almost imperceptible nod of acknowledgment. "This is going to be big news for a few days. People will talk about it and you may hear something. If you do, let me know and I'll make sure my department gives you a sizable reward for any information. You know I'm good for it."

Tony glanced back at the TV screen as an image of Remmy Chilton flashed up. "So, this guy they arrested. He's not the guy?"

Frost shrugged. "Nobody knows for sure. But if we've got the wrong guy, people are going to talk. Everyone likes to boast when they know the cops have made a mistake. You may hear something and I'd appreciate knowing whatever you can find out."

Tony nodded once. "I can't promise anything, but I'll see what I can do." He slid out of the booth without another word and walked to the exit.

Frost took another sip of his soda water and glanced at his watch. He would wait five minutes before leaving, a lingering habit from his days in undercover when the rule was you never left at the same time as an informant. He didn't believe today's meeting posed any risks, but some habits he couldn't break.

Bridgette stepped into her apartment and instantly relaxed as she felt the warmth of her home wrap around her. She felt a sudden surge of energy as she checked her watch. Renée Filipucci would be here any moment. On the drive home, she had decided they would eat an Asian stir fry tonight. Partly because it was healthy, and partly because she had all ingredients. Her call with Hector Thorne had delayed her and she had been late getting home. Normally she would have slipped on some music—Harry Styles was getting plenty of airtime at present—but getting the meal ready had to be her priority. After removing the ingredients from her refrigerator, she organized them on her kitchen countertop. As she sliced garlic with expert speed on a wooden cutting board, she thought back over the day.

She still couldn't believe the Vancouver police had disregarded Delray's advice and were pressing ahead with charges against Remmy Chilton. She frowned as she reviewed her conversation with Delray. The evidence said it was almost impossible for Chilton to have committed the murders and he didn't seem the type. If Chilton was innocent that meant the killer was still out there and they would need to start from scratch. Delray would normally provide her with help on such a murder case—with Frost at least coming back to partner with her. However, this wasn't an ordinary case. Assistant Commissioner Cunningham had made his intentions clear to her boss. Chilton was to be charged and no further resources were to be allocated to the investigation. Delray knew he could get away with leaving Bridgette on the case for a few more days, but she would have to be discreet. If word got back to Cunningham that Delray was defying him, all hell would break loose.

That meant going back over all the evidence and re-interviewing everyone she could find. Her heart sank as she thought about all the additional work ahead of her. The thought that Chilton's trial would be fast-tracked, leaving her with limited time, made her stomach churn. If that wasn't difficult enough, Delray had instructed her to be discreet about whom she interviewed and when. She couldn't blame him. If the media were to find out that the police were still investigating and unsure if they had the right person in custody, it would become a fiasco.

A knock at the door interrupted her thoughts. She knew before she opened it that it would be Renee Filipucci. Filipucci worked in the media, but they rarely discussed work. And after what had occurred today with the Chilton case, tonight would be no different.

Bridgette opened the door and said, "Hi," as the two embraced.

The two were polar opposites. Bridgette was softly spoken, quiet and thoughtful. She observed the world around her with a calm appraisal and considered each moment carefully before speaking or acting. Filipucci was brash and loud; her words spilling out as rapidly as they came into her head. Tonight was no exception as she asked

Bridgette how her day had been, declared she had had an exhausting day herself, was famished, and couldn't wait for dinner before they were back inside the apartment.

Bridgette did her best to keep up with the answers to her friend's rapid-fire questions. It was only when she went to Bridgette's refrigerator to retrieve a bottle of Vanilla Coke that the conversation momentarily paused. After drinking about half the bottle, Filipucci said, "I needed that."

Bridgette smiled as she turned on an electric fry pan. "Chicken stir-fry tonight. You good with that?"

Her friend pulled up a bench stool near to where Bridgette was working and said, "Sounds great. Thanks for having me over."

The two talked for a few minutes about their work days. Bridgette was deliberately vague, only saying that Delray had her working on an old case before finding her something new to do.

Filipucci quickly steered the conversation towards Levi Frost. "Have you heard from Levi today?"

Bridgette shook her head as she diced the chicken. "No. We've exchanged a couple of texts, but that's all. I wasn't in the office until late this afternoon—and he was out most of the day."

After taking another sip of her coke, Filipucci said, "So, what are you going to do, BC? Are you going to let this drift or what?"

"I don't know," said Bridgette as she tipped the chicken into the fry pan. As the meat sizzled, she added, "I've never been good with relationships. I don't even know if he likes me."

Filipucci laughed. "He took you to Black and Blue, didn't he?"

"Yes, but that's not the first time we've—"

"Who paid?"

Bridgette didn't answer straight away. She made a point of adding all the vegetables to the stir fry before she responded, "He wouldn't let me pay. He said it was his treat, being my first day back."

Filipucci raised an eyebrow. "He probably dropped close to two hundred dollars on that meal. Trust me, he likes you!"

Tony Staples mind raced as he walked along the inner city streets of Vancouver. The two-hundred and fifty dollars Frost had given him would buy him a thick steak and a nice hotel room for the night.

He mulled over his conversation with Frost from earlier that evening. He'd heard stories about the murder on Gulf Beach many years earlier, but he hadn't mentioned that to Frost. Staples took out his cigarettes and lit one while he walked. He drew in a deep breath of the smoke, letting it settle in his lungs for a moment before he blew it out into the chilled night air. He weighed up the offer. The police reward would put him back in the black for several weeks. It was tempting, but not without risk.

Staples frowned. He knew if he were discovered, it could be the last thing he ever did. Was it worth risking his life for? Informing on a drug dealer was far different to informing on a murderer—the stakes were much higher. Staples took another long draw on his cigarette as he continued to walk. Maybe there was another way to take advantage of this situation? A sly grin spread across his face as one person came to mind. He knew things that probably no one else outside the Vancouver police knew. He would need to be cautious. And discrete. But he knew the person would be willing to pay him handsomely to know that one Vancouver cop was still investigating.

Chapter Twelve

Bridgette stared out of the office window, watching as the first faint rays of sunlight colored the morning horizon. She had spent another restless yet not sleepless night tossing and turning, unable to settle as she relived the day. After speaking with Renee Filipucci the previous evening, she came to the same conclusion as her friend. She would need to talk to Frost about their relationship, or friendship, or whatever the hell it was. Her stomach tightened. Those kinds of conversations were not her strong suit. She felt like a giddy schoolgirl, but it had to be done. She would try to be subtle; skirting around what may or may not be happening between them. Hopefully, Frost would pick up on it and declare his hand. One way or another, they needed to resolve it to move forward.

She sighed and returned her attention to the Halloran case file. Delray's words, "You have to be discrete," echoed in her mind. Today was going to be tricky. Gathering evidence for a double homicide usually meant drawing attention. But this balancing act would take all her skill.

One misstep could mean disaster and put both her and Delray's careers in jeopardy.

She chewed on the end of her pen as she studied a list of potential interviewees. The list was a photocopy of the original one used by the detectives who worked the case thirteen years ago. She immediately crossed off the twins' parents. There was no way she could re-interview them without arousing suspicion. They would rightly ask: 'Why do we need to be re-interviewed? and, 'Isn't he in jail already?'

She decided she would start with the neighbors at the house where the girls had been staying. They might ask questions, but she could always allude to the fact a trial was coming up and they might need to testify.

For now, she planned to refocus on the evidence in the case file. It was one thing to go over it when you thought you had the killer in custody, but quite another when the killer was likely still on the loose.

She started by spreading everything out on her desk and organizing it into piles. She sorted the investigators' file notes into one pile and the witness statements and interview transcripts into another. Bridgette made a third pile for photographs. Besides the murder scene and the morgue, there were a few others that intrigued her. She sifted through the collection. There were photos of Gulf Beach Park, the marina, and the burger place where she met Mac. She found a few photos of the holiday house and put them in a separate pile. It was the final few photos that intrigued her most. These photos were in a separate plastic bag, and it seemed like someone had taken them all with a Polaroid self-developing camera. The 4x4 photographs all had a purple hue; partly due to their age and partly because of the technology used by Polaroid.

Bridgette spread the photographs out on her desk, running her fingertips over each of them as she went. They were mostly shots of the girls laughing and playing at the beach or lounging at their holiday house. Bridgette felt an ache inside her. The girls were young and happy, and completely oblivious to the cruel fate that awaited them.

She noticed a note tucked away in the plastic bag. It had been handwritten by a 'Detective Roussard' who had retired many years earlier. The note said Fiona had taken the photographs a few days before her death. She felt a tingle of excitement as she examined the last photo in the collection. It was of one twin—she presumed her sister, Tessa—standing next to a young man. They had their arms around one another as they smiled at the camera.

Bridgette picked up the photo and studied it closely. The backdrop was ocean. It might have been taken at Gulf Beach, but she couldn't be sure. She studied the boy in the image. She guessed he was in his late teens or early twenties. According to the parent's statement, neither twin had a boyfriend. She studied the photo for a moment and then murmured, "Who are you?"

After placing the photo back on her desk, she snapped an image of it with her smartphone. It was too soon to consider it a lead, but it was worth investigating.

Bridgette drove up the winding hill in her car, a cape of sea mist streaming around her. She pulled into a parking lot just off Marine Drive and checked her watch after switching off the engine.

She sat for a moment, listening to the tick of the engine as the motor cooled. She had spent almost four hours going over the case file at police headquarters, but found very little to go on. The investigation had been completely focused on Remmy Chilton and proving his guilt. No one had considered the possibility that someone else might have been responsible and there were no other suspects listed in the case file.

She grimaced as she realized how tough the job was that Delray had given her. She had narrowed the witness list down to seven people—all locals whom Delray agreed she could interview. They were mostly neighbors, people who were around on the day of the murder who might have seen or heard something. But she knew it was a long shot. Who would remember seeing the girls on a specific day thirteen years ago? And who would remember any conversations they'd had with them? And even if they did remember anything, would it help with the case?

She pulled out her phone and studied the photo she had taken of the Polaroid of Tessa with the unknown young man. She wondered again why the girls were in the woods. Had they been meeting up with this young man or someone else? Had they been lured there? Or ambushed? Perhaps something else?

Bridgette likened murder investigations to jigsaw puzzles. Every tiny detail was like a piece of the puzzle that had to be fitted together for the image to become clear. She was sure uncovering the girl's motive for being in the woods was one of the pieces.

Her thoughts were interrupted as her phone buzzed in her hand. Her heart raced a little as Levi Frost's name flashed up on caller ID.

She took a deep breath as she pressed answer. "Hi, Levi."

"Hey, Bridgette. I thought I would catch you in the office today, but you're gone already?"

"I left about ten AM. I'm up in West Vancouver today on the Halloran case. I'm re-interviewing some of the locals. I'm hoping someone might have seen or heard something that wasn't in the original report."

"Yeah, I spoke to the chief. You're in a tough spot." Frost paused a moment and then said, "Also... there was something I wanted to talk to you about."

Bridgette's heart skipped a beat. *What does he want to talk about?* She said nothing and waited. To her disappointment, Frost took a tangent she hadn't expected.

"I saw someone last night that I haven't seen since my days in undercover. He's got a pretty good network inside the Vancouver crime scene. I asked him to let me know if he hears any talk about the Halloran murders now that it's back in the news again. I hope you don't mind me reaching out to him. I don't think he trusts any other cops, so..."

Bridgette frowned as Delray's words, "We need to be discrete," echoed in her mind again. She would have preferred Frost to talk to her first, but what was done was done.

She chose her words carefully. "Probably nothing will come of it, Levi. But thanks for trying. Have you told the chief?"

"No. Not yet anyway."

Bridgette walked Frost through the sensitivities of the case now that the Vancouver police were planning on charging Chilton for the second murder.

"Yikes. I don't want to get you or the chief in trouble. Sorry, I should have checked."

"Don't worry about it, Levi. Right now, I can use all the help I can get."

There was a pause before Frost said, "Are you coming back into the office later?"

"Maybe. I don't know. It depends on how my interviews go here and what I can turn up."

"Perhaps we could get together tonight, then? The other night… there were things I wanted to talk to you about, but I got sidetracked…"

Bridgette's mind screamed, *'What things do you want to talk about?'* but she wasn't about to ask that question. Instead, she said, "That sounds nice," and then rolled her eyes at her lame response.

"Do you want to pick the restaurant this time?"

Bridgette didn't fancy another restaurant meal and knew Frost only had a studio apartment. "How about you come over to my apartment? We can order some takeout and talk without any distractions?"

"Okay… but I don't want to impose."

"You're not imposing, Levi. And I think it will be good for us to talk."

"Yeah… I agree. For me, this is… overdue."

"Let's aim for seven if that's okay? If anything changes on my end, I'll call."

"Sounds great. I'm looking forward to it already."

Frost disconnected and left Bridgette to her thoughts again. She smiled, little knowing it would be the last time she would experience such joy for an extended period.

Chapter Thirteen

Bridgette stepped out of her car and made her way along Kew Road to a large two-story colonial house with an imposing facade. Set back from the road, the house was encircled by tall trees and had one unique feature that separated it from others in the neighborhood. Tessa and Fiona Halloran were on vacation in this house when someone murdered them.

She paused for a moment and let her thoughts wander as she stared up at the dwelling. The curtains were drawn, and the towering trees around the building cast a permanent shadow over the structure. Bridgette didn't believe in evil spirits, but the house had a vibe that seemed to know about the past misfortunes of its residents.

Bridgette knew it was pointless interviewing the new owners. The house had sold six years earlier and was no longer available for rent. She turned her attention to the neighboring houses and walked back up the road to the first house on the left. This house was a brown two-storey colonial and was set back from the road in a mature garden. Bridgette walked up the driveway and checked her watch as she reached the front door. It was just before eleven AM on a Wednesday. Not a good time to be door-knocking when most people were at work. She took heart from a white, late model Mini Cooper parked in the driveway as she knocked.

A woman in her early fifties opened the door a moment later. She was wearing a pink and gray knitted top over a pair of denim jeans. Her hair was streaked with gray and her expression was one of wariness. Bridgette guessed she was expecting to be pressured into buying something or receiving salvation.

"Can I help you?" she asked.

Bridgette flashed her badge and introduced herself. The woman frowned when Bridgette mentioned she was re-interviewing neighbors about the Halloran murders.

"I'm sorry, Detective. I don't think I can be of much help to you. This is my mother's house, and I only moved in four years ago after my divorce."

"I see," said Bridgette with a nod. "Your mother… does she still live here?"

"Yes, she does. But she's had a stroke and is quite frail. She's sleeping at present and I'd rather not wake her."

"That's alright. I'm in the area for most of the day. What time would be convenient to come back?"

The woman checked her watch. "She normally wakes for lunch around mid-day." The woman frowned and added, "I'm positive my mother was interviewed all those years ago when that awful business happened. I'm not sure she can tell you anything more."

Bridgette half smiled. "I'm sure you're right, Ma'am. But we have to check." She explained how Remmy Chilton had walked free at the end of the first trial and added,

"We're just being thorough. We don't want any surprises the second time around."

The woman nodded. "Well… we don't want a murderer roaming around free, so if you think it will help, I'll make sure she's ready around lunchtime. Her name is Dorothy."

Bridgette thanked the woman for her time and promised to return after mid-day. She murmured to herself, "At least its something," as she walked back down the driveway. Although it wasn't an ideal start to her interviews, it was hopefully a small step forward.

Bridgette spent the next hour knocking on doors of the other witnesses in the neighborhood without success. Most people weren't at home, which forced her to leave business cards with a handwritten request to call her ASAP.

She trudged back to the house where she had started and murmured, "Well, Dorothy, let's hope you can remember something," as she walked up the driveway.

After knocking, she was greeted by the same woman as last time. This time, the woman introduced herself as Alice as she led Bridgette inside. She showed Bridgette into a formal living room. "My mother has just woken up, Detective, so I'll need a minute."

Bridgette told Alice to take her time and then sat down to wait. The living room was about twenty feet long and featured two sofas, a piano and a sideboard with stained-glass doors. Several landscape paintings hung on off-white walls and there was a navy rug on the floor to complete the decor. Its musty smell, like old books, made Bridgette think everything belonged to Dorothy and not her daughter.

A moment later, Alice wheeled Dorothy into the living

room. Bridgette guessed Dorothy was in her early seventies. The woman's frame was slight and her pale hands trembled as they clutched the edges of a black and white checkered shawl, that she wore draped across her shoulders. Despite her frailty, her gaze was clear and sharp as it focused on Bridgette.

Alice brought the wheelchair to a stop in the middle of the room and introduced Bridgette to her mother. Bridgette rose from her chair and exchanged a handshake with Dorothy, letting her know that she was pleased to meet her.

When Bridgette had settled back in her chair, Alice said, "Well, this is a work day for me, so I'm going to get back to it."

As they waited for Alice to leave, Dorothy said, "She's a company accountant but she mostly works on her computer. I'm darned if I know how she gets her job done, because she doesn't go into the office much."

Bridgette was surprised by Dorothy's remark. Despite her frailty, it seemed clear the woman still had her senses about her. She smiled politely and said, "Alice seems a very capable woman."

Dorothy grimaced. "I'd be lost without her. She does everything for me."

Keen to steer the subject onto the Halloran murders, Bridgette said, "So, have you lived here for long, Dorothy?"

The woman nodded. "Almost forty years. When my husband and I bought this house, we were one of only a few in the area."

"I guess a lot has changed."

"And not all of it good," said Dorothy with a frown. Her expression darkened further as she added, "Alice tells me you're here to talk about the murder of those girls?"

"I hope that won't be to upsetting for you."

Dorothy clutched at her shawl again. "They were so young… it was such a tragedy."

"Did you know them very well?"

"Not really. The family used to hire the house next door for a couple of weeks each summer. They'd been coming since the girls were babies, but we never got to know them very well."

"Do you remember much about the last time they were here?"

Dorothy frowned. "We never saw them much. They were mostly grown up by then and would go out a lot on their own."

Bridgette clarified, "When you say '*we*,' who do you mean?"

"I'm sorry honey, I meant my husband, Jim. He lived here with me until eight years ago." Dorothy's lip quivered as she added, "Heart attack. One minute he's out the back working in the garden, and the next, he's in an ambulance on his way to hospital."

"I'm sorry to hear that."

"He was dead before they got him out of the ambulance. I never really recovered. I think that's what caused my stroke."

Bridgette nodded and gave Dorothy a moment to compose herself and then said, "I guess you and Jim followed the murder case thirteen years ago?"

"Yes, we would watch all the reports on the TV, and Jim would read the paper each day. We couldn't believe it when the man who did it walked free."

"Yes, it was quite a shock for a lot of people."

"My daughter tells me the man is going to be retried? I didn't think you could do that?"

Bridgette explained how only one of the murder cases

had gone to trial and Chilton had been recently recaptured at the border. She chose her words carefully as she told Dorothy that both the detectives who had investigated the murders had retired and that she was familiarizing herself with the case for the impending trial.

"Well, I'm not sure I can tell you anything more than I told the other detectives, but I'd like to see that man put away behind bars where he belongs."

"Did you ever see him around here?"

"No. That's what the detectives wanted to know. Had we seen him before, or anyone else suspicious. We told them it was a quiet neighborhood and we kept to ourselves."

"Did you see the girls on the day of the murder?"

"Not exactly…"

Bridgette leaned forward. "Not exactly?"

"Jim and I were out in the backyard watering some plants. The house next door has a gate in the rear fence that you can use as a short cut to go down to Gulf Beach. The twins used it often. But we can't see it on account of all the bushes and trees."

"So what happened."

"The girls had an argument at the back fence is what happened."

"What were they arguing about?"

Dorothy frowned. "They had a big row about going down to the beach." Dorothy closed her eyes as she tried to remember. Bridgette had many questions, but she didn't want to disrupt the woman's thoughts.

Dorothy opened her eyes. "They were arguing about something one of them didn't think was right. One of them said, he's going to get us in trouble. I remember Jim said to me later, it sounds like one of them has a boyfriend because he heard them saying 'him' several times too while they argued."

"So what happened next?"

"Well… the yelling went on for about a minute. It was quite uncivilized. They were still screaming at each other as one of them left and the other stormed back into the house."

"One of them went back inside?"

"Yes. I've never heard a door slam so hard in my life. Jim said it's a wonder it didn't come off its hinges."

"And what time was this?"

"I'm not sure, Detective," said Dorothy with a shake of her head. "The parents had gone out for the day and weren't home yet. My guess is it was close to five, but we weren't watching the time. We were so disgusted we both went back inside."

Bridgette's frown deepened. She hadn't remembered reading about the argument in Dorothy's original testimony. "Did the detectives ask about any of this when they questioned you?"

"I don't remember," said Dorothy with a frown. "They mostly wanted to know if we had seen the man they arrested anywhere in the area. We said 'No,' and they didn't ask us much else. I don't think the argument came up. And we were in so much shock about what happened we forgot to mention it. I'm sorry, Detective."

"That's okay, Dorothy," soothed Bridgette. "This is helpful information." Bridgette pulled out her phone and flicked through her photos to the picture she had taken of the Polaroid photo. She held her phone up and said, "This is a photo that was taken by one of the girls a few days before their deaths. Do you recognize the man?"

Dorothy studied the image for a moment and shook her

head. "No. I don't believe I've ever seen him. Is he a suspect as well?"

Bridgette replied, "Not at this stage," but her mind was racing ahead. Dorothy's information had been invaluable. Although there were still many missing pieces, she now had a clearer sense of where the investigation should be heading.

Chapter Fourteen

Bridgette walked across the marina parking lot, her mind still processing the things she had learned that day. She walked up a set of steps that led to Mac's diner, her mouth salivating a little at the unmistakable aroma of food cooking coming from within. It was nearly closing time and only two customers remained with almost empty coffee cups in front of them.

Bridgette was happy the diner was close to empty. That meant she could interview Mac quickly and be on her way. He saw her approach and raised a quizzical eyebrow. "I didn't expect to see you back so soon, Detective?"

"Hi, Mac. I hope you don't mind, but I've got a couple more questions for you."

"Sure thing," said Mac with a shrug, "But I don't know if I can tell you any more?"

Bridgette pulled out her phone and scrolled through until she found the copy of the Polaroid of the young man standing with one of the twins. She handed it to Mac and said, "Have you ever seen him before?"

"This is one of the twins, right?" said Mac with a frown. Bridgette nodded.

Mac scratched his chin. "The girls mainly came in on their own. Maybe a few times each week when they were up here on holiday. I got to know the family quite well." He handed the phone back and said, "He looks familiar, but it was a long time ago."

"When you say familiar, do you mean you think you've seen him here, or he just looks like someone who may have come in?"

"I mean, I *think* I saw him here one day… with the twins."

"Was this just before they were murdered?"

Mac pursed his lips while he thought. "I guess. They ordered burgers and sat at one of the tables here while they ate."

"Did it seem like they were just friends, or was there more going on between them?"

"Like boyfriend and girlfriend?"

"Yes."

"I don't recall. Summer's are busy here and I'm run off my feet. So, I don't really notice what goes on out there unless someone's making a nuisance of themselves."

"You don't recall which twin he was hanging out with?"

Mac laughed. "The girls looked identical to me, so I couldn't tell you that. All I know is, he seemed to be close to one of them, and the other guy seemed to be teamed up with the other one."

"The other guy?" said Bridgette with a frown.

"There were four of them here. The twins and two young guys."

Bridgette checked her watch and sighed as she got into her car. She realized she couldn't brief Delray at the office and be home for dinner with Levi Frost by seven PM. Her gut tightened; the girl's murder deserved her full focus, but she couldn't ignore Levi's plea to meet. She dialed Delray's number from memory and crossed her fingers, hoping he would pick up.

Delray answered a moment later with his usual economy of words. "I've got five minutes, Bridgette. Then I have a meeting with Cunningham."

"Thanks for taking my call, Chief. I'll try to keep this brief."

Bridgette recounted her meeting with Dorothy, and how she had learned about the argument between the two girls shortly before they were murdered. Her words tumbled out in a rush as she explained how they were meeting someone.

Delray listened without interrupting. There was a pause before he replied, "So, lemme get this straight. The girls had a fight and only one of them went to the meetup?"

"That's correct, Chief."

"So how come we have two dead girls if only one of them left the house?"

"I've been giving that some thought. According to Dorothy, the disagreement may not have been about the meeting, but what they would be doing once they were together. One twin said words to the effect that they we're going to get in trouble."

"So, what are we talking about here? Underage age drinking, drugs, sex?"

"I don't know yet, Chief. That's going to need more investigation."

"But that still doesn't explain two dead girls. Didn't you say one stayed at the house?"

"The bond between twins is very strong—typically a lot stronger than normal siblings. It's not hard to imagine the twin who stayed behind, having second thoughts about letting her sister go on her own. She may have cooled off and then went to find her. Dorothy and her husband would've been inside by then and probably didn't hear her leave."

"Okay, that makes sense. And it may explain why they weren't discovered together."

"There's one other thing you need to know."

"Better make it quick."

"I went back to the burger place and showed the owner the photo of one twin with the young man."

"Did he recognize him?"

"He was reasonably confident he'd seen him at his diner with the girls."

"Okay, now we're getting somewhere."

"But that's not all." Bridgette then recounted her conversation with Mac and how he had informed her that the girls had met with two young men, not one.

"When was this?"

"He's not sure of the date, but it was a day or two before they were murdered."

"And none of this is in the original case file, right?"

"Right."

Delray grumbled, "This is what happens when you only follow one line of inquiry. They had the cap and when they matched Chilton's voice to the caller who reported the murder, they thought they had their murderer."

"I think I'm only scratching the surface, Chief," said Bridgette.

Delray let out an audible sigh as he murmured, "What a mess."

"Also, I asked Dorothy what time she thought the argument occurred."

"And what did she say?"

"She thinks it was close to five PM."

"And they were both dead about half an hour later…"

"Yes."

There was a long pause. Delray said, "If this is true, and the girls were supposed to be meeting up with two guys, it's hard to see how Chilton is responsible. Particularly if he didn't leave the burger place until shortly after five."

"I agree, Chief. I think Remmy Chilton has been telling the truth all along."

"We need to figure out the identity of those two young men. The photo is a good starting point, but it's going to require a lot more work."

"I agree. It will be my focus tomorrow."

Delray let out another long sigh. "I have to go. I'm late for my meeting with Cunningham. And boy, is it going to get ugly."

"Because you're going to be late?"

"No. They've got a press conference organized for tomorrow morning to give the start date for the Chilton trial."

"They? As in the commissioner and Richard Temple?"

"No. As in Assistant Commissioner Cunningham and Richard Temple. He and Temple have known each other for a long time and the commissioner is leaving for a conference on Friday. He thinks it's better if Cunningham takes the lead on all the press conferences for this case for continuity."

Bridgette knew Cunningham liked to talk about himself and would enjoy the opportunity provided by a press conference.

"He's not going to like what you have to tell him."

"No. But he's pig-headed. I doubt this is going to make any difference."

"You think he'll press ahead? Surely the evidence—"

"I've worked with Cunningham for twenty-five years and I know what he's like. If Temple gets himself elected, he could quickly become a key political player in law and order in this town. And if that happens, we could wind up with Cunningham as commissioner."

"Wow. I'd never thought about it like that."

"Cunningham's not a very good police officer. But as someone who knows how to play political games to climb the ladder, there's none better."

"Well… good luck, Chief."

"Thanks, I'm gonna need it."

Chapter Fifteen

Felix Delray had never liked his boss. He pondered what he would say while riding the elevator to the fourth floor. He had a bad feeling about the Halloran case. It didn't matter how he approached it, Cunningham was not going like what he had to say. Delray had seen several good police officers forced from their positions because they had defied him. He wouldn't go that far, but he would stand his ground. Cunningham was hoping to gain favor with Richard Temple, but he would be quick to pass the blame on to his team if things went awry.

Delray was used to arguments with his boss and decided on his strategy as the elevator door opened on the fourth floor. He steeled himself for what was ahead as he walked along the corridor of the executive suite. Despite Cunningham's threats, he wasn't afraid of him. But their constant bickering had worn him down. He would need to control his language and his temper. He admonished himself to hold it together as he knocked on Cunningham's open office door.

Cunningham sat at his desk. His boss was in his late forties with thinning light brown hair. His Adam's apple stuck out a little, accentuated by his slim frame, which rumor suggested resulted from a picky diet. Cunningham had relished his six-year tenure as assistant commissioner. His office was large and featured its own en-suite bathroom and original oil paintings on the walls. By comparison, Delray's office was the size of a phone booth, but he couldn't have cared less—he had no desire for an office or a role on the fourth floor. As usual, Cunningham busied himself looking at something on his computer screen, even though he had clearly heard the knock. Delray rolled his eyes. He knew making him wait was another one of Cunningham's petty mind games to show who was boss.

Finally, Cunningham looked his way. "Come in, Chief Inspector."

Delray walked in and sat in one of the three visitors chairs on the opposite side of Cunningham's desk.

Cunningham swiveled away from his computer and looked at Delray. "We're holding a press conference tomorrow at ten AM for the Halloran case. I need an update on the prisoner to pass on to Senior Prosecutor Temple. Has he revised his testimony?"

"No, Sir. It's pretty much word for word to the original he gave thirteen years ago."

"That should make it simple."

Delray felt his gut tighten as he responded, "I'm not so sure, Sir."

"What do you mean?" demanded Cunningham.

Delray let out a long breath. "We don't think Chilton killed the girls, Sir..."

Cunningham's eyes widened. "What the hell are you talking about? We have charged him murder."

"I've had one of my team go back over his original statement. The timeline is too tight for Chilton to commit two murders. He couldn't have made it from the marina to the woodlands and back again to make the nine-one-one call in the time window."

"I'm not interested," bellowed Cunningham. "And who authorized you to spend resources on this?"

"Sir, this was my decision."

Cunningham raised an eyebrow. "And what gives you the right to make such a decision?"

"I made it because the original detectives are no longer on the force and we need familiarity with the case."

Cunningham clasped his hands together and leaned forward. Barely able to control his anger, he said, "I'm not sure if you're aware, Chief Inspector, but the decision to prosecute Remmy Chilton was made on the basis that nothing about the case has changed. We still have two dead girls, and we can prove Chilton was at the crime scene. He left his DNA there, for God's sake. And the commissioner approved the charges. What more do you want?"

Delray attempted to explain that Remmy Chilton had likely just found Fiona Halloran's body, but Cunningham silenced him by raising his hand. "I'm not interested. And I forbid any further use of police resources on this. We have a man in custody, a man who we would have put in jail thirteen years ago if the lab had done its job properly."

"Sir, I respectfully disagree. I think we need to investigate this further, just to be sure. We don't need a repeat of the embarrassment that happened—"

"And if the press finds out we're not sure we've got the right man, you don't think that's going to be embarrassing?" thundered Cunningham.

"We've been discrete so far, Sir."

"This stops now! And that's an order!"

Delray took a deep breath. He knew what he was about to say could cost him his career. "Sir, I'll put what I have in writing to you and the commissioner, so that it's on the record. If you decide to over-rule, that's your decision."

Cunningham's face turned red. "You need to respect the chain of command, Chief Inspector. This is not your call."

"Sir, with all due respect, I think the commissioner deserves to see that report."

Cunningham pointed a finger at Delray. "This is my first and final warning. If you bring the commissioner in on this, your career is as good as over."

"Noted, Sir."

Cunningham held Delray's gaze and said, "Close the door on your way out."

Bridgette shifted on her kitchen stool and checked the time on her phone again. It was now just after nine and there was still no sign of Frost. She frowned as she wondered what the hold up was. Frost rarely sent text messages, but he would always call and apologize if he was running late. She wondered if he had forgotten about their dinner, but quickly dismissed that idea as she replayed their last conversation over in her mind. No, Frost was keen to talk and he wouldn't have forgotten.

She wondered if the battery in his phone was flat as she checked her messages again for about the tenth time in as many minutes. Only one new message had come in and that was from Renee Filipucci. Bridgette swiveled her phone around in her hand as she weighed up what to do. She had already sent Frost two messages—gentle, tactful messages reminding him of their dinner date.

She frowned again. Perhaps a call would be best? She dialed his number from memory and felt butterflies in her stomach as it connected. After eight rings, the call went through to voicemail and Frost's baritone voice greeted her and asked her to leave a message.

Bridgette debated disconnecting until she heard the beep. "Hi Levi, it's Bridgette. Just calling to… let you know that dinner is in the oven keeping warm. You must have been held up, so… come when you can or… call me. Okay, talk soon."

Bridgette shook her head as she disconnected, and then cursed herself for leaving such a lame voicemail message.

She sighed as she sat for a moment, contemplating what she should do next. She glanced across at the oven and realized it had been at least fifteen minutes since she had checked their meal. Bridgette removed the warming dish that contained the spicy chicken meatballs in rice that she had cooked earlier and lifted the lid. It was one of Frost's favorites, but it looked a little dry, so she added half a cup of water and stirred it through the ingredients. After returning the dish to the oven to keep it warm she sat on her stool again and contemplated what she would do while she waited.

She knew she could call Filipucci, but she didn't want to be on another call just in case Frost called her back. She contemplated responding to Filipucci's previous text message, but what would she say? If she told Renee that Frost hadn't arrived yet, that would spark a flurry of messages from her friend—questions that she didn't want to answer.

She looked at her front door again, willing Frost to

knock. As if by magic, she heard a sharp three knock rap. Bridgette smiled as she got off her stool and headed for the front door. She had a security peephole, but didn't bother to use it. She was sure Frost would have a good a good excuse for being late as she flung the door open and said, "Hi, Lev—"

Bridgette's face dropped as she stared into the eyes of her boss, Felix Delray.

Delray wore a grim expression, a grimmer one than she had ever seen him wear before.

"Chief, this is a little… unexpected."

"You mind if I come in?"

Bridgette showed Delray through to her small living room and offered him a seat on her couch. She pulled up a chair and said, "I guess the meeting with Cunningham didn't go so well?"

Delray grimaced as he shook his head. "This has nothing to do with Cunningham."

"Okay… then what?"

Delray's features grew even darker. "There's been an accident."

Bridgette felt her gut tighten. "What kind of accident?"

"It's… Levi. He's been involved in a hit-and-run."

"He was hit by a car?" asked Bridgette with a frown.

Delray nodded. "It happened in Gastown about six this evening. I don't have all the details yet, but it looks deliberate."

Bridgette stood up. "Is he badly hurt?"

Delray sighed and nodded at the same time. "He's in emergency right now. I think they're operating on him, but I don't have much information."

"How bad?"

"It's pretty bad, Bridgette," said Delray with a grimace. "They're not sure he'll pull through."

Bridgette closed her eyes and threw back her head as she screamed, "No!"

A moment later she felt herself falling and then felt Delray's arms wrap around her. They stood in the middle of her living room for a long time. The silence was only broken by Bridgette as she wept uncontrollably on her boss's shoulder.

Chapter Sixteen

Bridgette stared at the monitor, her breath catching in her throat as she watched the green line rise and fall with each of Frost's heartbeats. His breathing was labored and his pulse weak. She held onto hope with each beep that this wouldn't be the way her partner met his end.

She switched her gaze back to the bed. Frost's body was motionless beneath the sheets, oblivious to the tubes and cables that connected him to various machines. He was alive, though barely. Choking back a sob as she stared at his almost completely bandaged face, she murmured, "This doesn't get you out of our date, Levi. When you're better, I'm holding you to it."

She checked her watch; it was eleven-thirty five PM. She and Delray had rushed to the hospital directly from her apartment, but when they arrived, they only got as far as the waiting room. Delray was able to sit and wait. But Bridgette paced as she awaited news of her partner's condition.

After two hours, a doctor emerged and told them they had moved Frost to the intensive care unit, but refused to give them any more information because they weren't next-of-kin. Bridgette had gone straight to Frost's room, while Delray had gone in search of more information about his condition. Now, as she sat alone at his bedside, she realized how fragile life was as Frost hovered between life and death.

Delray interrupted her thoughts as he walked into the room. He came and stood alongside her as he murmured, "How is he?"

"No change," said Bridgette without taking her eyes off Frost. "The nurse took his vitals a few minutes ago and said he was weak, but stable."

Delray grimaced. "Well, at least he's not going backwards."

"What did you find out?"

Delray rolled his eyes. "I had to pull my badge before they'd tell me anything. I spoke to the orthopedic surgeon first—he says he's got a cracked pelvis, five broken ribs, and a broken femur. The pelvis and ribs shouldn't require surgery, but his left leg took the brunt of the hit from the car. It's broken in two places and requires plates and screws…" Delray grimaced and then added, "But that's not the worst of it. He fractured his skull when he hit the pavement and its now the swelling on the brain that they're most worried about. Surgery could kill him, so they've put his leg in a splint for now."

Bridgette bit down on her lip as she nodded.

Delray continued, "I also caught up with the neurosurgeon. They've got him in an induced coma and are monitoring him closely."

Doing her best to hold back tears, she asked, "Did they say anything about his chances of pulling through?"

"They're more cagey than a bunch of politicians," growled Delray. "The best I could get out of them was the next twenty-four hours are critical. Whatever the hell that means."

"Did anyone see it?"

"The accident?"

Bridgette nodded.

"Not that we know of."

"So, we don't know if it was an accident or deliberate?"

"No. We have detectives working on it, but so far they're just collecting statements and CCTV footage to piece together what happened."

Bridgette took a deep breath to calm her nerves. Normally, her brain would be in analytical mode by now; assessing the facts in a structured, logical and organized manner. She felt the muscles in her neck tensing as she wrestled with her emotions. A tear trickled down her cheek as she gazed back at the bed. She couldn't believe it was an accident; Frost's years of working undercover had left him highly attuned to his surroundings, no matter where he was.

Delray added, "The neurosurgeon is going to check in on him in about half an hour. If the pressure on his brain gets worse, they'll have to operate. But no one wants to do that right now, because…"

Delray's voice trailed off. Bridgette didn't need him to complete his sentence to know none of the doctors were confident he would live through the night.

"I guess all we can do is wait," said Bridgette.

"Levi's a fighter. He's not gonna give up easy."

"Have we contacted his mother?"

Delray nodded. "She's the legal next-of-kin, but she lives in Toronto. She took the news pretty hard, but is on the first flight out tomorrow. We don't expect her here until mid-afternoon."

They were quiet for a while before Delray said, "I think

I'm gonna head for home. I gotta be back in the office for an eight o'clock meeting with Cunningham about this."

Bridgette said, "I'd like to stay with him. He shouldn't be on his own tonight."

Delray nodded. "I figured you'd say that. I talked to the head nurse. Since there's no next-of-kin here, you can stay if that's what you want. They're happy to give you a blanket and a pillow for your chair, but they'll be in and out all night taking observations."

"I won't sleep anyway, so that's fine."

Delray said his goodbyes and left Bridgette alone with Frost and his monitors. Bridgette's mind was in overdrive. She knew him better than most and agreed with Delray; Frost was a fighter and wouldn't let go easily.

She moved her chair a little closer to his bed. Gently, she squeezed his hand and murmured, "I'm here, Levi. You're not doing this on your own."

She said a brief prayer and then returned her gaze to the monitor. The green line continued its rise and fall. It was going to be a long night.

Chapter Seventeen

Delray tossed and turned for most of the night. Bridgette had promised to call him if Frost's condition worsened, but he had received no calls. Every hour or so, he had picked up his phone from his bedside table to see if he had any text updates from Bridgette. There had only been one at 6:45 AM as he was getting ready to hit the shower:

'Hi Chief. Levi has made it through the night. No real change to report. The neurosurgeon will be in just after 7 to check on him. I'll give you an update when I know more. Regards BC'

Delray had skipped breakfast—a meal he usually relished. But the worry of one of his team still hovering between life and death had robbed him of his appetite. His wife knew about the meeting he was to have with Cunningham and encouraged him to remain calm and not get emotional. Now, as the elevator opened on the executive level of police headquarters, Delray was unsure if he could follow her advice. He knew Cunningham would pepper him with questions and the threat of firing him for telling the truth weighed heavily on his mind. He wondered about the questions. Cunningham would no doubt frame them so that he could use Delray's answers to distance himself and the force from whatever happened to Frost should the need arise.

As he walked to his boss's office, his mood darkened. His watch read 7:56 AM—too early to knock, so he sat in reception, mumbling a "good morning" to the efficient, Executive Assistant Kathy Rayner.

Rayner looked up from a document she was reading and said, "You can go in, Chief Inspector. The commissioner is expecting you."

Delray frowned. "I'm actually here to see Assistant Commissioner Cunningham."

Rayner shook her head. "There's been a change of plan. The commissioner wants to be a part of this meeting. Weren't you informed?"

"Not that I'm aware of," grumbled Delray as he got up from his chair.

Delray knocked twice on the commissioner's door and was greeted by a "Come in" from inside.

Delray opened the door and walked into the spacious office. Commissioner Underwood was seated at his desk as expected, but there was no sign of Cunningham. Underwood was a man in his late fifties with a close-cropped salt and pepper haircut, with salt now the dominant color.

Delray had a great deal of respect for Underwood and was relaxed in his company, particularly on the few occasions when Cunningham wasn't present. He said, "Good morning, Sir," as he sat down and added, "Is the Assistant Commissioner joining us?"

Underwood removed his glasses. "He will be in a few

minutes. I've asked him to delay this morning's press conference until mid-day. Given what happened last night to Detective Frost, I'm sure the reporters will have questions about his condition as well, and I want to make sure we're fully briefed before we say anything."

Delray nodded. "I think that's wise, Sir."

The commissioner leaned forward. "I learned of Detective Frost's accident last night, but I have no details except that he was struck by a car. How's he doing?"

"He's still alive, Sir, but it's pretty bad," said Delray. "I'm expecting an update from Detective Cash any minute now."

Underwood nodded. "If she calls during this meeting, feel free to take it. I'd appreciate the update as well."

"Certainly, Sir."

Underwood grimaced. "I know I'm putting you on the spot here, but do you think it was deliberate?"

Before Delray could answer, they were interrupted by a knock at the door. Underwood said, "That will be Cunningham," and then added, "Come in," in a louder voice.

Delray heard the door open behind him but didn't turn around. His skin almost crawled as he listened to the nasal twang of Assistant Commissioner Leo Cunningham's voice as he said, "The press conference has been pushed back to noon, Sir," as he walked into the room. He added, "I'll give you a briefing about it as soon as it's finished," as he sat beside Delray without acknowledging him.

Underwood said, "Thanks, Leo, that's appreciated. However, given recent events, I have decided to hold the press conference with the senior prosecutor myself."

Delray waited until he was in the elevator heading back to the second floor before he allowed himself a smile. With Frost hovering between life and death, there wasn't much to smile about today, but seeing Leo Cunningham humiliated by his boss was a moment he would savor for a long time.

The meeting turned sour for Cunningham when Underwood insisted on doing the Halloran press conference. It only worsened when the commissioner asked Delray for an update on the case.

Cunningham had tried to gag Delray by giving the update himself. He was insistent that everything was on track to proceed to trial. However, Underwood seemed less than convinced and wanted to hear from Delray directly. Despite Cunningham's protests, Delray had given Underwood his honest appraisal of Bridgette's investigation. It was clear from the commissioner's body language that Cunningham had not told his boss about the possibility that Remmy Chilton was innocent. Delray had only lasted another sixty seconds before he had been excused from the meeting.

He sighed as he headed down in the elevator to level two. There would be payback from Cunningham for embarrassing him in front of the commissioner, but Underwood had a right to know all the facts. At least he could make informed decisions about how he wanted to proceed. Delray checked his watch and frowned as he stepped out onto the second floor. He expected to have heard from Bridgette by now and decided he couldn't wait any longer. Upon entering his office, he reached for his phone and dialed her number from speed dial.

Bridgette had spent the night in vigil beside Levi's bed. Her eyes were heavy from lack of sleep and her movements sluggish with exhaustion as she now waited outside Frost's room. Her heart skipped a beat as she checked her watch. The neurosurgeon had been in with Levi for over ten minutes. Was this a good sign, a bad sign, or just a doctor being thorough?

As far as she could tell, Levi seemed no better or worse than when he had entered the ICU the night before. She had watched him carefully; each breath, each twitch, each flicker of his eyelids. She figured if his condition had worsened, the nurses, who made half-hourly observations, would have called for assistance.

She stared at the door to Frost's room, willing it to open. Life had thrown her some unexpected curve balls, but never before had she felt so helpless. She sighed as she tried to block out negative thoughts. She knew that so much of what would unfold over the coming days was beyond her control —all she could do now was focus on staying calm despite the overwhelming uncertainty of Frost's condition.

The door opened, and the doctor walked out. Her heart raced as she walked towards him, bracing for what would come next. The neurosurgeon, a man in his early forties with thinning blonde hair, stopped and gave her a curt nod. Bridgette tried to read his body language, but he gave nothing away.

She asked, "How is he?"

"I've run some more tests and examined the data," he said solemnly. "It appears he's no worse, but his condition is still critical."

The doctor sighed heavily and warned that if Frost's condition worsened even slightly, he could be gone within an hour or two. Bridgette held back tears as she asked about his chances of survival and whether he would have brain damage, but the doctor was coy with his response.

"All we can do for now is wait. We won't really know much more until the swelling goes down. Until then, we need to keep him in an induced coma."

The neurosurgeon reassured Bridgette that Frost was getting the best of care and told her he would check in again around lunchtime. In a daze, she returned to Frost's bedside, clinging to the doctor's words, 'he's no worse.'

As she stared down at her partner, Bridgette's phone buzzed. It was Delray.

Bridgette pressed answer and managed, "Hi."

Delray got to the point, just as she had with the neurosurgeon. "How is he?"

Bridgette bit down on her bottom lip as she looked at Frost through eyes that began to fill with tears again. She managed, "He's alive, Chief. The surgeon says he's stable but still critical."

There was a pause before Delray replied, "Well... I guess that's something."

Bridgette relayed her conversation with the neurosurgeon as best she could.

When she finished, Delray said, "How are you holding up?"

Bridgette let out a long sigh to compose herself. The truth was Levi Frost meant more to her than she had ever cared to admit. But she wasn't ready to share that thought with anyone, not even Renee Filipucci. She responded, "I'm going okay. A little tired, but... this is where I need to be."

"Well, hopefully you'll have some support there shortly. I got a text from Frost's mother to say she's arriving early afternoon."

Bridgette nodded. "That's good. Whatever happens, his mom should be here."

"I'm organizing an airport pickup for her. I'm assuming you'll stay with Levi until then?"

"Yes. If that's okay? I know I should be working the Halloran case, but—"

"Don't bother about work, Bridgette. Stay there until Levi's mother arrives, and then maybe you can head home for a few hours sleep."

"Thanks, Chief. I'm sorry about the case. I know—"

"Don't worry about it, Bridgette. I had a bit of a breakthrough with the commissioner on that one…"

Delray filled her in on the details of his meeting with the commissioner, but Bridgette heard very little. She ended the call after promising to call her boss if Frost's condition deteriorated.

She glanced at the blue line on the monitor before returning her gaze to Frost again. She gave him a reassuring smile as she gently squeezed his hand. "It's going to be alright," she whispered softly. "Your Mom is on her way. Just hang in there a little longer."

Chapter Eighteen

Bridgette stared down at Frost, who remained motionless apart from the subtle rise and fall of his chest as he breathed. She took comfort from the constant beep of the monitors, which reminded her he was still alive and fighting.

She took a sip from a bottle of water, which the nurses had kindly provided her, along with an egg sandwich and a cup of coffee at lunchtime. She had quickly drained the coffee but had lingered with the sandwich—her appetite almost non-existent.

Bridgette craved sleep as she checked her watch. It was just after three PM, but she was unwilling to close her eyes even for a second. She wasn't naturally superstitious, but she had decided that staying awake gave her a special connection to Levi—a bond that was keeping him alive. She was unsure what would happen if she fell asleep. Would the bond be broken? Would he slip away peacefully and be gone before she awoke? She wasn't about to risk it and urged herself to stay vigilant.

She was conscious of a figure standing in the doorway.

In her near-delirious state, she initially thought it was a nurse, but as she focused, she saw a woman in her late fifties dressed in jeans and a black travel jacket. The woman had long gray hair tied back in a ponytail. She cupped her hand over her mouth as she stared at the bed. Bridgette rose to her feet as she realized this was Levi Frost's mother.

Frost's mother dissolved into tears. She dropped her bag and rushed into the room, seeming not to notice Bridgette's presence. Bridgette hung back a little and watched as the woman stood beside her son's bed, sobbing as she took in the sight of the tubes and cables that connected her son to various machines.

She gave the woman a few moments to process the shock of what she was seeing before coming forward. "You must be Levi's mom?"

The woman turned to Bridgette and wiped tears from her eyes. "Yes, I'm Eleanor. And you are?"

"I'm Bridgette. Levi's work partner. I'm so sorry..."

Eleanor Frost returned her gaze to her son. She shook her head and said, "I knew it was bad. They told me over the phone, but I didn't think it would be like this."

Bridgette paused, debating with herself how much to tell Levi's mother. After a deep breath, she decided Eleanor needed to hear everything. Her voice was gentle but firm as she told her the extent of her son's injuries and his chances of survival. She concluded by saying, "Levi is a fighter—I'm sure you know that. He's made it this far, and we have to remain positive for him. The neurosurgeon said the first seventy-two hours are critical. If he survives that long, he has a chance of making a recovery."

Eleanor nodded as she blinked back more tears. "You're right. We have to be strong for him." She let out a long sigh and then said, "How long have you been here?"

"I got here about nine last night. I came in with Chief Delray when we heard the news."

"So, you've been here all night?"

Bridgette nodded. "I didn't think it was right to leave him here alone. I've talked to him a little to reassure him that he's not on his own and he has people in his corner."

"Thank you, Bridgette. I really appreciate that."

Bridgette bit down on her bottom lip. "No problem."

They were silent momentarily before Eleanor said, "Levi doesn't have much family. His father left us when he was quite young. I've tried to contact him but only got as far as leaving a message."

Bridgette had never heard Frost refer to his father. Perhaps this was why, she thought. Tactfully, she said, "He talks about you all the time."

Eleanor dissolved into tears again. "He's a sweet boy. I'd be lost without him."

Bridgette motioned to the only chair in the room. "Would you like to sit? I know seeing him like this must be a shock."

Eleanor Frost sighed as she sat down. "I wasn't sure who to contact about Levi's accident. I thought I'd wait until I got here to see how he was." She glanced at Bridgette and added, "He's lived over here on the West Coast for almost ten years now. He comes home to see me a couple of times a year, but I really don't know who his friends are anymore. And there are no close relatives apart from me."

"It's alright, Eleanor," soothed Bridgette. "Most of his friends here are with the Vancouver police. My boss has made sure they all know about the accident, but only family are allowed to visit at present."

"I guess that's for the best."

"Now that you're here. I'm going to step out into the

hallway and call my boss if that's okay? I'm giving him regular updates, and he'll want to know you've arrived safely."

Eleanor Frost nodded once. "Thank him for organizing everything for me."

Bridgette struggled to stay awake during the next hour. After talking to Delray, she got a second chair brought to the room so that she could sit alongside Eleanor Frost. But conversation had been difficult. Eleanor was tense and Bridgette knew she was going through the same emotions she had experienced the night before. She had wondered if Eleanor would view her as a threat and try to push her away. But that hadn't happened—at least not yet. Even though she had been subdued, Eleanor had seemed glad for the company.

At close to five PM, Bridgette said, "The neurosurgeon should be here soon to check on Levi."

"He checks in regularly?"

Bridgette explained the routine. She concluded by saying, "They took Levi off for more scans at lunchtime, and the doctor thinks the swelling has stopped."

"I guess that's good?" said Eleanor with a frown.

Bridgette nodded. "Levi's condition appears to be stabilizing. The doctor was all doom and gloom yesterday, which is understandable. But today, he's a little more positive."

"I can't thank you enough for staying with him," said Eleanor, as her eyes welled up again. "Levi talks about you all the time. I was worried about him while he was in undercover. And then I wondered if he would ever fit back into regular police work."

Bridgette nodded. "It's a mother's prerogative to worry, Eleanor."

Eleanor stared down at her son. "He was just getting his life back. After his divorce, it seemed he had really lost his way. The job offer from Chief Delray came at just the right time, and he grabbed it with both hands."

"That he did," said Bridgette with another nod. "The chief has been thrilled with his work."

Eleanor's voice wavered a little as she said, "I remember he was very anxious when he first transferred to homicide. I'm sure you knew that. I could tell he still wasn't sure if he'd made the right decision. But as the weeks passed, I began to hear a joy in his voice that I hadn't heard in years. He enjoyed working with you and I know he was happy."

Bridgette felt a lump forming in her throat, but she didn't want to show her emotions to a woman she had just met. She kept her gaze firmly fixed on the monitors as she murmured, "We were both happy."

Chapter Nineteen

Bridgette felt her gaze becoming heavy. Her eyes were dry from lack of sleep—even attempting to blink was leaving them sore. It was close to six PM, and she had trouble focusing even for short moments.

The voice of Eleanor Frost cut through her dazed numbness as she asked, "How long have you been awake, Bridgette?"

Bridgette struggled to do the math. She responded, "I'm not sure. Maybe forty hours."

"I think you should take a break. It doesn't make sense for us both to be sitting here trying to stay awake. If we take it in shifts, someone can always be here with Levi."

Bridgette stared down at Frost's bed. "I didn't want to leave him, but now that you're here…"

Eleanor shifted in her chair and placed a hand on Bridgette's shoulder. "I know how much he means to you. If anything changes, I'll call you straight away. I promise."

Bridgette nodded, appreciative of Frost's mother's sincerity. She watched Frost's chest rise and fall as she pondered. She realized she couldn't stay up all night, and it would be better for Levi if someone were always there. "If you don't mind, I think I'll go home and get a few hours sleep."

"I think that's wise. I've been awake for about thirty hours and should be okay for a few more. Come back when you're rested. We can take turns to have someone here by his bedside."

"Do you have anywhere to go?" asked Bridgette with a frown. "You're welcome to stay at my apartment."

Eleanor Frost's eyes creased as she smiled. It was clear to Bridgette that her sentiment was one of gratitude. "Thank you, Bridgette, but they've offered me a bed here in the hospital since I'm from out of town." She reiterated her promise to call Bridgette if anything changed.

After getting home and showering, Bridgette slept for six hours and woke a little after two AM. She texted Eleanor Frost as soon as she woke to see how Levi was doing and got a prompt reply to say there was no change. They agreed Bridgette should return to the hospital to relieve Eleanor, who was having difficulty staying awake.

The twenty-minute drive back to the hospital gave her time to think. It was now close to thirty-six hours since Levi's accident. With each passing hour, she knew—or at least hoped—that Levi's chances of survival were improving. Refreshed from sleep, her analytical mind kicked back into gear. Delray had told her that security camera footage of the incident showed the hit-and-run looked deliberate but that none of their inquiries to date had yielded any leads. She wondered if they were taking the right approach. But it wasn't her case, and Delray had told her to stay on leave at least until Levi regained consciousness. Still, she might suggest to him her strategy when they next spoke.

Bridgette thought about the hospital again. She was ready for another long beside vigil and thankful for her friendly relationship with Eleanor. After stopping for a set of traffic lights near the hospital, she wondered what the woman had meant as she recalled her words, "I know how much he means to you."

Bridgette frowned as she shifted into gear and set off when the lights turned green. She was usually very careful with her words and rarely told anyone how she really felt. But perhaps it wasn't anything she had said? Maybe sitting by Levi's bedside for hours had given Eleanor a window into her deeper emotions, almost as if she could read her thoughts. She sighed as she pulled into the hospital parking lot. Since losing her parents, she instinctively kept people at arms length until she was sure she could trust them. But that was difficult with Eleanor Frost, who was uncovering things about her that she wasn't ready to share.

The next few hours passed slowly for Bridgette. Eleanor Frost had been grateful for her return and had immediately retreated to the room provided by the hospital to sleep. Bridgette was thankful for the time alone with Levi and had quietly talked to him while holding his hand. She started by telling him of her pride in his perseverance. She urged him to continue his fight and then spoke fondly about his mother, admitting that she had enjoyed Eleanor's company.

At just after seven AM, Frost's neurosurgeon appeared with two hospital orderlies. After a brief examination, the surgeon announced they would be taking Levi for more tests. Bridgette was initially alarmed until the neurosurgeon assured her the tests were just routine.

She had debated contacting Eleanor but decided to let her sleep. She would wait until the neurosurgeon returned hopefully with an update.

Bridgette stared at her watch again as she paced around Levi's room. It was nearly nine AM, and Levi had been gone for almost two hours.

Why is it taking so long? she thought. The tests the day before had only taken twenty minutes. *Had Levi suddenly deteriorated? Had they uncovered something that they had missed earlier?* She felt a knot in her stomach and admonished herself to stay calm. She heard footsteps in the corridor and turned to see the orderlies wheeling Levi's bed back into the room. Bridgette stared down at her partner. He was still unconscious but appeared to be breathing normally. A moment later, the neurosurgeon and a senior nurse entered. The neurosurgeon had his usual serious expression tattooed across his face, which revealed nothing.

Bridgette asked, "Everything okay?"

The neurosurgeon said, "Where's his mother?" while he kept a watchful eye on the nurses as Levi was hooked up to his monitors again.

Bridgette felt a rush of adrenaline course through her body as she feared the worst. "She's sleeping," she stammered. "We're taking it in turns so that someone is here with him all the time. Is he alright?"

The neurosurgeon frowned. "I should only be sharing this with his mother."

"Doctor, I've been here from the start. I can go and wake her if you like. What's happening?"

"I think that would be best. The swelling in Levi's brain is starting to subside."

"What does that mean?"

"I think we should wait for Levi's mother before I continue."

Bridgette rushed out of the room and returned five minutes later with Eleanor Frost. Eleanor had slept in her clothes, and her hair was a mess. But this was the furthest thing from her mind as she asked, "What can you tell us, Doctor Gibbs."

"As I said, the swelling in Levi's brain is starting to subside. That means it's now highly unlikely we'll need to do any emergency surgery."

Eleanor's hand came up to her face. "You think he's going to pull through?"

The neurosurgeon raised a cautious eyebrow. "It's early days, but we've adjusted his medication. We're removing the drugs that keep him in a coma and replacing them with painkillers."

"So... he's going to wake up soon?"

"It could be just a few hours, but I've seen some patients take up to seventy-two." The surgeon explained they had already made the changes to his drugs and had been closely monitoring Levi for the past hour.

Bridgette felt her breathing return to normal as Gibbs added, "Keeping Levi in an induced coma is a two-edged sword. On the one hand, it means he remains comfortable, and is in no distress. On the other, if there is any neural damage, it's best to determine what that is as soon as possible." Gibbs explained that diagnosing brain injuries wasn't an exact science and that Levi's brain scans were inconclusive. He indicated more tests would be required after Levi had regained consciousness. It would then take time to determine what treatment, if any, beyond bed rest was needed.

A million questions swirled through Bridgette's mind. But she deferred to Eleanor Frost, who said, "How soon will you know, Doctor Gibbs?"

"He's under constant monitoring from the nurses station and the anesthesiologist will continue to check in on him." The doctor was deliberately vague with the rest of his answer as he concluded, "Multiple factors are in play."

Bridgette said, "So, once he's regained consciousness and you've done your initial examination, you should know more?"

Gibbs nodded. "You could put it that way. I've been in touch with the orthopedic surgeon as well. It will be several days before the swelling goes down enough in his leg for surgery, but we need to factor that in as well."

Gibbs outlined the steps ahead, but Bridgette barely heard them as a wave of relief washed over her. She couldn't hold back her tears as she realized Levi was now likely to survive. But her relief was tempered. Broken bones were one thing, but brain damage was quite another. She hoped they would have an answer to that question later in the day.

Chapter Twenty

It was no secret that Blaine Underwood loved his job. He thrived on the pace and pressure of being Vancouver's police commissioner. Sixty-hour weeks were typical, but he avoided the office on Saturdays, preferring to work from home after an early morning round of golf.

But today was different. Underwood glanced up at the wall clock in his expansive office. It was almost nine AM, and he knew the crown prosecutor would be arriving shortly. He sighed and opened the brief prepared for him by Cunningham and Delray the previous evening.

He ignored the executive summary, which was solely the work of Cunningham and focused on the main report that Delray had prepared. He skimmed over the findings of the Halloran murders and focused on the summary about Remmy Chilton. He grimaced when he had finished. Despite Cunningham's protestations, he had to agree with Delray—the case against Chilton looked thin in light of the new evidence uncovered by Detective Cash.

Underwood closed the file and leaned back in his chair.

He loved most aspects of his job, but despised dealing with politicians and the media. The Halloran murder case had now become political due to Richard Temple's attempts to use it for publicity to promote his own political campaign.

Today's meeting would be challenging and he had to be careful. Temple was already more politician than prosecutor. He'd heard rumors that the man regularly pulled seventy—hour weeks and was highly ambitious. But the rumors didn't stop there; Temple had survived three internal investigations on charges of bullying and harassment. Underwood knew the rumors were likely true because the Vancouver Crown Prosecutor's office had the highest turnover of junior staff of any jurisdiction in the country. Still, it also had one of the highest success rates in prosecuting criminal cases. Underwood knew Temple's political masters were always keen to look the other way if he got the results that made them look good. He was almost untouchable and used to getting his way. Underwood expected the meeting to turn sour quickly. He was okay with that. He might get his game of golf in after all.

A knock on his open door broke his thoughts. A uniformed officer in his early twenties leaned in and said, "Excuse me, Commissioner. Crown Prosecutor Temple is here to see you."

Maintaining his neutral expression, Underwood said, "Show Dr. Temple in."

In his early fifties, Richard Temple had a round face, accentuated by the extra pounds he carried. He had a full head of hair, which had allegedly turned white in his early forties. Underwood had never seen him out of a suit, and today was no exception.

Temple nodded once and said a curt, "Good morning, Blaine," as he sat down opposite Underwood.

Underwood returned the nod. "Good morning, Richard."

Temple didn't mess around with pleasantries and got straight to the point. "Thanks for meeting me on a Saturday. I hope I haven't interrupted your game of golf."

Underwood leaned back and said, "Well, that depends, Richard. If this is a short meeting, then no, you haven't."

Temple ignored the subtle jibe. "I'll do my best to be brief. I got word from Assistant Commissioner Cunningham that your organization was having second thoughts about the guilt of Remmy Chilton in connection with the murder of the two Halloran girls."

Underwood nodded and summarized the details of Delray's report.

Temple remained passive until Underwood had finished. "None of that changes anything, Blaine. We can still place Chilton at the crime scene—he's admitted he was there—and his movements show he had time to commit the murders."

"But he has no motive, and the timelines are extremely tight. We are now investigating a separate line of inquiry. We believe the girls were due to meet someone. We even have a photograph—"

Temple held up his hand and calmly said, "I'm not interested. This case should have been completed thirteen years ago. And it would have been if it weren't for the incompetent bumbling of the Vancouver Police and the lab with the DNA evidence."

Underwood felt his blood pressure rising as he leaned forward. "You know as well as I do that Vancouver Police had nothing to do with that. That was all the labs fault—"

Temple chided, "You seem to forget the police commissioner at that time lost his job shortly afterward."

"That case had nothing to do with it," corrected Underwood shaking his head. "Peter Stillwell saw out his contract as police chief and took early retirement."

"I'm not interested in your petty arguments. Like it or not, this case was an embarrassment for your department and Vancouver's public administrators. And we're not going to have a repeat of it. How do you think this will play out in the media if you change your mind? Vancouver police are now not sure they've arrested the right man. I don't think so."

"It's a media fiasco I'm trying to avoid, Richard. Suppose this thing goes to trial, and we suddenly turn up evidence that exonerates Chilton and points the finger at someone else. How is that going to look?"

"We have a man in custody. The media is expecting a trial; the good citizens of Vancouver are expecting a trial, and that's exactly what I'm going to give them."

"All I'm asking for is a postponement until we examine this new information. And then we can proceed with the appropriate trial, whether it's Chilton, or someone else."

Temple shook his head. "You don't seem to get it, Blaine. That ship has sailed. I'm resigning in three months to run for public office. I'm sure you're aware of that. This is one of the few cases that is a blot on my CV, and I fully intend to rectify it. I promised justice for the parents of Fiona and Tessa Halloran thirteen years ago, and that's what I intend to give them."

Underwood held Temple's gaze for a few moments. "You and I are very similar in many ways."

"How so?" said Temple as he raised an eyebrow.

"We both want the parents of Tessa and Fiona to be able to sleep at night, knowing that someone is now behind bars for their murders. But there's one huge difference between us."

"And what's that?"

"I want the right man behind bars. And I'm not convinced it's Remmy Chilton."

"Like I said earlier, Blaine, this is out of your hands now." Temple stood, adding, "If you want to drop the charges, I suggest you speak to your superiors first. Your contract is up in eight months, and if you want to see it extended, you'll let this one play out."

Temple headed for the door and called out over his shoulder, "All future communications on this matter will need to be in writing." He turned back when he reached the doorway and added, "Enjoy your golf," before disappearing.

Underwood remained expressionless, but his anger was boiling inside. As he pondered Temple's warning, he started to plan how he would spend the day ahead. He knew Temple would be busy with calls, persuading the politicians, journalists, and his superiors that the Vancouver police chief was wavering. Underwood was not bothered by this. He had played political games before and knew this wouldn't be the last scuffle he was involved in. He looked at his clock and sighed. There would be no time for golf. His day would be consumed by phone calls, the first being to Felix Delray.

Bridgette could barely contain her excitement when she had first learned that Levi was being withdrawn from his induced coma. But the rest of the morning dragged for her as she waited anxiously for a change in his condition. There had been hints all morning that he was beginning to regain consciousness. At first, it was just the occasional flutter of his eyelids and a murmur or two. But as it approached midday, Frost began to move around a little in his bed. Bridgette wondered if this was due to the change in his medication, and he was now starting to feel the pain of his injuries or simply a sign that he was getting closer to a conscious state.

Eleanor, too, had found the waiting frustrating. At about one-thirty PM, she declared she needed to eat and headed to the hospital's canteen to grab her first meal of the day.

It was the first time since early that morning that Bridgette and Frost had been alone together without his mother or any of the hospital staff present.

She cherished such times with him and called, "Now would be a good time to wake up, Levi. We've got so much to talk about, and you still owe me that dinner."

To her surprise, Frost's eyelids fluttered open as he murmured, "Bridgette?"

Bridgette couldn't hide her smile as she stood up and leaned in closer to him. "Can you hear me?"

Frost closed his eyes again and nodded once. In a croaky voice, he said, "Where am I?"

Bridgette took his hand and squeezed it gently. "You're in the hospital. Do you remember your accident?"

Frost said, "No," as he briefly opened his eyes again. He murmured, "I feel dizzy," then drifted off again.

Bridgette was unfazed. The doctors had told her the process of coming entirely out of a coma could take days, and it would be normal for Levi to start with only minor bouts of consciousness. She debated pressing the buzzer to call the nursing staff but secretly enjoyed the few moments she had with him alone.

"You gave us quite a scare. Your mom's here—she's just

gone to get some lunch, but she'll be back shortly. The doctors are hopeful you'll make a—"

Frost murmured, "What day… is it?"

"It's Saturday, Levi."

Frost opened his eyes again. "Saturday?"

"Saturday," said Bridgette with a nod. She smiled and added, "You had us all a bit worried there for a while."

"What happened?"

"You were hit by a car. You don't remember?"

Frost closed his eyes again. "No…"

"The doctors say it may be some time before you get your memory back," soothed Bridgette.

Frost tried to nod but winced with pain. "I remember… I was coming to your apartment… dinner."

"Well, I'm glad you remember that part," Bridgette joked, "Because I'm holding you to our date."

Frost opened his eyes again. He glanced at the machines he was hooked up to and asked, "How soon until they'll let me out?"

"You're pretty banged up," said Bridgette with a grimace. "I think you'll be here for a while."

Frost held Bridgette's gaze as he squeezed her hand a little. "Thanks for staying…"

Bridgette smiled and did her best to hold back her tears. "I wouldn't be anywhere else."

Chapter Twenty-One

Bridgette kept vigil at Levi's bedside throughout the weekend. She and Eleanor barely left his side and were buoyed by his extended periods of consciousness as the weekend wore on. The doctors seemed pleased with his progress, although they remained concerned about his broken leg and the need for surgery as soon as possible.

At first, Frost didn't seem to grasp the extent of his injuries and was puzzled by all the machines. Bridgette patiently explained what had happened, and even though he had no recollection of the incident, he accepted that he had been involved in a hit-and-run.

Because he was still in a critical care unit, no other visitors had been allowed. However, the nursing staff made an exception for Felix Delray, who visited Frost briefly on Sunday afternoon. They had shared a pleasant ten minutes together before Frost waned and needed more sleep.

It was now close to six PM. Bridgette stood alone at the window in Frost's critical care unit and watched the sunset while he slept.

Her thoughts were interrupted by a murmur from the bed behind her. "Where is everybody?"

She returned to Frost's side and told him that Delray had gone home and his mother was eating her evening meal in the canteen.

They were quiet for a moment before Frost said, "Did I hear right earlier from the doctors?"

"About what, Levi?" asked Bridgette as she sat down.

"That I could be in here for… months."

There was no sugarcoating Frost's condition. Bridgette had been present when the doctors had outlined the surgery required for his leg. Repairing the multiple breaks in his femur would require numerous surgeries and Frost would have to be fitted with an external metal frame to hold his bones in position while they healed. She did her best to explain this to Frost in simple terms.

"Sounds like I'm pretty banged up."

"But you're alive, Levi." Bridgette frowned and then added, "It could have been a whole lot worse."

"Worse than this?"

"Everyone was worried about your skull fracture. You could have been left with permanent brain damage, but the doctors are now confident that's not the case." She pointed to his leg and added, "This will heal with time and surgery along with your other injuries. We have to be patient and take it day by day."

Frost squeezed her hand gently. "I feel guilty. You're spending so much time here."

"I wouldn't be anywhere else," she said with a tired smile.

"Is the chief okay with you taking all this time off?"

"He thinks it's best for your recovery," she said with a nod. "And I've got plenty of leave."

"You're making a lot of sacrifices."

Bridgette mused, "How would you feel if the roles were reversed? If it was me in the bed instead of you?"

"I'd want to be sitting where you are," declared Frost.

She found it hard to hide a smile as she responded, "Touché."

"But what about your case—the Halloran girls? That's not going to solve itself."

"I spoke to the chief just before he left the hospital. He's going to assign it to someone else tomorrow."

"Is that what you want?"

"I can't be in two places at once."

Bridgette then explained how Delray had told her about the clash between Underwood and Richard Temple over prosecuting Remmy Chilton. She concluded by saying, "The commissioner doesn't want to see a repeat of what happened with the first trial, but neither does he want to see an innocent man go to prison. So he's given the chief another week. If we can find the killer, he'll step in before Chilton goes to court for his preliminary hearing."

"And when's the hearing."

"It's scheduled for Tuesday next week, so we've got eight days."

"And if we can't find the killer by then?"

"We know Richard Temple will turn Chilton's trial into a media circus. Withdrawing the charges after it's officially started is going to cause a lot of political flak. The chief thinks it might even cost the commissioner his job."

"You're the best hope the chief's got to solve this."

Bridgette raised an eyebrow. "You'd prefer me out there solving crimes than being here with you?"

"Maybe that didn't come out right," said Frost with a frown. "The dinner we were supposed to have the other night… I was going to tell you…" He pointed at his monitoring equipment and added, "And this accident changes nothing…"

Bridgette said, "Well… that's good," but tensed up a little as she wondered where Levi was headed with the conversation.

"I'm stuck here whether I like it or not," sighed Frost. "But you can make a big difference to where Remmy Chilton spends the next twenty years."

"A week isn't much time to solve a cold case."

"But if anyone can, you can."

Bridgette considered Frost's words as he added, "I'm having surgery this week, and it's my guess I'll be bombed out a lot of the time. My mom is here for at least another week, so she can look after me during the day."

"So… you think I should work the case?"

"It's your call. Maybe speak to the chief? At least giving him a few hours each day might help." Frost managed a wink from his one eye that wasn't bandaged as he added, "I'll miss you of course."

Bridgette realized they were now engaging in banter. She found it hard to imagine that just a day ago, the doctor's still had grave concerns about his survival. She kept those thoughts to herself as she responded, "It's nice to know I'd be missed."

Frost's mood grew serious again. "I'd prefer you stay here all the time. But, right now, I think Remmy Chilton needs your help as much as I do."

Chapter Twenty-Two

After declaring she was tired, Eleanor left the hospital early Sunday evening to stay at a nearby hotel. Bridgette wondered if she had feigned her tiredness to give her and Levi time alone. Even though Levi dozed for much of the time, she enjoyed their time together. During his lucid moments, Bridgette had steered the conversation away from their relationship. She figured it best to wait until after his surgeries before discussing the topic.

Frost wanted to discuss his accident. He had no recollection of why he was in Gastown and was troubled by the fact that it looked deliberate. "Who would want to do that to me?" he had asked.

They had discussed motive. Frost thought it was unlikely to be linked to his current case as he worked in the background rather than as a lead detective. They went over all the cases they had been involved in together and drew a similar blank—the guilty parties were either dead or in jail.

That left either his work in undercover or a personal grudge. Apart from his ex-wife, who seemed happy in her new relationship, Frost couldn't think of anyone on a personal level with whom he'd fallen out. They discussed his undercover work and agreed it couldn't be dismissed.

Frost finally succumbed to his fatigue at just after ten and drifted off into a deep sleep. Bridgette had then driven home and enjoyed sleeping in her own bed. Despite the roller coaster of emotion of the last four days, she slept soundly and woke to her alarm at six AM.

After calling the hospital, Bridgette learned that Frost had a peaceful night and was improving steadily. Feeling encouraged, she hit the gym for a workout and grabbed a bagel on her way to work.

After arriving at police headquarters a little after seven-thirty AM, she spent most of the next hour preparing for an eight-thirty meeting with Delray. She made notes about her conversations with Mac and Dorothy as well as observations from her interview with Remmy Chilton and her visit to the crime scene in the woods. It was only when she got to the photo of one of the twins with the young man that she paused to chew on the end of her pen. She studied the image and wrote more notes and questions on her scratch pad.

Now, as she made her way to her boss's office, she had a better feel for what she wanted to investigate. She paused in Delray's open doorway to knock, but Delray beat her. "Come on in, Bridgette. How's Levi doing?"

Bridgette explained how she had called the hospital earlier and got a positive update.

"I gotta say, that's a remarkable turnaround, "said Delray with a scratch of his chin. "On Friday, it looked like we would lose him."

"I agree, Chief. He's got a long way to go, but fingers crossed."

"And you, how are you doing?"

"I'm okay," she said with a nod. "I got a good night's sleep and am ready to get back into it."

"Well, I appreciate you coming in. But if anything happens and you need to return to the hospital, that's fine with me."

"Thanks, Chief."

"So," said Delray as he put on his glasses, "This thing goes to court next week. And even though it's just a preliminary hearing, it's like the starter's gun at the beginning of a race."

"And now the media has a hold of it, we won't be able to stop it."

Delray winced. "Not you, not me, and not even the commissioner after their blowup on Saturday."

Bridgette recalled Delray telling her this would be Temple's last case before he ran for public office. "I can't believe how dirty this is getting."

"That's politics for you. Temple doesn't want this derailed, and he's got people in high places in his pocket. A few well-placed words of complaint and the commissioner won't get his contract renewed."

They were quiet momentarily before Delray added, "I don't like this any more than you do, Bridgette, but we have to play this carefully. We've got a week to find something solid, but Underwood has asked me to be very discrete. That's code for not telling Cunningham anything because he'll only report it back to Temple."

"That's going to make it tough."

"I agree," said Delray with a nod. "I can give you a junior analyst to help, but other than that, you're on your own."

Bridgette walked back to her desk, her movements deliberate and measured. She was fully aware of the immense pressure that was bearing down on her, and she couldn't help but feel a sense of unease. As she sat down, she took a deep breath and tried to steady her nerves. The weight of expectation was heavy. She had studied a few cold cases as part of her criminology degree. She knew that finding a killer in a cold case typically took a team of investigators months, if not years, to solve.

She tried to push an image of Remmy Chilton sitting in a cell to the back of her mind but found it challenging. Interviewing him had been the right thing to do, but it now made this more personal. He was no longer just a mugshot and a name in a computer file associated with the case. He was now a real person, someone of limited intelligence who was about to be screwed over by powerful men all because he had been in the wrong place at the wrong time.

Bridgette picked up her phone and stared at the photo of the young man with his arm around one of the twins. There would be no time to investigate multiple leads. She had to gamble on one line of inquiry, and finding out who this man was had to be it. She sucked in a deep breath as she thought about her dilemma. How do you find out someone's identity from a grainy thirteen-year-old photograph?

If the photo had been better quality, she could have gotten one of the analysts to search for digital matches on social media. But the quality of the image was poor, which meant she would have to go 'old school' and figure it out on her own.

She studied the image for a few minutes as her mind processed possibilities. She figured the boy was between sixteen and eighteen when the photo was taken, which probably meant he was still in senior high school. Finding his identity would be virtually impossible if he was just on holiday like the twins. But if he lived locally, she figured there might be a chance, particularly if he had gone to a private school like most kids did in the Gulf Beach area.

Bridgette swiveled her chair and unlocked her computer. She let her fingers dance across the top of the keys on her keyboard for a few seconds while she thought and then rapidly keyed in a few search words and pressed enter. In less than a second, Google returned her a list of matches—yearbooks for private schools in Vancouver. She opened the first one on the list—Wynyard Academy in West Vancouver. She clicked through to the school's yearbook page and then selected the archives.

Bridgette scrolled through several web pages and then nodded to herself as she picked up the handset for her desk phone. She had seen enough and knew this was worthy of further investigation.

Chapter Twenty-Three

Bridgette pulled into the parking lot of the Chetwynd Academy and glanced at the car's clock. It was already a few minutes after five PM, and she hated being late for appointments.

After grabbing her notebook and phone, she got out of her car and stood for a moment to get her bearings. As she surveyed the buildings within the hedged perimeter of the manicured school grounds, she understood why Chetwynd was considered one of Vancouver's most prestigious private schools. There were six buildings in total. All were constructed using a striking combination of two-tone bricks that lent them an air of majesty. She noticed a large brass plaque which read 'Administration Block' on the front of the building to her left and headed for its entrance.

She cut across a manicured strip of grass and up a set of steps before opening a heavy wooden entrance door that led into the building's foyer. The area was large and imposing. She marveled at the exquisite ceiling moldings and the thick oak window frames—a far cry from the architecture in the public school buildings where she had been educated.

Bridgette looked to her left and right as she walked forward before stopping again. The reception area was dim, with most of the lights switched off. She could see no one and as she wondered what to do next, a voice called out from a hallway on her left. "Detective Cash?"

Bridgette turned and saw a tall man in his early fifties walking towards her. He was wearing a dark blue suit and could have passed for a lawyer or accountant, but she guessed this was the school's principal and the man she had come to see.

"Mr Longmire?"

"Call me Lance," said the man, extending his hand.

"Sorry I'm late," said Bridgette as they shook hands.

"It's only a few minutes. And this sounds important, so I didn't mind waiting." He gestured down the hallway. "My office is this way."

She followed him down a hallway with highly polished floorboards to his office. The office was large and comfortably accommodated his mahogany desk, two easy chairs, and coffee table. The office was stately and in keeping with the rest of the building—its only concession to modernity being an Apple laptop on his desk.

Longmire motioned Bridgette toward the easy chairs. "I'm sorry I can't offer you coffee or tea, but the office staff all go home at five."

"No problem, Lance. I don't drink coffee or tea this late in the day anyway, or I'll never sleep."

Longmire politely laughed as he sat in an easy chair opposite Bridgette. "Now, how can I help you?"

Mindful of her need for discretion with the Halloran case, she chose her words carefully, "I'm currently working on a cold case, and some new information has come to hand in the form of a photo that was taken about thirteen years ago."

Bridgette pulled out her phone and scrolled through to a photo of the young man seen with one of the twins. This image was a zoomed-in copy of the original Polaroid and only showed the teenage boy.

"We're trying to locate this young man," she added as she passed her phone across. "He would have been about sixteen or seventeen when this photograph was taken. We believe it was taken here in Vancouver. Normally, we would use our software to search for a match against police records or social media images, but the image quality is too poor."

The man studied the image. "Which is why you're here, I guess?"

"Old school policing," said Bridgette with a nod. "We've been searching through online photos that we know are about thirteen years old. Private school yearbooks and sporting photographs have been our first targets."

"Why private schools, if you don't mind my asking?"

"We believe he may have been a private school student."

Longmire nodded. "I wasn't available when you called earlier, but this explains why you've been searching through our online records."

"We came across the photo of a former student that bears a striking resemblance to the photo you're currently looking at. His name is Andrew Thornton and he graduated thirteen years ago."

"I'm afraid there's been a mistake," said Longmire as he returned her phone.

"A mistake?" said Bridgette with a frown.

Longmire peered over his glasses. "Where did you get that name from?"

"It was the name associated with the photo in your yearbook."

Longmire stood. "I've been at this school for sixteen years…" Bridgette watched him walk across to a bookcase as he added, "Back then, I was deputy headmaster. Part of my role was to work closely with each graduating class in their final school year. I got to know each student quite well."

"I'm not sure I follow?"

Longmire seemed to ignore Bridgette's question as he searched a row of books with an index finger. He mumbled, "Here it is," and withdrew a book that looked the size and shape of several books Bridgette had on her coffee table in her apartment. As he walked back, he added, "I keep in contact with a large number of my old students. Andrew was one of them until his tragic accident."

"Accident?" said Bridgette with a frown.

"Andrew died in a car crash about eight months after leaving school…"

Longmire sat down and added, "It was a desperately sad time for his family and this school."

"I can imagine."

"This is the yearbook for Andrew's graduating class…" Longmire opened it to a specific page and handed it to Bridgette. "And you've alerted me to an error." He pointed at the photo of the student who was a match for the boy in the Polaroid. "This is who you are looking for?"

"Yes, but I'm confused. The caption below that photo says Andrew Thornton."

"Indeed it does," said Longmire. He pointed to the image of the next schoolboy in the yearbook. "This is actually Andrew."

Bridgette stared down at the photo of the real Andrew

Thornton. He had a narrow face and looked nothing like the other student.

Longmire added, "It appears whoever put the yearbook together got these two photos and names mixed up. You're not after Andrew Thornton at all."

Bridgette let out a gasp as Longmire told her the student's real name. "Are you sure?"

Longmire said, "Yes..." but Bridgette barely heard the rest of his answer as she began to think through the ramifications for her investigation.

Bridgette arrived at the hospital shortly after six PM. She had attempted to contact Delray before she left the school, but he was unavailable. She didn't want to be taking calls from her boss once she entered the hospital, so she pressed speed dial and murmured, "Please pick up..." as the phone connected.

To her relief, Delray picked up on the fourth ring. "Sorry, I couldn't take your call earlier. It's been a mad house here."

"That's okay, Chief. I'm just glad I got through to you."

"Where are you?"

"I've just arrived at the hospital but I'm still in my car."

"Give Levi my best. How's he doing?"

"I talked to his mom earlier. He's continuing to improve, and they've scheduled surgery for tomorrow."

"Well, that's a good sign. How about you? Did you make any progress with that photo today?"

"As a matter of fact, I did."

"Okay, tell me."

"I met with Elly, the analyst you assigned me, shortly

after our meeting. We figured if the young man lived in the neighborhood where the murders occurred, he probably went to a private school."

"That makes sense. Real estate is super expensive in that area and if you can afford to live there, you usually send your kid to a private school."

"I tasked Margot with searching through online school yearbooks from that era for any students who resembled the guy in the Polaroid."

"Sounds like a smart place to start."

"While she was doing that, I drove up to the West Vancouver Yacht Club. I figured if the young guy in the Polaroid was a local, maybe he hung out at the marina, or his parents had a boat?"

"And how did that go?"

"Not great. Nobody I talked to seemed to be there thirteen years ago, except the guy from the burger shop, who didn't know his name. I spoke with the yacht club's general manager but he's new and he didn't recognize the boy in the photo."

"Another dead end then?"

"No. He does know the former GM and gave me his contact details. I called him and he's agreed to meet with me tomorrow morning."

"Okay, well that's progress. How did Margot go?"

"Better than me. She found seven photos from yearbooks that looked like a possible match to the boy in the Polaroid. She's getting residential addresses for six of the men using our license and vehicle registration databases. We'll start interviews hopefully tomorrow."

"What about the seventh guy?"

"Margot couldn't find anything about him in any of our

databases. So I went to his school late today and asked about him."

"And what did you find out?"

"He died eight months after graduation and before he got his driver's license."

"So that explains why he's not on any databases. But, he was still alive when the girls were murdered."

"True, but it's more complicated than that."

"How so?"

Bridgette explained the mix-up in the photographs in the yearbook.

"So what's the problem? If the principal has given us the correct name for the student in the photo, surely we investigate him?"

"It's not going to be that easy…" said Bridgette grimly.

"And why is that?" demanded Delray.

"The student's name is Jacob Temple."

"Jacob Temple? I don't know anyone by that name."

"Maybe not, but you do know his uncle…"

After a moments silence, Delray growled, "You gotta be kidding me?"

"I wish I was. The principal knows the family and confirmed that Jacob Temple, now thirty, is senior prosecutor Richard Temple's nephew."

Chapter Twenty-Four

Felix Delray sat in his office studying the two images before him. It was still early on Tuesday morning, but he was already sipping on his third coffee. The two images were both photocopies provided by Bridgette to help discuss the new developments in the Halloran case.

Pointing to the photo on the left, Delray said, "So, this is a copy of the Polaroid?"

"Yes," responded Bridgette. "I got Margot to do some digital enhancement. It's about as good a quality as we can make it."

Delray picked up the other photo and said, "And this is the one from the yearbook?"

"Yes."

Delray put the photo down and stared at each one in turn. "They look like the same guy."

"I agree."

"Let me see the other photos again."

Bridgette handed over a handful of photographic

images that she had similarly copied from other yearbooks. "I can pull up the originals on your computer if you like?"

Delray murmured, "No, this is fine," as he perched his glasses on the end of his nose.

After a few moments of studying each image Margot had collected, he handed them back. "Okay, they look a bit like the guy in the Polaroid, but nowhere near as close as this..." added Delray as he pointed to the photo on his desk.

Bridgette glanced down at the yearbook photo they now knew to be a seventeen-year-old Jacob Temple. She knew Delray was in a bind and asked, "So, what do you want to do?"

Delray grimaced. "This is a mess. I had a conference call with both the commissioner and Cunningham last night to tell them that Richard Temple's nephew was a person of interest. Cunningham went off his nut and said under no circumstances was Jacob Temple to be interviewed."

"I'm not surprised. And the commissioner?"

"He was a little more circumspect. He said he wanted to sleep on it. I'm meeting with them both at nine-fifteen to get their decision."

Bridgette knew Jacob Temple was their best lead, but her hands were tied. "What do you think he'll say?"

"I have no idea," said her boss with a shrug. "For once, I kind of agree with Cunningham. All we have is a photo likeness. It's a good likeness, but that's all it is."

"But surely it's worth investigating. Surely it's worth interviewing Jacob—"

"But we don't call the shots. And sadly, this thing will play out in the media."

They were momentarily lost in their thoughts before

Bridgette broke the silence. "So what do you want me to do?"

Delray leaned back in his chair. "We need more. A photo isn't going to be enough. If we drag Jacob Temple in here and he denies it's him in the photo or that he knew the girls, his uncle will make sure the commissioner loses his job. Underwood knows that. We need something else."

"You mean other evidence that Jacob Temple knew the girls?"

Delray nodded. "Or that he hung out at the yacht club during that period. Maybe he was a junior sailor?" Delray pointed at the Polaroid photo and added, "Anything that ties him to the location or the girls will make this a lot easier to sell up the line."

Bridgette already had a couple of ideas in mind and said, "I'm on it," as she rose to her feet. As she headed for the doorway, Delray asked, "What time is Levi's surgery?"

Bridgette looked at the clock on Delray's wall, which showed the time was close to nine AM. "He's being prepped now. I called into the hospital on my way to work this morning and spent a few minutes with him. I passed on your best wishes."

"Thanks. I appreciate it."

"No problem."

As she turned to head out the door, Delray said, "Hey, Bridgette. Should you be here? Wouldn't you rather be at the hospital?"

"There's not much I can do there right now, and... I've never been good at waiting around in hospitals."

"What time is he due to come out of surgery?"

"They're not sure—his leg is a mess. So probably not until early afternoon... If it's okay with you, I'll head back to the hospital when I get word he's in recovery."

"We all have to prioritize what's important," said Delray with a nod. "And I can't think of anything more important than that."

Floyd Geddes lived in West Vancouver, about a two-minute drive into the hills from the ocean. Bridgette didn't know much about Geddes other than that he was the retired general manager of the Eagle Park Yacht Club. But as she drove along Falcon Road past a row of imposing two-story colonial houses, she figured he was wealthy. She slowed to check house numbers before pulling to a stop and parking on the street behind a late-model black Mercedes.

Bridgette got out of her car and surveyed Geddes' residence. The house was painted a light gray with white trim. She could see no fences—all were covered by either neatly trimmed hedges or deep manicured gardens with mature trees and bushes.

After making her way up a pebbled drive and onto the house's front veranda, she pressed the doorbell. Bridgette smiled as somewhere inside the house, she heard an electronic chime play a short stanza from Beethoven's 'Ode to Joy.' A moment later, a man in his late seventies opened the front door. Floyd Geddes wore a blue cardigan over cream corduroy pants and brown loafers. He had thinning white hair that was possibly red in earlier years. He had a ruddy complexion and an alert demeanor despite the large bags under his eyes.

Geddes smiled at her and said, "You must be the detective."

Bridgette smiled back as she introduced herself and

flashed her badge. Geddes invited her in and made small talk as she followed him into a formal living room.

"Can I get you a coffee or tea," asked Geddes as she settled.

"No thanks, I had one earlier," she responded as she sat on a plush leather sofa.

Geddes grinned. "I'm sure you're not here to arrest me."

"No. Certainly not." Bridgette said with a shake of her head. "I'm hoping you can help us."

Bridgette pulled out her phone and scrolled through her photos until she found the image of the young man taken on the Polaroid. She handed her phone to Geddes. "This photo was taken about thirteen years ago. We're unsure of the young man's name, but we want to interview him about a case I'm working on. We have reason to believe he may have hung out occasionally at the yacht club you used to manage."

Geddes held the phone close to his face and murmured, "He looks familiar." He paused and lifted a pair of reading glasses that were dangling from a strap around his neck. After settling them on his nose, he said, "If I'm not mistaken, this is Jacob Temple. But like you said, it's an old photo."

Bridgette suppressed a smile. She deliberately avoided giving Geddes any clues about the young man's identity. The fact that he had identified Temple without prompting helped her cause. "What can you tell me about him?"

Geddes frowned. "Where do I start?"

"Anywhere you like really. Did you see him very often?"

"Well, in the summer months when I used to be president, quite a lot. His father owned a half-share in a boat they used to berth at the marina. They would take it out most weekends in the summer as a family. That went on until about ten years ago."

"And what happened then?"

"Jacob's father, his name was Payne Temple, was a developer in real estate. But he had a falling out with his business partner, who also owned a share in the boat. It all got nasty, and the boat got sold when their partnership dissolved. We never saw the family after that."

Bridgette nodded. "Would you have any records of Payne Temple's membership at the yacht club? It will help my investigation if I can produce something in writing."

Geddes nodded, "Sure, but not here. That would be all down at the club's office." He grinned and added, "Although I do have copies of the minutes and attendance at all our annual meetings. Payne Temple was at every one of them and always had a lot to say."

"That would be great, Floyd. I'll take you up on that before I go. For now, let's get back to Jacob Temple. What can you tell me about him?"

"Well, he was a pain in the ass as a child, and it only got worse the older he got."

"How about you start with your first memories," said Bridgette with a smile.

Chapter Twenty-Five

Bridgette got out of the elevator and walked straight to Delray's office. Her boss had messaged her earlier to say he needed to meet with her urgently. They had agreed on eight AM, but Delray had been cagey about the meeting. She figured it had to be about the Halloran case and wondered if it was all getting too political. Was her investigation going to be shut down?

As she knocked on his door, she noticed him putting on his coat to leave, which added to her confusion.

"Hi, Chief. I thought we were having a meeting?"

"We are. But it's in the commissioner's office."

"The commissioner's office?" said Bridgette as she followed him out the door.

Delray called over his shoulder as he strode toward the elevator, "I called the commissioner last night after I got off the phone with you. We had a long talk."

Delray pressed the button on the elevator and added, "You know all hell is going to break loose if we bring in Jacob Temple for an interview."

"You mean with his uncle?" asked Bridgette as they stepped into the lift.

"One false step here, and Underwood can kiss goodbye any extension to his contract. He wants to hear from you firsthand before he makes a decision."

Bridgette understood Underwood's dilemma. Richard Temple could ruin his career with one well-placed phone call. Her chest tightened as she realized the commissioner was relying on her investigative work to decide. Suddenly, she found it difficult to breathe.

Delray seemed to sense her stress. As the elevator door opened, he said, "Just tell him like you told me. Keep it simple, and let him ask all the questions."

"Will Assistant Commissioner Cunningham be attending as well?"

"You ever see the movie, The Godfather?"

"No. Long before my time."

"You should watch it sometime. There's a line in it, 'Keep your friends close and your enemies closer.'" Delray lowered his voice as they approached Underwood's reception area and added, "Cunningham will be there and I think that's why."

Delray put on a smile for Underwood's assistant and said, "Good morning, Kathy."

The greeting was returned by Underwood's assistant, along with instructions to knock and enter the commissioner's office.

Bridgette followed Delray into Underwood's office after her boss briefly paused at the door to knock. Rather than heading for Underwood's desk, Delray veered right to a conference table with six chairs that the commissioner had in his office.

Along with Delray, she murmured a greeting to Underwood and Cunningham as they sat down. Underwood had a neutral expression, while Cunningham looked ready to explode.

Underwood thanked Bridgette and Delray for coming at such short notice and then looked directly at Bridgette. "The chief has been keeping me informed on the developments with the Halloran case. I understand there's been some concerns about Remmy Chilton's guilt, and a discrete investigation has been underway."

Bridgette glanced at Delray, who motioned for her to answer.

"That's correct, Sir."

Underwood opened a file and pulled out a copy of the Polaroid picture. "This photo of one of the twins with a boy was found in Fiona's belongings shortly after her death?"

Bridgette nodded. "That's correct, Sir." She glanced sideways at Cunningham, who seemed ready to pounce on any answer he didn't like. She ignored his glare and added, "It was part of the original collected evidence."

Underwood stared at the photo. "And up until now, we've never been able to identify this young man?"

"That's also correct, Sir."

"And you believe you've identified him?"

Cunningham exploded, "All she has is a theory, Sir. A theory and no more. And if we allow this to proceed, it will likely cause significant embarrassment for this organization!"

Bridgette resisted the urge to roll her eyes.

Underwood batted away Cunningham's outburst with a calm reply, "I'd like to hear from the detective herself."

Bridgette took this as her cue and summarized why she believed Remmy Chilton was innocent. Cunningham went to protest again, but Underwood shut him down with a wave of his finger. She then detailed how she had little to work with in the way of evidence or witnesses and had focused on the Polaroid photo.

After the commissioner had commended her initiative for using online yearbooks, Bridgette concluded by saying of all seven young men they had found, Jacob Temple had the most striking resemblance.

Cunningham had been biding his time but now exploded. "You're going to need a lot more than a likeness in a yearbook to an old, grainy photo, Detective. It's insufficient evidence to drag someone in for questioning, particularly on such a sensitive case."

Delray chimed in and explained how the principal of the school that Jacob Temple had attended also verified him as the young man in the Polaroid.

"Still not enough evidence," barked Cunningham. "And might I remind everyone, we're already proceeding with the prosecution of the original suspect, whose DNA was found at the scene."

Underwood looked at Bridgette for a response. She said, "I'm not sure if you're aware, Assistant Commissioner, but I also interviewed Floyd Geddes yesterday."

"Who's Floyd Geddes?" demanded Cunningham.

"He used to manage the Eagle Harbor Yacht Club before his retirement. I showed him the Polaroid, and he identified Jacob Temple as the young man with his arm around one of the twins."

"But what does that prove?"

"It proves Jacob Temple knew at least one of the twins and at a time close to their murders. Geddes told me that Temple hung out at the yacht club frequently throughout the summer months." She paused and looked at each of the three men in turn before she added, "The yacht club is less than two miles from the murder scene. I'm not saying Jacob Temple is guilty, but I am saying we should interview him to find out what he knows."

Twenty minutes later, Bridgette and Delray were back in Delray's office. The meeting with the commissioner had degenerated into an argument between Cunningham and Underwood, where Delray and Bridgette felt like spectators. In the end, Underwood had excused them when Cunningham had stated that all their careers were in jeopardy. They had retreated to the second floor and were now waiting for the commissioner's decision.

"How long do you think this will take?" asked Bridgette.

"I'm not sure," said Delray. "We're pretty much dead in the water if they won't let us interview Jacob Temple."

"After leaving the hospital last night, I thought about the case on the way home. I can't think of any other possible angles we can explore without tipping off the media."

Delray agreed and then asked, "How's Levi doing?"

"He was pretty bombed out last night, so I spoke mainly to his mom. The operation seemed to go okay, but he's going to need more surgery."

"Well, that's a step in the right direction, at least. Is he up for visitors yet? I've got some of the guys asking if they can go see him."

"I'm planning on heading in there later today. I'll ask the nursing staff—"

Delray's desk phone rang. He looked at the number and murmured, "This is it…" as he picked up the handset.

Bridgette waited patiently while her boss took a call from the commissioner. The call lasted two minutes. As

Delray put the handset back in its cradle, Bridgette asked, "How did it go?"

"Not great, but not bad either. The commissioner has scheduled a lunchtime meeting with Senior Prosecutor Richard Temple. He's going to explain to him there's been a development in the case and then drop it on him that we want to interview his nephew."

"That sounds like a fun meeting," said Bridgette as she raised an eyebrow. "I would like a front-row seat at that one to watch the fireworks."

"Be careful what you wish for, Bridgette," said Delray with a grimace.

Bridgette's eyes widened. "We got an invite?"

Delray nodded. "The commissioner wants you to tell Temple exactly what you told him this morning."

The rest of the morning dragged for Bridgette. She called the hospital shortly after she met with Delray and was able to speak to Levi for a few minutes. Frost sounded like he was in pain but put on a brave face. She apologized for not being there, but he reassured her that working on the case was a better use of her time.

After the call, she sat at her desk with her scratch pad in front of her. She used the time more for thinking than anything else. It was now Wednesday and less than a week until the preliminary hearing for Remmy Chilton's trial. She knew the chances of finding out who killed the Halloran girls before then were slim. Bridgette had spent an hour online learning all she could about Jacob Temple. Temple had followed in his uncle's footsteps, studying law at university and was now working as a junior partner in a local law firm.

She frowned. This didn't work in her favor. Jacob Temple would know his rights and would give nothing away in an interview. The Polaroid was evidence that he knew one of the twins only, but nothing more. Unless they could place him in the vicinity of the murder scenes or with the twins on the day of the murders, she knew the interview was a bust before it started.

She thought about the lunchtime meeting with Richard Temple. This was the first hurdle they needed to overcome. Delray had warned her that the senior prosecutor would inform his nephew immediately if the interview was to go ahead. And that meant questioning Jacob Temple as soon as possible before he had time to prepare a story. She wrote a big question mark on her scratchpad and scowled. She knew from experience the worst people to interview were lawyers. How do I get him to open up?

She then recalled how Mac from the burger shop had seen the twins with Temple and another young man a day or two before their murders. She nodded to herself and then wrote down her first question.

Chapter Twenty-Six

Bridgette and Delray had been instructed to wait in the fourth-floor executive conference room for the meeting with Senior Prosecutor Richard Temple. The room easily accommodated a twelve-seat oak conference table, sideboard, and another locked cabinet made of oak.

Bridgette glanced at her watch and asked Delray, "How long do you think they'll be?"

"I have no idea," replied her boss as he shifted in his chair. "We were all supposed to meet at half-twelve, but they're running almost twenty minutes late."

"Maybe Prosecutor Temple has had second thoughts?" mused Bridgette as she stared at the large original oil landscape paintings on the wall opposite.

"Who knows? Maybe—"

Delray paused as Assistant Commissioner Leo Cunningham entered the room. He sat on the opposite side of the conference table to Delray and Bridgette. In a low voice, he hissed, "Richard Temple is absolutely pissed. I want you two to keep your commentary to a minimum. I've already warned the commissioner this fiasco could cost us all our jobs, and I don't intend to be dragged down with him. Are we clear?"

Delray and Bridgette nodded unison as Blaine Underwood and Richard Temple entered the room.

Bridgette studied Temple as they all shared perfunctory greetings. She thought that his normally rosy complexion looked decidedly red today, possibly exacerbated by the need for this meeting.

Underwood thanked everyone for their attendance and, after introductions, quickly moved on to the reason why they were there.

Turning to Temple, he said, "As you are aware, Dr Temple, new evidence has come to light in the Halloran case that we'd like to discuss with you before the preliminary hearing next week."

"What kind of evidence?" demanded Temple. "And why the need for all this secrecy? Couldn't we have just discussed this on the telephone?"

Underwood opened a file he had carried in and withdrew a copy of the Polaroid image. As he slid it across the desk to Temple, he said, "Part of the original evidence we collected from the twin's holiday house was a Polaroid of one of the twins with a young man. We believe it was taken in the days before their murders."

The room was quiet for a moment while Temple studied the image. If he recognized it as his nephew, he wasn't letting on. "I remember that picture from the first trial. So what?"

"At the time of the first trial, nobody had any idea as to the identity of this young man, and given it clearly wasn't Remmy Chilton, it didn't seem to matter."

"You're saying it matters now?" said Temple with a scowl.

"It's a complication we'd rather get cleared up before the case goes to trial. The media will be all over this case, and we must manage every possibility."

Temple said, "I intend to prosecute Remmy Chilton. We found his DNA at the crime scene, and we have witnesses that prove he was in the area before and after the murders took place. I'm not interested in who the girls may or may not have been spending their vacation time with."

Underwood kept his tone even. "I think you are. Have a closer look at the image."

Temple picked up the copy of the Polaroid and studied it for a moment. "It looks like the grainy image of some boy standing with one of the twins at a beach. So what?"

Underwood nodded at Bridgette and said, "Detective Cash has spent the last two days on this. Would you mind telling the senior prosecutor what you've found?"

Bridgette swallowed and said, "Three witnesses, independent of each other, have identified the young man in this photo as Jacob Temple."

Temple's jaw momentarily dropped, but he quickly recovered. "My nephew?"

"That's correct, Sir," said Bridgette with a nod.

"There must be some mistake," barked Temple.

Bridgette patiently explained how the multiple witnesses had confirmed his nephew's identity. She added, "It's not surprising that he knew the girls, given he used to live in the area and spent much of his vacation time in or around the marina."

Temple glared at Underwood. "How dare you suggest that my nephew was in any way involved in this atrocity!"

Bridgette broke in before Underwood could reply. "Sir,

it's important to know the identity of this young man so that we're not ambushed at trial. The work we've done here—"

"Don't you go telling me my job, Detective!" snarled Temple as he pointed a finger at her. "I've been doing this longer than you've been alive."

Underwood calmly interjected. "Detective Cash raises a good point. We don't want a repeat of what happened last time, Richard. If you—"

Temple barked, "This is preposterous," and added, "I've heard enough," as he rose.

The prosecutor strode to the door and then glared back at Underwood. "It's not for me to interfere with a police investigation, however ludicrous it might be. But rest assured, I'll be making a formal complaint about your actions to your superiors."

Temple disappeared. The room was momentarily silent before Cunningham rose and mumbled, "I'll see the senior prosecutor out. He shouldn't be walking around here without an escort."

Underwood and Delray exchanged a look as Bridgette wondered if she had said too much in her challenge to Temple.

Underwood picked up his file from the table. "Now that we've extended that courtesy to the senior prosecutor, I want you to continue your investigation."

"What exactly would you like us to do, Sir?" asked Delray.

Underwood looked from Bridgette to Delray. "I want you to interview Jacob Temple."

Chapter Twenty-Seven

The receiver crashed against its cradle with enough force that it echoed through the cavernous office. Dr. Richard Temple remained motionless, his fingers still curled around the heavy plastic of the phone as if he might hurl it across the room at any moment. The lunchtime meeting with Underwood and his team had been bad enough, but Underwood's follow-up phone call when he got back to his office had been the final straw.

Who did he think he was? Temple looked around the sanctuary of power and privilege with painstaking care—walls lined with books whispering of his intellect and awards glittering with his ambition. Now, the news delivered by Underwood that they were going to interview his nephew threatened to dismantle it all.

"Bernice," Temple's voice cut through the intercom, "Hold all my calls for the next hour."

"Of course, Dr. Temple," came the obedient reply, her tone an unruffled contrast to the storm brewing within him.

Temple pushed back from his desk and stood. He did his

best thinking on his feet, whether in his office or on a courtroom floor.

His steps were measured at first, each footfall a deliberate punctuation to the racing thoughts as he assessed the problem. He had meticulously tailored his reputation and could not afford the slightest hint of impropriety. His campaign for office, the culmination of years of scheming and strategy, hung precariously in the balance.

With each pass between the mahogany bookshelves and his imposing desk, his pace quickened, agitation seeping into his gait. The media would be ravenous, and the thought that his nephew could bring it all undone by some juvenile act when he was a teenager was unacceptable.

He paused in front of his window and stared at the traffic below as he thought about Jacob. The thought twisted in his gut. The boy had always been impulsive, but to be implicated in something as heinous as the Halloran murders? It was inconceivable. Yet here he was, forced to initiate damage control, knowing the weight of public opinion could crush his career and obliterate his legacy without remorse.

A lesser man might have been paralyzed by such an unforeseen blow, but he was no stranger to adversity. It was a foe to be outmaneuvered, not feared. "Containment," he murmured, the word hanging in the air like a spell. If he could keep the story from leaking and maintain the facade of unblemished character, all his plans could still come to fruition.

He nodded once and returned to his pacing. Yes, he could navigate through this. As the minutes ticked by, Temple's mind sharpened to a point. He needed to have another conversation with Underwood. There would be pleasantries, of course, a veneer of cordiality and an apology of sorts for hanging up on the previous call. His excuse would be shock and concern for his nephew. He would weather this storm and bide his time until he got what he wanted. But as soon as this mess died down, he would call Underwood's superiors. Underwood had crossed a line, and it was time for him to go. It wouldn't take much —and they owed him more than one favor and would be eager to do his bidding.

His thoughts were interrupted by his desk phone. Temple strode across to his desk, lifted the receiver and barked, "I told you to hold all calls, Bernice!"

"It's your nephew, Jacob. He said it was urgent."

Temple grimaced and said, "Put him through," as he sat down.

A moment later, Temple heard the nasal twang of his nephew Jacob.

"Uncle Richard?" Jacob's voice came through, tinged with anxiety. "I didn't know who else to call. They're saying I—"

"Listen to me, Jacob," Temple cut across his nephew's worried babble. "I've already heard. Commissioner Underwood has already called me. I don't know what you've been involved in, but for now, don't say anything to the police or anybody else. Do you understand me? Not a word."

"I didn't do anything. I'm innocent—"

"Nothing!" Temple's command reverberated against the walls. "Get Michael Phipps to handle everything. Just do exactly what your boss says and keep your mouth shut."

The line was silent save for Jacob's ragged breathing.

Temple leaned forward and took a deep breath to compose himself.

"Jacob, this is important. Your future, my future—it all hangs in the balance. Don't do anything stupid."

"I won't, Sir. I swear."

"Good. Follow Phipps's instructions—do exactly as he says and we'll get through this." With that, Temple ended the call, the click of the receiver like a judge's final verdict.

As silence descended on the room once more, Temple steepled his fingers. Promises and perils lurked in the shadows, each waiting to claim their due.

In his mind's eye, Temple could see the courtroom: the jury hanging on his every word, the judge nodding in tacit approval. And there, on the stand, would sit Chilton, a pitiable creature, his testimony feeble and ripe for decimation. It was almost too easy. Temple's lips curled into a cruel grin. Winning the Halloran case would still be his crowning legal achievement, the final thrust propelling him into the political stratosphere.

Temple nodded to himself as he picked up the phone again. It was time to call Underwood.

Chapter Twenty-Eight

Bridgette spent the rest of the afternoon preparing for the interview with Jacob Temple. She agonized over every questions she would ask. Underwood's instructions had been explicit: no aggression, no accusations, stick to the facts and see where it leads. She had seen the wisdom of his words, *"If he's not guilty, he may have vital information…"* and had structured her questions to elicit as much information as possible.

In keeping with the low-key strategy, Underwood had personally arranged for Bridgette and Delray to visit Jacob Temple at his law office rather than requesting him to come to police headquarters.

As they rode up in the elevator to the offices of Phipps, Babbs, and Associates, Delray said, "Underwood tells me the senior partner, Michael Phipps, is going to act as the lawyer for Jacob Temple. I've not heard much about him other than he's a ball-breaker and doesn't like police."

"That's pretty much what I've heard as well."

As the elevator door opened, Delray murmured, "You're

as good as it gets with this kind of interview. Just relax, and you'll be fine."

The compliment did nothing to alleviate Bridgette's anxiety, but she thanked Delray for his confidence in her anyway.

The reception area of the law office had a luxurious feel to it, in line with the hefty fees that Phipps, Babbs, and Associates were rumored to charge. The waiting area featured a set of black leather chairs with brass legs, while a mahogany coffee table, also trimmed in brass, completed the ensemble. The overall look of the reception area was reminiscent of a high-end magazine. Bridgette glanced around. The burgundy walls provided a high-contrast backdrop for the gold lettering of the partners' names. The reception desk was unattended, so Delray pressed the bell.

Moments later, a young, clean-shaven man with a business haircut emerged. The young man wore a dark navy suit with a burgundy tie that almost matched the decor of the reception area.

In a haughty voice, he said, "Detectives, Delray and Cash, I presume?"

"Chief inspector Delray, actually," corrected Delray with a raised eyebrow.

The young man acknowledged the correction with a slight nod and said, "This way, please. Mr Temple and our senior partner, Mr Phipps, are waiting for you in the conference room."

Bridgette and Delray followed the young man down a short corridor. They passed a series of offices as they walked. The law firm had used floor-to-ceiling frosted glass panels to divide each office. While it was impossible to recognize anyone inside, Bridgette could see the blurred shapes of individuals working away behind their desks.

They followed the young man until he stopped at a frosted glass door marked 'Conference Room.' The man knocked once before opening the door and motioning them in.

The conference room seated eight. Bridgette made eye contact with Jacob Temple and Michael Phipps. Both men were seated on the opposite side of the conference table and wore surly expressions.

Phipps was a slim man in his late fifties with a full head of immaculately styled gray hair. He wore a dark blue suit, white shirt, and navy tie that featured an immaculate Windsor knot. Phipps exuded an air of refinement and superiority from every pore of his skin. Jacob Temple sat to his left. It seemed clear to Bridgette that he was trying to emanate his boss's look, but it was less than convincing. His dark blue suit was slightly too small and made his body look pudgy. His hair was a little greasy, and his slightly receding hairline caused him to part his hair a little lower on one side than was usual. He had a red complexion and sat with one elbow on the conference table. Bridgette wondered if she was staring into the face of a killer as she made eye contact. But it was impossible to tell—most killers look the same as everyone else. Temple leaned back slightly in his chair. Bridgette had studied body language as part of her criminology degree and knew he was trying to appear relaxed and almost disinterested. But the constant tapping of his index finger on the arm of his chair and rapid eye movement told Bridgette all she needed to know—Temple was nervous.

Neither Phipps nor Temple offered a greeting beyond a frosty stare. Bridgette figured her demeanor would have been similar if she was in their position. Delray ignored the hostility and made friendly introductions on behalf of them both.

After they settled in their chairs, Phipps said, "You realize, Chief Inspector, this is highly irregular and on very short notice. We have a very busy office here, and if it weren't for a personal request from Commissioner Underwood, we would have made you wait until a more convenient time."

Delray managed a cordial smile. "Well, Michael, we appreciate you seeing us at such short notice. It's just that with the preliminary hearing for the Halloran case starting next week, we're trying to get everything squared away, and we're hoping Jacob may be able to help us."

Temple frowned. "I'm not sure how I can help with a thirteen-year-old murder case?"

Bridgette took this as her cue. "Did you know the girls, Jacob?"

"I don't remember. It was a long time ago."

"But they were murdered, and it was all over the news. Surely you would remember something like that?"

"Look, I saw them on the news, like everybody else. I guess I did wonder if I had met them. But the marina and the beach were busy places in summer."

"Surely you would remember two pretty blonde girls who were identical twins?"

"There were lots of young people there, and I hung out with quite a few of them."

Bridgette slowly withdrew a copy of the Polaroid photo from her satchel. As she slid it across the table towards Temple, she said casually, "Have you ever seen this photo before?"

Temple's eyes widened a fraction as he looked down at the image. "No."

"Let me refresh your memory," said Bridgette as she withdrew a scratch pad and pen from her satchel. "It was taken thirteen years ago, right before the twins were murdered."

Temple shook his head in response.

"You can pick it up, Jacob," said Bridgette. "It won't bite you."

Temple studied the photo again as he shifted in his seat. Bridgette was positive he knew it was him in the photo even though he responded, "No, I don't believe I've ever seen this photo."

"You know where we got it, right?"

"I have no idea, Detective."

"It was found in a box under Fiona's bed shortly after her death. It was one of several Polaroids she'd taken while on holiday."

Bridgette noticed beads of sweat forming on Jacob Temple's forehead as he looked at the photo again. Finally, he managed, "Okay, I can see now that it's a photo of one of the twins."

"The boy in the photo... he bears a striking resemblance to you, don't you think?"

Temple shrugged. "I'm not an expert on old photographs."

"So you're saying this isn't you in the photograph?"

Phipps interjected, "I don't like your tone, Detective. Jacob has indicated he hasn't seen the photo before, so move on."

Bridgette ignored Phipps's outburst and kept her focus on Temple. "Take a close look at the young man with his arm around one of the twins. That's you, right?"

"I've never seen it before," murmured Temple.

Bridgette withdrew another photo from her satchel and slid it across the table. "How about this photo? Do you recognize the boy in this photo?"

Temple glanced sideways at Phipps and said, "That's a picture of me from my high school yearbook."

"Correct," said Bridgette as she straightened up the photo so that the two images were side by side in front of Temple and Phipps. "This photo was taken about three months after the murders. Notice anything similar about the two men in the photo?"

Phipps exploded, "This is ridiculous. It's a grainy image from a yearbook, and yes, it looks similar to the Polaroid, but that's all. There would have been hundreds of young men in Vancouver at the time who look similar to that Polaroid."

Bridgette kept her gaze fixed on Temple. "You don't live far from the Eagle Park Yacht Club, do you?"

"I live in the city."

"But, when you were in high school?"

"I guess," said Temple with a shrug.

"And you hung out at the marina and the beach while on vacation?"

"Sometimes. We did a lot of things during vacation time."

Bridgette made a note on her scratch pad as she responded, "We have two eyewitnesses who claim you spent a lot of vacation time at the yacht club and the marina."

Phipps interjected again. "Where are we going with this, Detective."

"One of these witnesses remembers you hanging out with the twins. Does that refresh your memory at all?"

"Like I said, I don't remember," said Temple sullenly.

"Both witnesses report you used to hang out with one young man in particular… someone about your age. Who would that be, Jacob?"

"I have no idea. I used to hang out with lots of people."

"Apparently, you were inseparable."

Temple shook his head. "I don't know what to tell you."

Bridgette raised an eyebrow. "How about the truth?"

Phipps exploded again, threatening to stop the interview. Bridgette kept her focus solely on Temple. When Phipps concluded by saying he would personally complain to Underwood, Bridgette swung her scratchpad around so that it faced Temple. She slid it towards him and said, "When I first asked you if you hung out at the marina, you said 'we.' I wrote it down."

"I meant my family."

"Are you sure you didn't mean your friend?"

Phipps rose to his feet. "This meeting is over! We have tried to cooperate, but this line of questioning makes that impossible."

Bridgette watched Temple rise to his feet and then said, "I'm going to do you a favor, Jacob."

"And what's that?" snarled Temple.

"I'm going to find out who your friend was. And after we've chatted, I'll come back and tell you what his name is so you don't ever forget again."

Chapter Twenty-Nine

The trip back to police headquarters gave Bridgette and Delray a chance to debrief before she returned to the hospital.

As Delray drove, he said, "The commissioner will want to hear all about this as soon as I return."

"Did I go too far?"

"You got it about right," said Delray with a grin. "We were never going to get a confession, and regardless of what happened, Phipps was always going to complain."

"What's your take on Temple?"

Delray frowned. "I'm not convinced he's a murderer, but he's definitely not telling us everything."

"I agree. Temple knew as soon as I put that photo on the table that it was him in the picture with one of the twins."

"Agreed. The thing that bothers me is, what is he trying to hide? He could've simply fessed up and said yeah, okay, I remember that was me. But he tried to hide it, and I want to know why."

"It would've been easier to brush off," mused Bridgette. "All he had to do was say I saw them at the beach, and one of them had a new Polaroid, and I had my photo taken. That was the response I was expecting."

"And that would've given us nowhere to go," said Delray as he changed lanes. "But the fact that he tried to stonewall us makes me wonder what he's hiding."

Bridgette nodded. "He's hiding something."

"That threat at the end," said Delray with a laugh, "About finding out who his friend is was pure genius."

"That certainly rattled him," said Bridgette with a smile. "I'm returning to the marina tomorrow to find out who that friend was. Even if I have to get a sketch artist involved."

"It's a good strategy. This could be the break we need."

It was close to eight PM before Bridgette arrived at the hospital.

She felt guilty as she walked into Frost's room. "Sorry, I'm late. How are you feeling?"

Frost managed a weak grin. "Excited!"

"Excited?" said Bridgette with a frown as she sat beside his bed.

"They're going to put me back on solid foods tomorrow."

"Well, that's exciting," said Bridgette with a smile as she glanced around the room. "Where's your mom?"

"She had a migraine and went back to the hotel room about an hour ago."

"I'm sorry to hear that. Is she okay?"

"Yeah. I think the last few days have finally caught up

with her. She said to say hello and hopes to catch up with you tomorrow."

Bridgette smiled. "I like your mom. I wasn't sure if I would, but…"

"She means well. And I've appreciated having her here. How's the case going?"

Bridgette gave Frost a brief rundown of the interview with Temple. She avoided discussing office politics as she could see Levi was tiring quickly.

Frost mused, "Well, with only five days until the preliminary hearing, let's hope you have a breakthrough."

Bridgette didn't want to talk about work anymore and changed the subject. "What did the surgeon say about your surgery?"

Frost looked down at his broken leg, which was now suspended in a sling about six inches off his bed. "They did more X-rays today, and he's happy with my progress." Frost grimaced and added, "He thinks it will take another two or maybe three surgeries to get it right and lots of rehab."

"I'm sorry, Levi."

"It is what it is," said Frost with a shrug. "At least I'm still here. I just hope we can catch the bastard who did this."

"Have you heard anything?"

"I got a call from the chief earlier today. The team is still on it, but so far, no leads."

Frost let out a long breath and laid his head back on his pillow. "I get tired just from talking for a few minutes…"

Bridgette reached out a hand and grabbed Levi's. "I'm here for a couple of hours, so if you need to rest, that's fine with me."

"Thanks," said Levi as he closed his eyes.

A thought popped into Bridgette's mind. "Your phone—would you mind if I take a look at it?"

"It's in the top drawer," murmured Frost. "What are you looking for?"

Bridgette murmured, "I want to look back through your calls. Maybe there's a clue about who did this to you."

"I still don't remember anything about that day apart from our dinner date, so be my guest," said Frost. "The screen's all smashed, but you can still read it."

Frost gave her the password and then closed his eyes again. By the time Bridgette unlocked the phone, Frost was gently snoring. She didn't hold out much hope that anything would come of her investigation, but it at least gave her something to do until Frost woke again.

Jacob Temple paced around his one-bedroom apartment. It was just after eight PM, and he'd already had three shots of whiskey. He was tempted to fill his glass again but knew he needed to be sharp for what he had to do next. The meeting with Cash and Delray had left him rattled. Michael Phipps had told him afterward that he had done well and the matter was effectively at an end. But he was not convinced. The look the young female detective had given him when she promised to find out who his friend was had stayed with him. If she carried through with her threat, he knew it would only be a matter of time before she found her answer.

Temple opened Evernote on his laptop and navigated to a file that he had stored in the Cloud. He tapped the number displayed on his screen into his phone and held his breath while waiting for it to connect.

A moment later, his call was answered. Loud background music was all he heard at first before a door slammed. A baritone voice barked, "I told you never to call me on this number!"

"This is important," said Temple. "Trust me, I have no desire to talk to you either, but there's been a development."

Over the noise of traffic, the baritone voice snapped, "What kind of development?"

"We have a cop asking questions."

"Hang on."

Temple heard footsteps, and then a car door open and shut. The background noise was negligible now, and he figured his contact was now sitting in a car.

The man continued, "What do you mean we have a cop asking questions? Isn't Chilton's trial starting next week?"

"It is, but—"

"But what?"

Temple swallowed. He had known the man he was speaking to since he was a teenager. He had witnessed his violence firsthand and didn't want to provoke him. "They came to see me today... to ask questions about the photo."

"Well, what's that got to do with me?"

"The cop has been asking questions at the marina. She knows I was hanging out with someone at the time of the murders and is hellbent on finding out who."

There was silence for a moment before the man responded, "Why would this cop need to be poking her nose into this. They've got someone behind bars already."

"I've asked around. It's only one cop—she doesn't think Chilton's guilty, so she's digging."

More silence. "What have you told them?"

"Nothing. The photo proves nothing other than I had my picture taken with Tessa."

"What did you say about me?"

"Nothing. I told them I had lots of friends and it was a long time ago. I doubt they'll be able to make a link to you."

"But you still called?"

Temple grimaced. "I thought you should know. You can't be too cautious."

"So what does your uncle think?"

"He thinks Chilton is guilty. The trial starts next Tuesday and he's told the police commissioner if he withdraws the charges after it starts, he'll get him fired."

"I don't like it. A nosy cop is a loose end we can't afford."

"Look, we got through this thirteen years ago, and we'll get through it again."

"This cop, who is she?"

"Her name is Bridgette Cash."

"I thought they worked in pairs?"

Temple wanted to keep his answers simple. He did not mention that Cash was working with her boss and simply said, "Her partner is in the hospital. She's working alone, and this is her return-to-work assignment."

"Return-to-work assignment? What the hell does that mean?"

"My uncle told me she had some psycho come after her about two months ago. She needed stress leave to recover."

"Is she suicidal?"

"I have no idea. And what does it matter?"

"That's not your concern."

Temple felt his gut tighten. "Listen, sit tight. This will all blow over in a week or—"

"You don't get to tell me what to do! Not now, not ever! You got that?"

Temple closed his eyes and gritted his teeth as he thought back to what happened thirteen years ago. A harmless meetup to smoke some weed with two pretty young girls had all gone horribly wrong when when only one of them had shown up. In the space of just a few minutes the man had flown into a rage and had taken the lives of two innocent young girls. Temple wanted to say, *'If you had listened to me thirteen years ago, we wouldn't be in this mess,'* but knew that would only make things worse. After composing himself, he said, "I've warned you. That's all I can do..." and disconnected.

Chapter Thirty

Bridgette slept soundly for the first time in weeks. Her anxiety about Frost's recovery was diminishing as she could see daily improvements in his health. She had stayed with him until close to ten PM the previous evening, enjoying his company and the short bursts of conversation when he was awake. After an early morning gym session, she had driven up to West Vancouver and treated herself to pancakes at a cafe recommended by Renée Filipucci.

She had used the time to mentally plan her strategy for the day. The goal was simple—find out the name of the boy that Mac had seen regularly with Jacob Temple at his burger place. As she considered her options, she decided the best person to ask would be someone with intimate knowledge of the marina thirteen years ago. Floyd Geddes was the obvious choice.

Now, as she parked out front of his house on Falcon Road, she did her best to temper her hopes for the meeting. Detective work typically required hundreds of hours of investigation and dozens of interviews to get the answers.

But she didn't have time to play the numbers game and had to be smart with her time. She had called Geddes earlier and arranged to meet him at ten AM.

Before she got to his front door, Geddes had it open to welcome her. She noticed he was wearing the same blue cardigan as last time, but his cream pants had been replaced by denim jeans.

Geddes smiled and said, "Good to see you again, Detective. I don't get many visitors these days, and I'm always happy to help the law."

As they walked inside, Bridgette thanked Geddes for seeing her at such short notice.

When they were settled in the sitting room, Bridgette showed Geddes a copy of the Polaroid of Temple and one of the twins again. "We interviewed Jacob Temple yesterday."

"Well, that must have been interesting for you."

Bridgette knew she had to be careful about what she said and simply responded, "Yes," and then added, "As you know, the trial starts next week, and this photograph will be part of a larger body of evidence available for use by both the prosecution and the defense. "

"I'm not sure I can help anymore with the photograph, Detective. I'm pretty certain that's Temple, but I don't know what else to tell you."

"One of the other witnesses believes he hung out with one friend in particular during the summer months."

"Let me guess—he denies this?"

Bridgette frowned. "I can't give you specifics of any interviews we've conducted, Mr. Geddes. But let's just say I'm not sure he's fully cooperating. Did you ever see him hanging out with anyone in particular?"

"Well, let's see," said Geddes with a scratch of his chin.

"A lot of young people used to hang around at the marina back in the day. And also at the beach. But I didn't see much of that as I was busy with the yacht club."

"So, you don't recall him hanging out with anyone in particular?"

Geddes frowned. "Not really... but one incident has always stayed with me."

"And what was that," said Bridgette, trying not to get her hopes up too much.

"One day, I caught him and another boy on a boat in the marina. A boat they shouldn't have been on."

"They were trespassing?"

"Yes. We had quite a problem with it back in the day. People were complaining that things were being stolen off their boats."

"What kinds of things?"

"It was mostly alcohol and small amounts of cash. The locks on many of these boats aren't great, and it was easy to break in. But the thieves would leave instruments, depth sounders, and other stuff worth thousands of dollars and just steal small stuff. It made me think it was kids."

"Okay."

"I remember catching Temple and this other guy—he was probably a couple of years older—one day. I challenged them about what they were doing on the boat, and they gave me some BS about being there to pick up life-jackets."

"But you knew that was a lie?"

Geddes nodded. "They said they had permission, but I knew that wasn't the truth. I told them to clear off, or I'd call the police."

"Do you remember who the other boy was?"

"I knew that was going to be your next question," said Geddes with a grimace. He thought for a moment and said,

"I remember his father. He was a real asshole who thought he was better than everyone else. I didn't see much of him, but he had one of the biggest yachts in the marina then."

Before she could respond, Geddes pulled out his phone. "I'm going to call a guy called Gil Padano. Gil worked down at the marina and has a better recall of names than I do."

Bridgette waited patiently while Geddes made his call. He made small talk with Padano for a few moments before asking, "Do you remember the name of that real estate asshole? The one who had the big blue yacht?"

Geddes listened for a moment and exclaimed, "That's it. Mallory! I remember now."

After promising to catch up soon for a drink, Geddes thanked Padano for his time and disconnected. He turned to Bridgette with a smile and said, "John Mallory is the name of the guy who owned the boat. I don't remember his son's name, but hopefully, that's a start. The son was a piece of work, now that I think about it. I had a couple more run-ins with him after that but I haven't seen him in years."

Bridgette did her best to hide her excitement as she responded, "I'm sure that's more than enough to start with."

Geddes frowned. "Aren't you going to write down his name?"

"No need," said Bridgette with a smile. "John Mallory is a name I'm not going to forget."

Chapter Thirty-One

Bridgette returned to the police headquarters as soon as she had completed her interview with Floyd Geddes. Buoyed by the breakthrough she had made with the name, she had hoped to quickly determine the identity of John Mallory's son, but that task had proved more challenging.

Delray had made Margot James, a young analyst in the homicide team, available to help Bridgette with her search. Eventually, they learned that John Mallory had died six years earlier while running a real-estate business in Seattle. There was little information on the public record about his death apart from a coroner's report that said he had died of a heart attack most likely brought on by heavy cocaine use. At the time of his death, he had been divorced for three years and lived alone.

Bridgette had worked until almost six PM before leaving the office. She felt guilty about leaving Margot, who had volunteered to continue the search. Still, Bridgette also wanted to spend time with Levi Frost. She arrived at the hospital just before seven PM and was pleased to see Frost sitting up in bed with most of the bandages removed from his face.

Eleanor Frost stayed with them for a few minutes before excusing herself to go and have her evening meal.

When they were finally alone, Bridgette said, "You know, I think your mom is a very switched-on lady."

"How do you figure that?" said Frost with a frown.

"She didn't go for her evening meal until I arrived. I think she wants to give us time alone. I'm beginning to think last night's headache may have been more about giving us time together than anything else."

"I never thought about it like that."

"I'm glad you're doing better."

"Thanks for coming in. I know the chief is working you hard."

Bridgette wanted to squeeze his hand. But now that Frost was recovering, it felt slightly awkward. Instead, she smiled and said, "It's no problem, Levi."

"The doctor said I'll be moved to an orthopedic ward tomorrow. And I'll be able to have visitors."

"That's great. I know the guys back at the office are all keen to see you."

"You'll still come?"

"Of course."

Frost murmured, "Good," before his face became a scowl.

"What's wrong?"

"You know they lied to me."

"Who lied to you?"

"The nurses."

"The nurses lied to you?"

"The solid foods I was supposed to get. They weren't very solid. Soup, in fact."

"What were you expecting?" said Bridgette with a laugh. "Steak?"

Frost closed his eyes for a moment. "I keep thinking about our last meal together. Now that was a good steak."

Bridgette smiled. "It was a good night."

Without opening his eyes, Frost said, "Tell me about your day."

Bridgette kept it short and focused on how they had found out the name of the father of the young man they believed had been Jacob Temple's friend at the time of the murders. Bridgette added, "But the father died a few years back. And trying to find current family members, including the son, is proving a challenge."

"It's never easy."

Bridgette sighed. "We're running out of time, and I keep thinking about Remmy Chilton sitting in a jail cell."

"You're doing all you can."

Bridgette's phone buzzed as she went to respond. She looked down and read the screen.

Hi Bridgette, I think I've found John Mallory's son's identity. His name is Kurt Mallory, but he now goes by the name of Kurt Blackwood. It looks like he was living in Seattle but moved back to Vancouver eight months ago (address as yet unknown). Sending you a photo (taken 2 years ago) and then heading home. Feel free to call if you need anything further. C U tomorrow. Regards Margot

"Well, that's good news."

"What?"

"Margot's found out the name of the guy we think Jacob Temple used to hang out with."

"That's great. So... are you heading back into the office?"

"Maybe later. I want to spend some time with you."

"You know I don't mind. It's important work, after all."

"Our lives have to be more than police work."

The room went quiet as Frost closed his eyes again. Within seconds, he was breathing deeply and occasionally letting out a gentle snore.

Bridgette studied the image of Kurt Mallory on her phone. He looked to be in his early thirties with light brown hair that had probably been blonde in his youth. He had a square jaw and looked confident as he stared at the camera. The image was a head-shot and looked like it was taken as a professional profile for a website or similar. She debated calling Margot to find out where she got the image but decided it could wait until the morning. She used the time while Frost slept to do an online search for all she could find out. Kurt Mallory appeared to be a ghost. No one matching that name had a profile in Greater Vancouver, but Kurt Blackwood was another matter.

It was well after nine PM before Frost woke again.

He blinked sleep from his eyes and said, "Have I been asleep long?"

Bridgette smiled. "Almost two hours."

Frost grumbled, "Seeing you is the highlight of my day. I'm not happy about sleeping through most of it."

Bridgette felt a lump form in her throat. She knew she would hang on to his words long after she had left the hospital. "You're still on heavy painkillers, and your body is in overdrive trying to heal. Sleeping a lot is natural."

"Yeah... I guess," said Frost as he looked around. "Where's mom?"

"She's come and gone. Stayed for about an hour and then left. She'll be back tomorrow around eight."

They talked for a few more minutes about Frost's rehab

program and the future operations he would need. She sympathized with his journey ahead.

As they made small talk, she noticed Frost was struggling to keep his eyes open. "I think it's time for me to go and for you to sleep."

Frost frowned. "Sorry, I can't keep my eyes open."

"You're doing better every day."

Frost thanked her for her encouragement. They said their goodbyes, with Frost wishing her luck finding Kurt Mallory.

As she headed for the door, Frost added, "Hey, Bridge."

Bridgette paused at the doorway and looked back. It was the third time she could remember Frost shortening her name to 'Bridge', and she liked it.

"Thanks for coming."

Bridgette smiled. "It was the highlight of my day," and then headed for the exit.

Chapter Thirty-Two

Kurt Mallory cursed again as his phone buzzed. It was another message from Jacob Temple—his third in less than an hour—demanding that he call back immediately. The lawyer was starting to panic, and Mallory now regretted not disposing of him years earlier. It would have been easy to return and break into Temple's apartment while he slept. If he made it look like a burglary gone wrong, no one would have suspected a casual acquaintance who lived across the border.

But he never made that trip. Life in Seattle, working in his father's real estate business, and his side hustle of selling cocaine to high-end clients had kept him busy. After his father's death, and with no desire to work sixty-hour weeks to keep the business going, he sold up and returned to Vancouver as a multi-millionaire. On his return, he had again contemplated getting rid of Temple. But the risk of their crime over a decade earlier being discovered seemed negligible and not worth the risk. He realized now that that decision had been a mistake. A mistake he had to fix.

But for now, Temple would have to wait. He adjusted his rear-view mirror slightly to ensure he had the best possible view of Ackroyd Road, even though the gesture was overkill. Parked directly opposite the driveway that led into the cop's apartment block, he was confident he would see her '66 Mustang as it drove in.

Earlier in the evening, he had knocked on her door with a pizza box, pretending to be a delivery driver. But his knock had gone unanswered, so he had settled in his car to wait. The pizza box now lay open on the front passenger seat of his car. He gazed down at its contents, confident that he needed everything. He hoped the Glock 17 wouldn't be necessary. He was satisfied the sheer pantyhose would be an appropriate form of binding that wouldn't leave any bruising.

The sealed plastic bag that contained a soaked rag concerned him more. The Chloroform had been hard to come by, and his research suggested it didn't knock out the victim straight away like it was portrayed in the movies. He'd learned it took several minutes of application before it rendered the subject fully unconscious. Adjustments would need to be made, but it was the best he could do at short notice. He had planned out various scenarios around how he would administer it as he sat and waited for her return. He would need to keep her mouth covered for several minutes, which meant he would need an element of surprise.

The job had to be done tonight before she connected him to Temple. And the only way he could do that without arousing too much suspicion was to make it look like suicide. Just another cop who had gassed herself in her car because she couldn't cope with the stresses of the job.

His gaze settled on a coil of clear plastic hose next to the pizza box. He had cut off a small length earlier in the day and tested that it fit snugly over a standard car exhaust pipe. He found it ironic that he would use her own car, a '66 Mustang, as her murder weapon.

He'd learned she was a formidable cop, and his plan was far from foolproof. But he liked living in Vancouver and didn't want the life of a fugitive if he could avoid it. It was worth the risk, but it would take all his skill to subdue her without leaving any bruising or other telltale signs of a struggle. Once she was out of the way, he would focus on Temple. He figured that would be tomorrow's job.

After leaving the hospital, Bridgette decided to head straight home. It was now after ten PM, and she was tired. She planned to spend an hour at her apartment searching online for more information about Kurt Mallory, AKA Kurt Blackwood, before bed. But she wasn't confident she could focus as her mind replayed her last conversation with Levi Frost.

As she changed lanes to take an exit to her apartment in Richmond, his words, "Seeing you is the highlight of my day…" echoed in her mind. She smiled as she recalled the moment and how it made her feel. She was clearly falling for him, and she was okay with that.

She was also certain Eleanor had picked up on it, so she was giving them time alone. She allowed herself to dream about a future for the two of them. If it developed into a relationship, one of them would need to be redeployed—Vancouver Police disapproved of couples working in the same team.

Bridgette frowned. If everything played out as she hoped,

that decision was clearly some time off—Frost was in for months of rehab before he would be well enough to return to work. She thought about what lay ahead for them. Eleanor had told her she could only stay a few more days before her leave ran out, and she would be forced to return to her job on the East Coast. This would leave much of the care beyond what the hospital could provide to her, and she was okay with that, too.

Her phone buzzed. She glanced at the screen and saw it was an incoming call from Renée Filipucci.

She pressed the answer on her hands-free kit and said, "Hi, Renée. This is a bit late even for you."

"Hey, BC. Just thought I'd check in on you. You've been awfully quiet these last few days."

"Sorry. Work's been full on, and I'm at the hospital if I'm not there."

"How's Levi?"

"He's doing okay. The first surgery on his leg was a success, so they're moving him to an orthopedic ward tomorrow."

"Sounds great. Hey, we should try and catch up; I'm forgetting what you look like."

"How about Saturday. Tomorrow is full on with work, but I hope to have some downtime on the weekend."

"Sounds good."

"I'm looking forward to it."

"So… how are things going with you and Levi?"

Bridgette smiled to herself. She knew the question was coming, and while Filipucci could be nosy, she meant well.

"No change, really. I'm just focused on his recovery for now and putting my own feelings on the back burner."

"Well… if you need to talk, I'm always here."

"Thanks, Renée. You're the best."

Filipucci promised to call again tomorrow and then disconnected.

It occurred to Bridgette that regardless of whether a relationship developed, she was committed to helping Frost with rehab. He would be her priority, and she figured there would be less time for Filipucci and her other friends. She made a mental note to talk to her friend about it when they caught up next. While Renée was fiercely independent, she still had anxiety attacks stemming from a domestic violence incident with a previous partner. Bridgette had become her sounding board and promised to be there for her always, and that wasn't about to change.

Five minutes later, Bridgette pulled into the parking bay beneath her apartment building on Ackroyd Road. She mulled over what she would do. Starting an online search for more information about Kurt Mallory now would mean she would be up until midnight. And then her brain would be too active to allow her to sleep. After parking in her designated bay and switching off the engine, she sat for a moment and massaged her neck. Tomorrow would be Friday and time was running out for Remmy Chilton. If she could track down Mallory's address, there was a slim chance they could interview him tomorrow or over the weekend to learn more about Temple's relationship with the twins.

She grimaced and murmured, "We're running out of time," as she got out of her car and walked towards the stairwell. She decided to spend an hour or two tonight searching online for more information before going to bed. Hopefully, she might find Mallory's address to give the investigation the jump start it needed in the morning.

As she walked towards the stairwell, her body ached with fatigue. Usually alert when alone, Bridgette didn't notice a shadowy figure lurking in the darkness when she had parked her car. And she hadn't seen the figure slinking closer and closer to her as she made her way towards the stairwell. Only when she reached out to open the door did she feel a cold presence behind her. But by then, it was too late.

A man in dark clothing and a ski mask lunged at her from behind. Before she could respond, she felt a bunched-up cloth being shoved into her face. The sweet smell emanating from the fabric covering her mouth and nose was vaguely familiar. She screamed and tried to push away as the man wrapped one arm around and shoved her hard up against a wall.

Bridgette's heart pounded as she struggled to break free. Her eyes began to sting as she twisted and kicked. But she was no match for the man's strength. She felt herself getting dizzy. Everything became a blur as she continued to struggle. Suddenly, she felt herself floating as her world began to spin.

Chapter Thirty-Three

Bridgette felt a buzz in her head as she woke. It was soft at first but grew louder as the seconds passed. She wanted to puke. Where was she? And what was that noise? And why was she so uncomfortable?

She blinked, but the darkness remained. Had she fallen? Was this a dream?

She lay on her side, willing her brain to re-engage. Her arms were uncomfortable—like she had slept on them wrong. But they refused to move. It was as if they were pinned behind…

Bridgette let out an audible groan as she realized her hands were tied behind her back. She tried to move her legs, but they were also tied together. She wondered where she was and why she was lying on her side? And what was that strange droning sound? And what was that dull red light switching on and off above her head?

She fought back an urge to vomit. She wished the rocking motion would stop. And then she realized she was in a vehicle. But whose vehicle? And where was she being driven? She tried to break free of her bindings, but they held firm.

The vehicle downshifted gears—definitely a manual, she thought. And then it accelerated, and she heard a familiar burble from the engine. Bridgette swore as she realized she was being held captive in her own car. The red light appeared above her head again, just momentarily, before her world turned dark again. She knew this was her car's brake lights and that she was bound up in the trunk. She wondered how long the journey would take before they stopped. She thought back briefly to when she had been attacked. The man had been strong and was able to overpower her with the element of surprise. And then she remembered the sweet smell of a rag being placed over her mouth and nose—chloroform. But what was his motive? Rape, murder, both? Whatever it was, she knew she probably wouldn't survive the night. Sucking in a deep breath, she willed herself not to panic.

As the fog cleared, she began to think clearly. She needed to get out of her bindings. She twisted her wrists backward and forward in a scissors motion, trying to break the bindings. But whatever the man had used to tie her up with held firm. She stretched out her arms as best she could and wiggled her hips, hoping to slip the her bound hands under her butt and down over her legs to at least get the bindings in front of her. But she was a tall woman, and the cramped conditions in the trunk made that impossible.

Bridgette felt herself go dizzy. There was little air in the trunk, and she needed to be thoughtful about her actions so she wouldn't pass out again. Using the tips of her fingers, she explored the bindings. At first, they simply felt like some sort of material. She continued her exploration and found the knot. It didn't take her long to figure out her captor had used pantyhose or similar to restrain her. Easy enough to cut if you had a knife, but almost impossible without. Bridgette tried to free the knot with the tips of her fingers, but she couldn't get the leverage she needed.

She implored herself, *'Think!'* as her car rumbled off a sealed road and onto dirt. Realizing the vehicle could stop at any second, she needed another strategy.

Bridgette wondered if she could use anything in her trunk to cut the bindings. She only had a small tool kit with pliers, a flashlight, a wrench, and a screwdriver. But they were wrapped up in a towel and wedged into a cavity in the floor at her feet. Bridgette tried maneuvering her feet for several minutes to dislodge the tools, but nothing worked. Now, a ball of sweat, she knew any further effort would be a waste of time.

She lay on her side, contemplating what to try next. The brake light came on again, illuminating the rear part of the trunk as the car rumbled along. Her '66 Mustang Fastback, like most cars of its era, was simple in construction. The trunk space was little more than painted sheet metal with carpet as a floor mat. The wiring for the tail lights was exposed, as was the fuel pipe that led from the gas cap above the rear bumper through to the fuel tank.

It was the fuel pipe that caught her attention. She had seen it hundreds of times when she had opened and closed the trunk, but it never held any significance for her until now. Even though the trunk had returned to darkness, she thought about the clamp that held the pipe to the car's gas-filling cap assembly. The clamp was held in place by a quarter-inch steel bolt. The bolt was worth less than a dollar in any hardware store, but now, it might save her life.

Bridgette dared to hope as she pictured the bolt in her mind. It wasn't the original bolt—the man who had restored her car had fitted a replacement that was slightly too long. She knew about half an inch of thread stuck out beyond the nut when the clamp had been fitted. If she could get her hands to it, there was a chance she could rub the bindings across it, using the thread of the bolt like a small saw. But she was facing the wrong way. With her back to the front of the car, there was no way she could get her hands near the bolt without flipping over. And the trunk of her Mustang was small. She knew turning over would be almost impossible, but it was her only hope.

Bridgette stretched out to flatten her body. Then she tried to roll onto her back, but her legs got caught on the trunk's roof. She needed to flatten out more and inched back as far as she could to the side of the vehicle to give her more room. With her head pressed hard up against the side panel, she tried to roll again, but her knees still got caught on the roof. Bridgette shifted her hips a fraction and breathed a sigh of relief as she was now able to complete the roll over maneuver.

Now facing the front of the car and conscious that every minute could be her last, Bridgette used her hips and legs to inch backward until she was hard up against the gas pipe. Bridgette ignored the sweat stinging her eyes and, by feel, positioned the binding around her hands over the bolt thread.

She noticed the car start to bump as it hit a rocky surface. Bridgette wondered how much longer she had before the car stopped. With a precise motion, she rubbed the nylon material backward and forward across the bolt's thread. Tiny motions. Backward and forward. At first, it didn't feel as though she was making any progress, but she kept at it. After about a minute, the binding stretched. She implored herself to remain calm as she continued the tiny back and forward motions. A moment later the binding snapped.

She rubbed her wrists together to regain circulation but stopped when she heard the car change gears again. Bridgette cursed as the brake lights came on and stayed on—the driver was definitely stopping the car. If she had more time, her focus would have been on getting her feet unbound, but she couldn't afford to take that risk. She needed a weapon, and she needed it now.

With her hands now free, Bridgette reached into the storage well. She felt the car stop and heard the engine switch off as she fumbled around for the tool kit. As she heard the car door open, she pulled out the tool kit. Not caring about the noise she made, she unraveled the towel and desperately felt around in the dark. First, pliers, and then a flashlight. As she heard the trunk unlock, she found what she was looking for. Bridgette gripped the screwdriver and braced herself for what was about to come.

Chapter Thirty-Four

Bridgette lay in the dark, not daring to breathe. With no time to formulate a plan, she gripped the screwdriver tightly and braced herself as she heard the man's footsteps as he walked around to the back of her car. With her feet still bound and groggy from the Chloroform, she knew the odds of survival were still slim, particularly if the man had a gun. But she wasn't about to give up without a fight.

Instinct took over as the trunk lid rose. She looked up over her shoulder as the man's shadow loomed above her. She waited a fraction of a second and then launched herself upward, swinging the screwdriver in one motion. A stab wound to the chest could have been fatal, but if the screwdriver hit a rib or breast bone, it might deflect off and only do minor damage. She needed to disable her attacker and aimed for the man's stomach.

Bridgette swung the screwdriver through a vicious arc. The man let out a bloodcurdling roar and doubled over as the shaft of her weapon penetrated his lightweight pullover and buried itself deep in his flesh. Bridgette let go of the screwdriver and reached for the shifting spanner at her feet while the man attempted to remove the driver.

After taking a step back from the car to examine what he had been stabbed with, he roared, "You little bitch!" and raised the screwdriver like a knife. Bridgette raised her left arm to deflect the blow as the man rushed forward. She waited a fraction of a second and swung the spanner at the man's head. She let out a groan as the screwdriver dug deep into the flesh of her upper forearm. The spanner continued on its arc, smashing into the man's head at the top of his left ear. Bridgette watched the man stagger before slumping to the ground beside her vehicle.

As he lay writhing on the ground, Bridgette removed her boots and slipped off the bindings around her feet. She managed to get out of the trunk and swung the spanner a second time just as the man rose to his knees. The weapon connected with the man's skull with a dull thud. She jumped to one side as the man collapsed forward on his face.

Keeping a firm grip on the spanner, Bridgette slammed the trunk down, raced around to the driver's door, and jumped in her vehicle. She felt for her keys and was relieved they were still in the ignition. After turning the key and gunning the engine to life, she shifted into first gear and dropped the clutch. The rear wheels spun briefly before they gripped the rocky surface and catapulted her car forward. Bridgette didn't look back as she shifted into second gear and accelerated into the night.

It was just after two AM when Delray walked back into the Emergency department of the Lions Gate Hospital in

North Vancouver. An uneventful evening at home with his wife had turned frantic when he got a call from Bridgette as he was getting ready for bed. It had taken several minutes to get her to the point where she was calm enough to talk coherently while she drove out of Cypress Park. When she explained that she had been abducted and bound up in the trunk of her own car, Delray immediately sprang into action.

While on the drive to Lions Gate Hospital, he had summoned two of his teams to Cypress Provincial Park just north of Vancouver, where her abductor had taken her. Based on Bridgette's advice, he believed her attacker would be on foot, and it was worth the time to try and find him.

Delray had arrived at the hospital shortly after Bridgette had checked herself into the emergency ward to have her wounds treated. After ensuring she was getting the best of care, Delray made an inventory of her car. He had taken photographs and would get a forensics team to review the vehicle from top to bottom before it was returned to her. As he made his way back into the Emergency department, he shook his head—she was lucky to be alive.

Delray waited just outside the cubicle where Bridgette was being treated until a nurse gave him the all-clear to enter.

He found Bridgette lying on a bed with a large bandage wrapped around her left forearm when he entered. "How are you feeling?" he asked as he sat beside her bed.

Bridgette managed half a smile. "It's shaken me up a little."

"Are you in pain?"

"I'm full of painkillers, so not in much pain at present."

Pointing to her arm, Delray asked, "Is the arm going to be okay?"

"Yeah," said Bridgette with a nod. "Four stitches. They spent most of the time cleaning the wound to stop infection."

Delray shook his head. "I'm not sure many cops in the same position would have survived."

"When I woke up in the trunk of my own car, I thought that was it for me…"

Delray had been given a brief explanation of how Bridgette had escaped when he first met her at Emergency. He would get more detail in time, but for now, he wanted to focus on catching whoever was responsible. "Do you have any idea who did this to you?"

Bridgette picked up her phone with her good hand and flicked through her messages. "I got a message from Margot earlier this evening. She said she'd found out the name of John Mallory's son. His name is Kurt Mallory, and this is his picture."

Delray studied the image for a moment. "This is Jacob Temple's friend?"

Bridgette nodded.

"And you think this is the guy who attacked you?"

"I *know* this is the guy who attacked me. When he went to lift me out of the trunk, I got a good look at him. Even though it was dark, that's definitely the guy."

"I'll call Central Command and get his picture circulated." Delray paused momentarily and added, "You wanna hear what I found in your car?"

Bridgette grimaced. "I tried not to look. I just wanted to get the hell out of there just in case he had a gun."

"He was going to make it look like suicide," said Delray with a grimace. He explained how he had found a length of hose, a couple of towels, the Chloroform, and stockings. "Because you've got an old car, I think he was going to run the hose from the exhaust pipe in through a window blocked with towels."

"That's why I was tied up with stockings, not cable ties."

"Yep. No bruising if you hadn't woken up. I figure he would have given you another dose of Chloroform and then untied you and slumped you in the driver's seat. With the engine running, you would have been dead in minutes."

"And it would have looked like suicide."

"What I want to know is, why not just shoot you? We found a Glock in the car."

"I'm positive Mallory was afraid I would make the connection to him. If it looks like suicide, nobody goes looking for a killer."

"Well, let's just hope we find him. I've got two teams searching Cypress Park as we speak. If he's badly wounded, we might—"

"I doubt you'll find him. At least not there."

"Why do you say that?"

"He would have had a car somewhere close by. He drives out there in my car and leaves me for dead. He has to have some way of getting back."

"We need to find out where he lives. I'll get someone on it straight away."

"He'll have to run now," said Bridgette with a nod. "I'm sure he was planning on staying if his plan had worked. But he knows I got a good look at him…"

"Do you think he's badly wounded? I've got all the hospitals in the local area, including this one, on the lookout."

"I don't know, Chief. But if I were in his shoes and could walk or drive, I'd be looking to get out of Vancouver first."

Chapter Thirty-Five

Kurt Mallory limped back to his Jeep Wrangler that he had hidden in the forest earlier that day. It had taken him over two hours to make his way back. Walking had been difficult, and the pain in his head and stomach was intense. He was also worried the bitch cop may have discovered his Jeep and lay in wait for him. After unlocking the vehicle, he crawled into the driver's seat and locked the doors. He sat for a moment to catch his breath. The pain in his stomach had subsided a little, but he knew he needed to check the wound before he drove off.

Gingerly, he lifted up his sweater and shirt to examine his stomach. The puncture wound was not much larger than the screwdriver shaft. It wept more than bled and looked like a bullet wound. He would need to see a doctor to see if it required surgery. And then there was the issue of it turning septic. But that would have to wait. He was certain the cop recognized him and that meant he needed to get out of Vancouver tonight.

Mallory opened the glove compartment and withdrew a

pack of Tylenol. He swallowed four tablets and closed his eyes for a moment. He would have loved to sleep, but he figured the cops would be crawling all over the forest shortly and he needed to get away. Mallory started his Jeep and shifted it into gear as he made plans. He figured Vancouver Police would have his identity sometime in the next few hours. And then they would know where he lived. It was too risky to go back to his apartment. It was a good thing he always had a plan B. But first, he needed to visit Jacob Temple. The meeting was long overdue, and they had a lot to talk about.

At just after four AM, Bridgette was advised by the Emergency doctor that she was being discharged. After signing her discharge papers, she found Delray in the waiting room, talking on his phone.

She presumed he was talking to one of his detectives in Cypress Park. As she approached, he mumbled, "I gotta go, Bridgette's here. Call me back if you find anything."

After disconnecting, he turned to Bridgette with a raised brow and said, "They're releasing you?"

"Yep. The wound's been cleaned and stitched, and I have a course of antibiotics. They just want me to take it easy for a few days."

"Well, let's get you home. You need to rest up."

"I'd like to keep working the case, Chief. I was a little shaken up, but—"

Delray raised an eyebrow. "You could have died tonight."

"But I didn't. And I know more about this case and Mallory than anyone else in the VPD. Who knows, he may have already run. But if he hasn't, he won't be hanging around for long, and we need to make every minute count."

"It wouldn't be right, Bridgette. After *all* you've been through, you need to rest. The doctor said so herself."

"If I go home, the attack is all I'm going to think about. And I know I won't sleep. This way, I'm at least doing something constructive, and catching Mallory will be the best therapy of all."

Delray frowned. "I don't have time to stand here and argue."

"I agree. But we don't know where he lives. Margot didn't get that far in her search last night. If we go back to the office now, I can get onto that immediately. And then you can coordinate the guys in the field."

"Okay, you make a good point," said Delray, holding up a hand in submission.

"Thanks, Chief."

Delray shook his head and grumbled as they walked to the exit. "I hope I'm not going to regret this."

With no traffic, the trip back to police headquarters took less than fifteen minutes. They made a rough plan of what they needed to do. Both Delray and Bridgette were convinced that Kurt Mallory was involved in the murder of the Halloran girls and equally sure he would be making plans to leave Vancouver if he hadn't already left.

Delray left Bridgette alone with her computer while he returned to his office to call Cunningham and the commissioner.

As a police officer, Bridgette had access to all kinds of databases. She quickly learned that Mallory had a valid driver's license, but the address provided was a postal address for a real estate office in downtown Vancouver. She noted the address for further investigation but knew it was unlikely this would be where Mallory would run to. She knew from her background research that he was now wealthy and had made a lot of money out of real estate with his father. It was conceivable that he operated one or more shelf companies and had used them to hide his identify for any properties he had purchased.

By the time Delray had finished his calls and summoned her to his office, she had tracked down two addresses for Mallory.

Bridgette didn't bother to knock on her boss's door. It was just after five AM, and they were the only two working on the floor. As she entered, she asked, "How did the conference call go?"

"Neither was happy about being woken up that early. But the commissioner was on board pretty quickly when I told him what happened to you. We'll have to submit a report at some point—he's pretty concerned about your health."

"I'll write it up later. What about Cunningham?"

"Cunningham is still not convinced that Mallory is the right guy for the Halloran murders. Fortunately, the commissioner was on board and overruled. He's authorized extra teams to be assigned to the search. Hopefully, with some more resources, we might have some luck."

"I may be able to help out with that." Said Bridgette.

"You have an address?" said Delray with a raised eyebrow.

"Two, in fact." Bridgette explained how she had tracked them through shelf companies Mallory appeared to own and then added, "It appears he owns two inner city apartments. And I think that's where we need to be searching first."

Delray nodded. "The commissioner is getting three teams of uniforms to go out and help with the search in Cyprus Park. I'll leave one of my teams to do the handover and get the other guys to come back now and go check on one of the apartments."

"And what about the other apartment?"

Delray picked up his keys from his desk. "Are you up for some more fieldwork?"

"Of course," said Bridgette with a nod.

"Then let's go. Every minute counts."

Chapter Thirty-Six

Bridgette stifled a yawn. It was almost six AM, and they had been in place in front of Kurt Mallory's apartment block on Quebec Street for nearly twenty minutes. Delray's mood darkened by the minute as he continued to check his phone for the text to say the search warrant had been approved. He dropped his phone in the car's center console in disgust and picked up a police two-way radio. "Johnson, you copy?"

The two-way responded, "Still quiet here, Chief."

Delray thanked the officer for the update and gazed up at the fifth floor where Mallory had his apartment. The building had three entry and exit points. Senior Constable William Johnson and his partner were covering the rear exit. Delray and Bridgette had been able to park almost directly opposite the front of the building. They had a good view of the front door that led into the apartment block. Two additional uniformed officers were stationed in an unmarked sedan just south of the driveway leading to the apartment building's underground parking. They had seen three people enter and exit the building since arriving, but none looked like Kurt Mallory.

On the short trip over from police headquarters, Bridgette and Delray had discussed tactics. They both agreed it was better to wait until they had the search warrant before they proceeded. Delray reasoned if Mallory was on the premises, they had legal cover to search his apartment for incriminating evidence after arresting him. And if he wasn't home, as they both suspected, they could conduct a legal search to find clues to his whereabouts.

But the wait was agonizing, particularly for Delray. He rechecked his phone again and grumbled, "What's taking so long?"

Bridgette thought better than to remind her boss that getting a search warrant at this time of the day would always be problematic, even if the commissioner himself was calling in favors with the judiciary. As she went to tactfully respond, Delray's phone buzzed.

He murmured, "It's the commissioner," and pressed answer. The conversation lasted only thirty seconds. After disconnecting, Delray grinned and said, "We're good to go. We have search warrants approved for both apartments—the commissioner's getting them emailed through now."

"So, what's the plan?"

Delray was already punching numbers into his phone. "I'm calling the team at the other apartment to let them know they can move in too."

While Delray made the call, Bridgette got on the two-way to the two uniform teams. She arranged for one uniform officer from each team to remain in place to cover the exits, just in case Mallory slipped them and made a run for it.

After finishing his call, Delray checked his messages.

"The second team at Cypress Park is on its way back. They'll be here in about ten minutes."

"Are we going to wait?"

Delray shook his head. "No. Minutes matter—we need to move now."

Delray pounded on the door to apartment 5C and yelled, "Open up! Police!" He knocked again, but his patience quickly ran out when he got no response. Nodding toward one of the uniformed officers who was carrying a portal battering ram, he said, "Bust it open."

The officer stepped forward with the ram, which was little more than a steel pipe about as long as a baseball bat and twice as thick. He gripped the device's two handles and, with a pendulum motion, rammed one end into the apartment's front door next to its two deadlocks. The sound of the ram reverberated around the hallway, but the door held firm. The officer didn't need any encouragement and swung the pipe again. This time, the door burst open.

With his gun drawn, Delray walked in first, followed closely by Bridgette and one of the uniformed officers. They checked a closet, powder room, and laundry as they walked down the hallway to the living room. Bridgette stood for a moment scanning the living room with her gun drawn while Delray and the uniformed officer checked two bedrooms. The living room was about thirty feet long by twenty feet wide. It had a modern white kitchen and dining setting for four people at one end. Bridgette noticed the front of the dishwasher and refrigerator had paneling to match the kitchen cupboards to blend them in. She noted one bookshelf with two ornamental pots but no books. The other end of the living room contained two leather couches, a glass coffee table, and a flat-screen TV mounted on the wall.

Delray and the uniformed office reappeared a moment later. Delray said, "All clear. No one's here."

Bridgette moved to the kitchen area and opened several drawers on the island bench-top.

Delray frowned. "What are you looking for?"

"I don't think anyone lives here," she said as she opened the refrigerator. "There's no food here and little in the way of cooking appliances." She pointed to the walls and said, "There are no pictures or photographs—nothing personal at all, even for a minimalist."

Delray motioned to the uniformed officer. "Can you check the wardrobes in the bedrooms? Let's see if we've got any clothes in there."

The officer returned a moment later and said, "No clothes, but you better come check this out."

The officer led them to the master bedroom and into a walk-in robe. They stood for a moment in silence and stared at a SONY video camera screwed to a mounting bracket just in front of a cutout in the wall.

Delray walked back into the bedroom and murmured, "I'll be damned. He's got this set up for filming."

Bridgette followed Delray back into the bedroom and stared at the mirror on the wall that backed onto the walk-in robe. She didn't need to investigate further to know the mirror was two-way and that Mallory was using it to film his exploits in bed. She wondered if his partners knew about the camera as she said, "Well, we now know what he used the apartment for."

"And we're not going to find him here," growled Delray.

Bridgette opened several drawers on a bedside table and said, "They're all empty."

Delray instructed the two uniformed officers to start making an official search of the apartment and then said to Bridgette, "Let's hope the other team has more luck."

As she watched Delray hit speed dial on his phone, a knot formed in her stomach. The realization that they were at a dead end and no closer to finding Mallory left her feeling angry. She closed her eyes momentarily and breathed deeply to control her emotions. Images of the night before when he had attacked her surfaced. Bridgette felt a shiver run down her spine as she relived her ordeal in the trunk of her car and how Mallory had been intent on taking her life.

She opened her eyes just as Delray disconnected. He grumbled, "They've had no luck either. They've found some of his belongings at that apartment, but no sign of him."

Bridgette cocked her head as she pulled on her left earlobe.

"What are you thinking?" asked Delray.

As an idea popped into her head, she said, "I think I know where he is. Let me explain on the way."

Chapter Thirty-Seven

Kurt Mallory parked his Jeep in front of a three-story apartment building on Logan Street in South Vancouver. After switching the engine off, he wiped sweat from his brow and closed his eyes to let the pain in his stomach subside. The drive back from Cypress Park had been challenging. Every time he turned the steering wheel, the pain in his stomach had been excruciating. He had taken another four Tylenol, but they made little difference. He breathed in and out through his nose, willing the pain to subside while he rested. After several minutes, he opened his eyes again and lifted his shirt to examine the wound.

A large purple bruise about the size of a baseball now surrounded the wound. And while it continued to weep a little, the blood flow had stopped. Mallory lowered his shirt and stared up at the apartment block. It was made of cinder block, painted cream, and trimmed with charcoal gray timber beams that were badly in need of painting. It was a far cry from his apartments, and he figured Phipps, Babbs, and Associates didn't share much of their profits with their staff.

Mallory winced as he reached across and opened the glove box. He withdrew a small knife that had started life as a cheese knife before he had sharpened the blade to a razor's edge. Mallory would have preferred to use his Glock, but the knife wouldn't make a sound and alert Temples' neighbors.

Mallory checked the clock on the dash of his Jeep. It was just before six-thirty AM. He figured Jacob Temple would be getting ready for work but probably still at home—perfect timing. Mallory gingerly picked up a North Face backpack from the passenger seat and got out of the car. He quickly scanned the interior of the vehicle to ensure he wasn't leaving anything of value behind. It was too risky to continue driving the vehicle and he needed new wheels—something Temple was going to provide.

Mallory did his best to look casual as he walked up the pathway toward the apartment block. Realizing his blood-soaked sweater would draw attention, he slung the backpack over his shoulder and positioned it in front of his stomach to hide the worst of the blood stains.

He paused at the front entrance to the building and allowed himself a grin as he stared down at the broken door lock—finally, a lucky break.

After stepping into the building's tiny foyer, Mallory grimaced—there was no elevator. He trudged up the stairs and paused to catch his breath when he reached the third-floor landing. After a few moments, he pushed off the railing and walked down the hallway. The carpet on the floor was threadbare and in keeping with the rest of the building that desperately needed a face-lift.

Mallory paused outside apartment 3B. The door had two locks, but it was the peephole that bothered him most. Temple would be wary of anyone knocking on his door at this hour of the day, and he needed to have his story straight before he knocked. He thought for a moment and then knocked.

Mallory suspected he would have to wait and was surprised when he heard Temple's voice behind the door just a few seconds later.

"Who is it?"

"It's me, Kurt."

There was a moment of silence. Mallory imagined Temple looking through the peephole as he added, "Jacob, I don't have much time. And I need to give you something to take care of."

"What do you need to give me?"

"I'm not going to explain it out here. Let's just say what I've got in my bag will make us immune from prosecution."

Another moment's silence. "This is all highly irregular, Kurt. Do you know what time it is?"

Patience had never been Mallory's strong suit, but he needed to exercise it now to get Temple to open the door. "I know what time it is. I'm about to head back to Seattle, but seeing as you're staying here, you'll need what I have in my bag more than I do if they come after us."

"What's in the bag."

"Let's just say, something that will keep Remmy Chilton locked up for a long time."

More silence. Mallory knew Temple was wavering and added, "Look, I don't have time to wait. If you don't trust me, I'll leave it in the hallway, and you can collect it later."

"What on earth could you have that could keep Chilton behind bars?"

Mallory deliberately raised his voice. "I'm leaving the bag here. Suit yourself when you get it."

Mallory bent down slightly to remove the bag. He heard a soft click as the door unlocked. The door opened a fraction. Mallory was three inches taller than Temple and had a toned physique from years of gym work. Under other circumstances, he would have pushed the door open and barged his way in. But he wasn't confident he had the strength in his weakened condition.

He placed the bag on the ground about a foot from the door and stepped back. "Call me when you're ready to talk. And if I'm in a good mood, maybe I'll answer."

Mallory turned his back and pretended to walk away.

He took one small step before Temple opened the door and said, "Hey, wait…"

Mallory kept Temple in his peripheral vision. When the lawyer had taken two steps forward, he turned and lunged. He shoved the knife hard up against Temple's throat and hissed, "Now, that wasn't so hard, was it?"

Temple stammered, "What do you want?"

Mallory's face broke into a cruel grin. "I need your car keys and then we'll talk. Five minutes should do it, and then I'll be on my way."

Chapter Thirty-Eight

After leaving the two uniformed officers to continue the search of Mallory's apartment, Delray and Bridgette opted for the stairwell rather than waiting for the elevator. Bridgette explained above the clatter of their shoes as they hurried down the steps, "I'm positive Temple was part of this. And Mallory is wounded and needs to get out of town."

"So who better to turn to than your partner in crime," said Delray.

"Exactly."

"As they hit the ground floor, Delray said, "Do you have Temple's home address?"

"Logan Street, South Vancouver."

Delray handed Bridgette the keys to his car as they raced across the road. "That's about ten minutes. You drive and I'll make some calls. We need a couple of squad cars to meet us there."

The drive took eight minutes without lights and sirens. Delray had instructed the two squad cars to park further down the street and await their arrival. The tactical meeting before they approached the unit was brief, with Delray instructing one team to head around back. At the same time, the other team waited out front.

When they got to the third floor, Delray drew his weapon and murmured, "It's just after seven. Unless he's an early starter or a gym junkie, Temple should be home."

Bridgette pulled her weapon and followed Delray down the hallway to 3B. Delray knocked. When he got no response, he knocked again.

He waited a few seconds and then murmured, "I don't like it." He pulled his two-way from a coat pocket. "Constable Wade. You copy?"

"Yeah, Chief."

"Parking lot for 3B. Is there a car parked in it?"

"No car in the 3B, Sir."

Delray swore and then added, "He drives a late model white KIA Seltos. It's a small four-wheel drive and should be easy to spot. You see anything like that parked down there?"

When Wade responded, "No," Delray turned to Bridgette. "Let's call his office. If he's there, we'll go down and talk to him straight away."

"He might be at work…" said Bridgette as she pointed at the door. "But Mallory might still be here."

"We'll need a search warrant."

Bridgette turned the door handle. As the door opened, she added, "Maybe not."

Bridgette followed Delray inside. They only took three steps before Delray swore again, adding, "We're too late."

Bridgette grimaced as she stared down at Jacob Temple.

He was lying on his side in a pool of blood. His eyes were still open and it looked as if he was staring at the coffee table about six feet away. She had seen this vacant stare of death before but went through the motions anyway. She counted off three puncture wounds in his chest that had turned his white business shirt red. After closing the gap between them, Bridgette knelt beside Temple to check for a pulse. She grimaced and looked up at Delray as she shook her head. "He's still warm. This has only just happened."

Delray made a quick check to be sure Mallory wasn't hiding anywhere and then called up the two uniformed officers to help search for clues. Next, he called in the registration plate for Temple's car, which they assumed Mallory was now driving.

When he disconnected, Delray said, "I think this is a bust, but we'll search anyway."

"I can't believe we got this close, and he still gets away."

Bridgette breathed in deeply as she put on latex gloves. She was seething inside and didn't want anger to cloud her judgment.

Delray said, "Why don't you start with his bedroom?"

"I'm on it," said Bridgette as she walked into a small alcove. The door to the right led to the apartment's bathroom, and the one on the left to Temple's bedroom. The bedroom was painted off-white like the rest of the apartment. From the doorway, she could see Temple's bed was unmade, and a pile of dirty clothes was heaped in a corner. She moved into the room and scanned his bedside table. There was a small bedside clock that was a few minutes fast, a box of tissues, and a bottle of pills. She picked up the bottle and read the label—a prescription for sleeping pills. After putting down the bottle, she opened the table's top drawer. It contained more bottles and what looked like cannabis in a small plastic bag. None of this interested her, and she opened the bottom drawer. It contained several paperback books and a few more empty prescription bottles but nothing else.

Bridgette moved around to the other side of the bed and was about to open the wardrobe when she noticed a flat object caught in the bedding. She reached across and lifted the bed covers. She called out, "Found his laptop," as she picked up a late-model Mac Book Air.

Delray, who was currently searching drawers in the kitchen, called back, "Is it locked?"

Bridgette returned to the living room and placed the device on Temple's small dining table. She opened it up and was presented with a password lock screen. "It's locked."

"We'll get it to the IT guys at the lab. Hopefully, they'll be able to unlock it."

Bridgette studied the laptop momentarily and said, "Chief, do you mind if I try something?"

"Sure," said Delray with a frown. "What do you have in mind?"

Bridgette picked up the laptop and walked across to Temple's body. "This model has fingerprint security built into the power button. I use it on mine, but not everyone activates it."

Bridgette placed the laptop on the carpet near Temple's body, just back from the edge of the blood pool. She stood and took two photos of Temple's body before she moved his hand. She pressed his right thumb onto the power button but got an error message. Grimacing, she said, "It's usually the thumb or forefinger."

"What about his left hand?" asked Delray.

"The power button is on the right. Most people use their right hand even if they are left-handed." Bridgette placed Temple's index finger on the power button and allowed herself half a smile as the lock screen vanished. "We're in."

Bridgette moved back to the dining table with the laptop and sat down. She opened Temple's email program and checked his Inbox. There were over three thousand messages, but only the top seven were unread. She did a word search for 'Mallory' and then for 'Kurt' but drew a blank on both. She scanned his latest emails, but nothing jumped out at her as having any connection to Mallory. Conscious that every minute counted, Bridgette switched to the laptop's file manager application and scanned the folders and files on his hard drive. After several minutes, she murmured, "We're getting nowhere with this."

Finally, she switched to his browser. There were five tabs open. The first was for a news website, and the second and third were for porn sites. The final two tabs held some promise. Tab four was open on Google, and she checked his recent search history. Nothing jumped out at her that could lead to Mallory. She clicked on the last tab, which opened to Evernote. She knew Evernote was an online note-taking application even though she had never used it. She figured Temple must have used it recently because she wasn't prompted for a password.

Bridgette found the application's search bar in the top left-hand corner. She keyed in the word Mallory and pressed enter. She waited for a moment until the search refreshed. Three notes were listed under the search bar. Bridgette murmured, "I've got a hit."

Delray said, "Let's hope it leads somewhere," as he walked over to join her.

Bridgette opened the first of the three notes. She skim-read the contents. "It looks like a background document. Temple's been keeping notes on Mallory."

Delray, who was reading over her shoulder, said, "This is all early stuff. Where he went when he left school, university, working in Seattle."

Bridgette clicked on the second document. It only contained an email address and phone number. The email address was intelm4n@gmail.com.

"Does that email address mean anything to you?" asked Delray.

"I'm assuming this was how he would contact Mallory."

"And Mallory probably didn't want his details in Temple's phone," added Delray.

Bridgette clicked on the third note. It was as long as the second note was short. She started at the top and skimmed the contents. There were dates and short notes against each. "It looks like a journal of his conversations with Mallory going back ten years or more."

"I wonder why he would bother to record that?" said Delray.

Bridgette scrolled to the bottom of the document. There were several addresses in Seattle and addresses for the two apartments Mallory owned in Vancouver.

Bridgette flipped back to the second document and memorized the phone number. She then opened a new window, typed the number into Google, and pressed enter.

"What are you doing," asked Delray.

A moment later, the search screen refreshed. She clicked on the top search result and pointed at the screen. "That phone number wasn't Mallory. It's for a private detective."

"He's been tracking Mallory with a private detective?"

Bridgette looked at the body and said, "Not as closely as he should have been."

She returned to the bottom of the list and stared at the last address, which was also in Vancouver.

Delray said, "That last address. Is that an apartment we don't know about?"

"It's not on our list," said Bridgette. "But it's not an apartment. That address is in the inner city business district."

"Let's get going," said Delray. "If he's heading out of town, maybe this is our last chance at catching him."

Chapter Thirty-Nine

Mallory maneuvered Temple's KIA Seltos into an open spot on the rooftop parking of the EasyPark, behind a large Ford Transit van. The van would hide the KIA if someone came up to the rooftop and did a quick scan to check for his car. He had constantly checked for police cars in his rear view mirror on the drive over and was fairly sure no cops had followed him. He made one final check in the mirror and then twisted the mirror to look at his face—it was pale and sweaty.

Mallory turned the engine off and winced in pain as he stepped out of the car. Resting up against a concrete barrier, he shaded his eyes from the sun as he made a mental list of what he needed from his office. The office was little more than a small two-room facility that he used to store the drugs and cash from his side hustle. He operated it through one of his shell companies to mask who the actual owner was, should it ever be raided by the cops.

He figured it would be hours before anyone discovered Temple's body and realized that he had stolen his car, but he didn't plan on staying long anyway. First, he would clean out his safe. Inside, there was close to eighty-thousand dollars in cash—mostly profits from selling drugs to wealthy clients, plus another gun and ammunition. The money would sustain him until he could establish a new identity and start over somewhere else. The safe also contained close to fifty thousand worth of drugs, primarily high-end cocaine. He would take a little for the trip, but he would leave most behind to collect later.

He looked down at his clothes. They were now filthy and had fresh blood stains from his encounter with Temple. He had several sets of clothes in his office. He figured after cleaning up and with a change of clothes, he could pass any routine stop by a cop car.

Mallory inhaled deeply to ward off the pain. He had some more potent painkillers in his office and would take a few before he hit the road again. While his health was deteriorating, he was confident he was well enough for the drive to Seattle, but he would need to see a doctor as soon as he arrived. The thought of going to a public hospital bothered him. If some medical practitioner became suspicious and called it in, he could find himself running from the police all over again. On the drive in, he came up with an idea. He knew he could purchase almost anything on the dark web, even doctors. There was a computer in his office and he decided to connect with a physician who could help before he left.

Satisfied with what he needed to do, Mallory pushed off the barrier and headed for the stairwell.

Bridgette drove into Vancouver's business district with her lights on but no sirens while Delray organized two squad cars to go to Mallory's unit and guard the exits until they arrived.

When he had finished his calls, she was keen to talk strategy and asked Delray to bring up Google Maps on his phone and key in the address.

She added, "Can you bring up Street View, Chief."

Delray, who had always struggled with technology, grumbled, "Maybe I should have driven," as Bridgette told him how to change the settings.

Finally, he said, "Okay, we've got street view. What are we looking at here?"

Bridgette turned quickly into Twelfth Avenue and said, "I think there's an EasyPark next door. Can you see it?"

Under Bridgette's instructions, Delray pinched the screen and slid his left finger across it to change the view slightly. "Yeah, I see it."

"Good, I know exactly what building he's in. I interviewed a witness some months back in that building. There's no underground parking, so you either park on the street or you need a parking station."

"He's not likely to leave a car on the street."

"No. And the EasyPark won't be full at this time of the day."

"Let's hope not," murmured Bridgette as she swung onto Burrard Street.

"Less than two minutes, now," said Delray.

"How do you want to play this?"

"I'll get you to drop me at the front of the building. I'll organize the uniform guys to come up with me and see if he's in his office. I'd like you to drive into the EasyPark, cruise each level, and see if you can see his car. If you find it, call me."

"And if I don't find his car?"

"Park and come up and help me with the search. This is probably our last shot at figuring out where he might have gone."

The low hum of Bridgette's engine echoed through the first level of the parking lot, a concrete cavern aglow with the harsh fluorescent lighting that turned everything a sterile shade of blue. Rows upon rows of cars sat silent and still in the dim light. Bridgette guided her unmarked sedan past each one, her eyes flicking from car name badge to license plate, searching for the late model KIA.

She rounded another corner, her gaze sharp and hands steady on the wheel, though frustration itched at the back of her mind.

She murmured to herself, "Level one's a bust," and eased her foot on the accelerator, guiding the car up the ramp to level two.

The second floor felt almost as claustrophobic as the level below. Cars were packed tight, nestled together like sardines in a tin. Bridgette's senses sharpened as she prowled through the aisles with predatory caution.

"Come on, Mallory. Are you here? Are you hiding?" she murmured, her words barely audible as she came to the end of the first row.

With a practiced ease, Bridgette maneuvered the sedan around the tight corners of level two, her gaze missing nothing. A four-wheel drive caught her eye, but she realized it was the wrong make as she cruised past. A deep breath steadied her nerves as she approached the end of the final row and headed for the ramp to level three.

The third level greeted Bridgette with another wash of stark fluorescent light, just like on the lower levels. The concrete expanse was dotted with cars like scattered chess pieces—this level was only about half full. Bridgette continued her cruise, her eyes darting from one vehicle to the next. She could feel a clock ticking inside her head. With each second passing, Bridgette knew Mallory could be getting further away. An edge crept into her thoughts, one she knew well—the serrated blade of frustration. She circled the rows quicker and cursed as she got to the final row. There were only four cars here, none of which was the KIA.

She paused for a moment and tried to think like Mallory. *'Rooftop?'* Fewer eyes and fewer questions. She knew it was a move she would make.

As the ramp incline beckoned her upward, something flickered at the edge of her vision—a presence in the stairwell. Her heart skipped a beat as she caught sight of him, the profile of a man only half-revealed in the artificial twilight. Tall, nondescript, and with light-colored hair that didn't catch the light right. The stoop in his posture that she saw for a fleeting second before he disappeared up the stairs to the roof caught her attention.

"Could it be?" Her voice was barely a breath as she gently applied the brake.

Bridgette picked up the two-way and said, "Chief, do you copy?"

A moment later, a crackly voice responded. "Yeah. We're up at the office. It all looks to be locked up tight. We've got a manager coming to unlock it and let us in. You find anything?"

"I've seen someone just go up onto the roof. But I only saw him for a moment."

"You think it's him?"

"I don't know. But there are car spaces free here on level three, so why would you park on the roof?"

"Stay put. I'm on my way."

Bridgette watched through the windshield as a woman emerged from the stairwell, glancing at her phone, before disappearing between a rows of parked cars.

"Keep it together," Bridgette muttered to herself. "This is no place for a showdown."

The thought of bullets flying on level three, endangering innocent bystanders, tightened her chest. With a decisive press of the gas pedal, Bridgette steered her vehicle up the spiraling concrete ramp that led to the rooftop. Sunlight spilled over the edge of the parking structure as she crested the final turn. Her eyes scanned the expanse of asphalt for the figure she'd glimpsed earlier. She spotted the man's silhouette about a hundred feet away as he walked towards a large Ford Transit van parked near the parking lot's rear left corner. Bridgette could only see one vehicle and assumed this was where the man was headed. His gait was measured, almost cautious. She couldn't tell if this was Mallory.

"Easy. Don't spook him," she murmured.

She let her car crawl forward, the tires rolling quietly over the painted lines. Every detail seemed amplified—the soft rumble of the engine and her own heartbeat thudding against her rib cage.

Her fingers tensed on the steering wheel as she thought through the possibilities.

"Come on," she breathed, eyes locked on the distant figure. "Turn around so I can see you."

When the man reached the van, he paused for a split-second as if sensing the tension in the air. Bridgette's grip tightened on the steering wheel, her knuckles white with anticipation.

"Turn around," she murmured fiercely.

As if hearing her silent command, the man turned and glanced over his shoulder—a sharp, piercing look that cut across the divide between them. Their eyes locked, and recognition flared like a struck match. As she stared into his cold, calculating eyes, Mallory's face twisted momentarily into a mask of surprise, quickly replaced by the hard lines of resolve as he ducked behind the van.

Bridgette picked up the two-way and screamed, "He's on the roof!" as the KIA Seltos burst forward from behind the van.

Bridgette jammed her foot down on the accelerator. She screamed, "Over my dead body," as the KIA accelerated across the rooftop towards the exit.

Her car's engine roared to life beneath her, a primal sound that mirrored the adrenaline pumping through her veins. She shot forward, closing the gap on Mallory's four-wheel drive as they neared the spiral exit ramp.

Chapter Forty

The concrete rooftop blurred as Bridgette narrowed her eyes, her gaze locked on the KIA as it barreled towards the spiral ramp. She gripped the steering wheel with white-knuckled determination as the roar of engines reverberated off the walls.

Bridgette jerked the wheel to the left, her heartbeat thundering in her ears as the KIA swerved to cut her off. She screamed, "Son of a—" as she fought with the steering wheel while her car skidded and fishtailed across the concrete. The scent of burning rubber infiltrated her senses, a pungent reminder of the razor's edge between pursuit and disaster.

"Come on!" she yelled, focusing on the KIA's taillights as they raced toward the exit. Her mind was working overtime; waves of strategy and instinct crashing together as she readied herself for whatever came next. Bridgette's vision tunneled further. She glanced at the fast-approaching ramp, knowing full well the reckless maneuver she was about to attempt could end in disaster.

The moment stretched, taut as a high wire. The gap closed between the cars as the edge of the ramp loomed. Her heart pounded against her ribs as she watched the KIA dive down the ramp. She could almost hear the squeal of its brakes over the cacophony of her own engine—a brief hesitation as it attempted to make the sharp turn.

Instead of braking for the ramp, Bridgette accelerated. Her world tilted, her stomach dropped, and for a terrifying second, she felt the police car lose its purchase as it hurtled down the ramp. And then came the crash. The world outside Bridgette's windshield transformed into an abstract painting of chaos and light as she collided with the KIA, the shock waves of the collision reverberated through her body.

A deafening bang erupted inside the cabin as the airbag burst. Her head snapped back, then forward, the seat belt arresting her flight with an abrupt and bruising embrace.

She coughed, spitting out the taste of gunpowder from the airbag propellant, and felt something wet trickle down her forehead. The wail of a car horn drilled into her consciousness, a relentless mechanical scream that seemed to come from everywhere and nowhere.

She groaned as she fumbled at the seat belt button, her fingers sticky with blood or sweat; she couldn't be sure. A sharp lance of pain stabbed through her chest as she moved, making her breath hitch.

Her curse was more growl than words as she shoved against the door. It gave way with a groan, her world tilting sickeningly as she tumbled onto the cold concrete.

She lay there for a half-second, catching her breath, watching the powder from the deployed airbags settle like gray snow in the stillness. With gritted teeth, she pushed herself upright, ignoring the fresh wave of pain that protested her every movement.

Staggering to her feet, she stumbled toward the KIA, which lay on its side in a sea of glass, a testament to the force of their collision. Bridgette withdrew her Glock and circled wide of the vehicle, expecting to see Mallory emerge at any moment. She stopped about fifteen feet from the front of the vehicle, its crumpled front end embracing a concrete pillar.

Her fingers were clasped tightly around the grip of her gun, her knuckles white with the pressure. She shifted her weight slightly, her muscles coiled and ready for any sudden movement. Every nerve in her body was wired, and she was acutely aware of every sound and movement around her. Bridgette edged forward to get a better view. Her eyes remained fixed on the KIA's interior as her mind struggled to process what she saw. Despite the shattered windscreen, she could see enough to realize that no one was behind the wheel. Without hesitation, Bridgette rushed forward and kicked in what little glass remained in the windscreen.

She leaned in and growled, "Damn you!" as she scanned the interior. The KIA was empty. Mallory had disappeared.

The acrid tang of burned rubber lingered in the air as Bridgette's boots crunched over shards of glass strewn across level three. She swept her gaze back and forth as she searched for Mallory, a frown etching deeper into her forehead. She kept her Glock steady with a two-handed grip, aimed forward and down. "Dammit," she murmured. "You can't just disappear."

Bridgette's mind raced as she strode to the stairwell. She cautiously peered over the edge, her gaze piercing the shadows of the spiraling descent. She saw no one and listened for the rapid fall of footsteps but heard nothing. Frowning, she pulled back, her mind working furiously. Mallory was cunning and resourceful. If he hadn't taken the stairs, he had to be hiding somewhere. *'But you can't hide forever,'* she thought, her grip tightening around her weapon again.

Bridgette moved with purpose down the first laneway. She sprinted from car to car before stopping and crouching to survey the vehicles in front of her.

The car horn suddenly stopped. She turned back but saw no sign of Mallory near either car. As silence descended like a shroud, her own breathing seemed loud in her ears. Bridgette sprinted low towards the next vehicle. She only got about halfway before three shots rang out. Despite the concrete perimeter walls being only half-height and topped with a heavy steel railing, the boom of the gunshots echoed around her.

Bridgette crawled forward until she reached the cover of a Toyota. Her heart raced as she positioned herself behind the front wheel. She peered cautiously over the hood, scanning the cars on either side of the laneway. Bridgette could see no sign of Mallory but gasped as she locked eyes with a woman sitting low in a car two bays down from her. The woman looked terrified as she gestured out the car's window with a finger.

Bridgette nodded to her as she understood the woman was signaling the direction that Mallory had taken. He was clearly edging around the perimeter towards a back exit—a second stairwell. Another two shots rang out, creating a cacophony of terror. Bridgette ducked again but didn't think the shots had been close. She counted off three seconds and cautiously lifted her head. The woman who had been signaling had ducked down out of sight. She studied each car in turn in the rear left-hand corner of the building but couldn't see any sign of Mallory.

Bridgette was just about to advance forward when her blood ran cold. It occurred to her that the woman who had signaled her was not the same woman she had seen walking up the stairs. She prayed the woman hadn't been taken as a hostage. *'Keep your head down,'* she coached herself and sprinted forward to the cover of the next car.

Two more shots rang out as she slid for cover behind an F150 Ford pickup truck. Positioning herself behind the front wheel, Bridgette breathed in deeply. Seven shots. She knew he wasn't using a six-shooter—he would be out of bullets—unless he had brought spare ammunition to reload. If it was a Glock, it would typically be seventeen or eighteen rounds. If it was a SIG Sauer, it could be twelve or fifteen.

"Keep counting," she murmured as she peered past the F150's front grill. Her glance was met by the sound of three more gunshots in quick succession, the last of which shattered a windscreen somewhere behind her. She murmured "Ten" as she heard a woman's muffled cry near the left rear exit.

"Damn it!" she hissed. Her heart hammered against her ribs as she realized Mallory now had a hostage.

Bridgette blew out a breath. A hostage changed everything. The parking lot was no longer their personal battlefield. She knew Mallory wanted the exit and would pay any price to escape, including taking the woman's life. She heard a wail of sirens in the distance. She figured Delray and the others would be out of the adjacent building and planning their assault on the EasyPark.

She flinched as two more shots rang out, and the woman whimpered again. "Twelve," she murmured. She heard more shuffling footsteps and knew Mallory was closing in on the rear exit.

The woman was now sobbing hysterically as Mallory shouted, "Shut up, or I'll kill you, bitch!"

Gritting her teeth, Bridgette knew innocent lives were at stake, and any wrong move could be catastrophic. *"Come on, think!"* she murmured under her breath. But her own thoughts were drowned out by the hostage's piercing screams, growing ever louder as panic set in. A glint of intuition—or desperation perhaps—sparked within her. Bridgette lay on her stomach and, using the cover of the truck's front wheel, peered out at the row of cars near the rear exit. The dim fluorescence of the parking garage cast long, quivering shadows. Inching out just a fraction from the cover of the truck's wheel for a better view, her eyes narrowed as she assessed the stretch of concrete that separated them. *'Sixty feet,'* she thought.

Bridgette lifted her gaze, carefully exploring the space under each car. "Come on, Mallory," she murmured. "Where are you?"

At first, she saw no movement and glanced at the gap between the last car and the stairwell exit—a fifteen-foot expanse of concrete. Her heart picked up speed. This was the gap Mallory would dread; it was open ground, a no man's land expanse of vulnerability he couldn't afford.

Her eyes flickered back across the concrete, skimming under each car again until—there. A pair of feet encased in black boots, another set teetering precariously atop high heels. They shuffled and pivoted, entangled in a macabre waltz just three cars shy from freedom. Bridgette's fingers twitched against the cool metal of her weapon, her instincts sharpening to a fine point.

Carefully, she shifted her weight, her mind whirring with

calculations, angles, and distances, just as she had trained for at the academy. As she watched the feet scuffle, she tried to picture their bodies above, hidden by the chassis of the car—a dance of desperation with Mallory orchestrating every step.

Bridgette's finger rested lightly on the trigger. Shooting prone offered her a high degree of accuracy. But as she channeled her intent through the gun sites at Mallory's left boot, the woman's screams were distracting as she tried to pull away. She waited almost two seconds until she had complete visibility of Mallory's feet beneath the chassis of an SUV. It was all the target she needed as she pulled the trigger three times in rapid succession. Boom, boom, boom!

The echo of gunfire was still ringing in Bridgette's ears when a new sound pierced through the reverberations—a high-pitched, guttural scream. She flinched as Mallory's feet shook before he collapsed to the concrete. The woman's screams intensified as more shots were fired by Mallory.

The sights of her pistol shifted to Mallory's right knee. Her finger caressed, tightened, then released—once, twice—the sound ripping through the EasyPark. The gun kicked against her palm with each declaration of her intent. Above the sound of her weapon, she heard the woman's screams continue unabated and the noise of men shouting in the background. Bridgette watched as Mallory fell to the ground and writhed in pain behind the SUV.

Her gaze flicked back to the woman. She gasped in horror as the woman's left ankle buckled beneath her as she sprinted away. She saw the woman collapse on the concrete, groaning in agony as she gripped her injured left ankle. Bridgette re-focused on Mallory and counted the number 'Fifteen' in her head as she watched his feet and realized he was attempting to stand. She knew the danger wasn't over as she jumped to her feet. The woman was only thirty feet from Mallory—too close if he still had bullets in his gun. Bridgette strode forward without regard for herself as she heard Delray's voice barking instructions to the uniformed officers behind her. She had no clear shot to disable Mallory, who was cunning enough to use the pillar between the front and rear passenger doors of the SUV for cover as he struggled to his feet.

Bridgette fired through the windows of the vehicle. Boom—her first shot shattered the driver's window. She veered right to open up the angle and fired again. This shot shattered the passenger window.

She pulled the trigger six times, her grip steady and unwavering as she advanced on the vehicle. Despite her racing heart, she could hear Mallory groaning in pain. Taking a deep breath, she cautiously stepped around the front of the SUV, ready to fire again if necessary. Mallory was on the ground, writhing in agony, with his gun lying four feet away from him. Blood oozed from a wound in his stomach, and she couldn't tell if it was a new injury or a reopening of an old one from the screwdriver.

"Stay down," she commanded as she approached and kicked away his gun.

A voice called behind her, "Are you okay, Bridgette?" It was Delray.

Still keeping her gun trained on Mallory, Bridgette replied between ragged gasps, "I'm fine, but Mallory needs an ambulance."

Chapter Forty-One

Bridgette knocked on the door of Felix Delray's office. Delray, who was currently on a call, beckoned her in and held up an index finger as he mouthed, "One minute."

Bridgette settled in a chair opposite. Her gaze flickered around the room, taking in the familiar awards and plaques adorning the walls, each a silent testament to Delray's dedication. She closed her eyes momentarily as a wave of exhaustion washed over her. The air smelled faintly of aged paper and the lingering ghost of black coffee. It was familiar and reassuring—exactly what she needed right now.

She wasn't sure if she drifted off to sleep but was soon aware of Delray's voice breaking through her fog.

"How'd you go at the hospital?"

"I got the all clear. My nose isn't broken, but I'm going to have two black eyes thanks to that airbag."

Delray winced. "But it might have saved your life…"

She nodded, though the muscles in her neck protested with a dull ache, a souvenir from the chaos at EasyPark.

"The guys are still at the scene processing everything," said Delray. "It's going to take hours."

"Do you need me to go back?"

"No. I'm not sure if you're aware of it, but you and I haven't slept in close to forty hours."

"Yep. That will do it. How's the woman?"

"The one hiding in the car was a little shaken, but she's okay. We've taken her statement and let her go. The other lady Mallory took as a hostage is not quite so good. She's got a badly sprained ankle and is in a lot of shock. They've got her sedated at present, so it may be a day or two before we get anything solid from her."

"And Mallory?"

"He's in surgery right now. Two bullets in one foot, a shattered knee cap, and a bullet in his pelvis." Delray grinned and added, "You did a good job."

Bridgette thought for a moment about Fiona and Tessa Halloran and then responded, "He got off lightly."

"At least you don't have his death on your conscience. The mayhem he caused in the EasyPark and the murder of Jacob Temple will be easy enough to prove."

Bridgette nodded. "But the murder of the Halloran sisters will be harder."

Delray leaned back in his chair, interlacing his fingers behind his head. "We know he killed Temple because he thought he was the weak link and would confess under pressure. And we have proof he knew the girls at the time of their murders, so…"

"Where does this leave Remmy Chilton?"

"I've got a meeting with the commissioner and Cunningham in ten minutes to give them an update on everything that's happened. It will be my recommendation that the charges against Chilton be dropped. He's been telling the truth all along, and thanks to you, we now know who's responsible."

Bridgette frowned. "I'd like to know why, though. Not knowing Mallory's motive for killing those girls is going to bug me forever."

"My guess is the girls were promised drugs or similar, but one decided to back out of the meet up. What sparked the actual murders, who knows? Perhaps there was an argument?"

"In the autopsy report, it stated they found fragments of rock in Tessa's hair next to a head wound. I've wondered about that... It made me think maybe she was trying to get away and fell and hit her head."

Delray mused, "And then Mallory and Temple panicked and killed her."

"Possibly. I've tried to piece it together in my own mind. If Fiona came along and saw what she saw, she would have tried to run for help."

"Which would explain the wounds to the back of her head if she was being chased."

"I guess we'll never know."

Delray unfolded his hands. "But we know enough. I'm sure the prosecutor will be able to convince a jury that Mallory was the murderer."

"Speaking of prosecutors, I'm guessing Temple's uncle won't be trying the case?"

Delray shook his head. "He's too close and it's a massive conflict of interest. They'll have to get someone else or bring in special counsel."

"I guess this will derail his political career."

Delray allowed himself a tired smile. "I'm not sure I believe in Karma, but times like this make you wonder." He paused, flicked around his computer screen, and pointed to an online newspaper article. "Senior Prosecutor Temple has already made a statement to the media. But I think it backfired. All they wanted to know about was his connection to his nephew. I'd say his political career is in the toilet, and he'll be looking for a new job."

They were quiet for a moment before Delray said, "You did a great job out there today… and a great job on the case in general."

Bridgette said, "Thanks," and then managed a tiny laugh.

"What's so funny," said Delray with a frown.

"Just a few days ago, you gave me the Halloran case and said, *I just want to ease you back in*."

"Yeah, I did say that," responded Delray with a grimace. "Well, that didn't work out quite as I planned." He studied her for a moment and added, "Seriously, how are you feeling?"

Bridgette's lips parted in a half-smile, half-grimace. "I feel like I've been hit by a freight train." As the smile vanished, she added, "But, strangely, I don't feel traumatized by this… more relieved than anything. And it's always nice to solve a cold case, and even better when an innocent man is released from prison."

Bridgette looked up at the clock on Delray's wall—it was almost three PM. She could feel the fatigue settling into her bones. "I think I'll finish my statement and then head home."

"Sounds like a plan. Hopefully, I won't be far behind you. And, needless to say, I want you to take a few days off. Go and see the doctor on Monday. I want a full report from her before you're allowed back at work again."

Bridgette nodded. She was too tired to argue and

secretly looked forward to spending a few more days with Frost while recuperating. "Thanks, Chief."

As if reading her mind, Delray said, "Have you called Levi yet?"

"No. I sent him a couple of texts. I figured he would hear about it from other detectives or the news soon enough, so I've let him know I'm safe."

"Good. He's got enough to worry about without wondering if his partner is still alive."

"I'm going to call him while I drive home. It will help keep me awake."

"You're not driving home," declared Delray. "You're way too tired. Take a cab and charge it to VPD; I'll cover it."

"Thanks, Chief."

"And when you talk to Levi, tell him I said, Hi."

Chapter Forty-Two

Bridgette slept soundly until ten o'clock the next morning. After savoring a breakfast of scrambled eggs, she climbed into her Mustang and headed for the hospital. It had been two days since she last saw Levi, and she could tell he was concerned because he sent her multiple text messages asking about her well-being, something that was out of character for him.

Despite the stiffness in her neck from the airbag's impact and still feeling like she had been hit on the nose with a frying pan, she was in good spirits. She had dabbed on a little makeup before she left her apartment, hoping to mask the worst of the bruising around her eyes, but after close to ten minutes at the task, she realized there was a little point, and no amount of makeup was going to hide her two black eyes.

She knocked on the door to Frost's hospital room and peered in.

Frost was reading something on his phone and smiled as he looked up. "Hello, stranger."

"Hi. Sorry, it's been so long between visits."

"How are you feeling?"

"Better. I slept for almost fifteen hours."

"The chief called about half an hour ago and gave me a rundown. He said you were a bit banged up…"

Bridgette shrugged as she sat. "I'll live."

"I'm not sure if you've seen the news, but you're all over it."

"I'm just thankful it's over. We've got two less scumbags running around than we had two days ago, and Remmy Chilton should soon be freed from prison."

"And the parents of the Halloran twins can rest easy, knowing they finally have justice for their daughters."

"Yeah. I think the commissioner himself is going to see them later today."

Frost smiled again. "It's good to see you."

"It's good to see you, too. Where's your mom?"

"She's saying goodbye to the nurses. She'll be back any minute."

"She's leaving?"

"Yeah. She's catching a flight home in a couple of hours. She also wanted to say goodbye to you, so your timing is good."

Bridgette, who had brought her Mac Book with her, placed it on a shelf next to Frost's bed.

"Are you going to work today?"

"No," said Bridgette with a shake of her head. "I've been given a week off, and I thought today maybe we could just hang out and watch some movies here if you're up for it?"

"I'm ready for that." He grinned and added, "I can go for nearly two hours between naps now. So, what movie did you have in mind?"

"Have you ever seen The Godfather? The chief recommended it."

"Maybe a long time ago. If memory serves, there's a scene with a horse's head in a bed."

Bridgette screwed up her nose. "Yikes, it sounds violent."

"It is, but I'd like to see it again."

"Do you have any favorites?"

Frost thought for a moment. "Well, if we're watching old movies, have you ever seen Midnight Cowboy? It's one of my favorites."

Bridgette cocked her head. "That's the one with John Voight and Dustin Hoffman?"

"Yeah. It's all about a quirky friendship. It won an Oscar back in the late sixties."

"I haven't seen it, so let's add it to the list." Bridgette moved in a little closer to the bed. "What are the doctors saying about your recovery?"

Frost grimaced. "I still need more surgery, but they're confident I'll keep my leg, which is great news. Also, the crack in my pelvis has started to knit, so it shouldn't need surgery if I keep off my feet for a few weeks."

"Well, that's a relief."

Frost glanced around his room. "But I'll be stuck in here for the foreseeable future."

"I'll come every day. We can work our way through the back catalog of your favorite movies if you like?"

Frost frowned. "Perhaps we should take a rain check on the movies today."

"Okay… Are you not feeling up to it?"

"No, it's not that. There are things I've been meaning to talk to you about. How I feel about you and… I'm not good with words, Bridge, but—"

Bridgette reached over and took his hand. "I'm not great at this either."

"Every morning when I wake up, you're the one I think about. And when I drift off to sleep at night, I wonder what you're doing."

Bridgette bit down gently on her bottom lip to hold back tears as she nodded. "It's kind of the same for me."

"Being here has given me a lot of time to think. I—"

Eleanor Frost strode into the room, announcing to Levi that she had to hurry downstairs to catch an Uber. She paused mid-sentence when she saw Bridgette and added, "Oh… I hope I'm not interrupting anything?"

Bridgette stood and reassured her, "It's quite alright, Eleanor. We were just discussing our favorite movies." She turned to Levi and smiled. "We plan on watching some of them tomorrow."

Eleanor winced as she noticed the bruise on Bridgette's face. "That must be painful. Are you okay?"

Bridgette joked, "Just a fight with an airbag that I lost. The doctor says it'll heal in a few days."

"I'm relieved to hear that," replied Eleanor as her phone buzzed. She checked the screen and announced she had to leave soon as her Uber would be arriving in a few minutes.

She hugged and kissed Levi goodbye, promising to call him every day before turning to Bridgette to hug her as well.

As they embraced, Eleanor whispered, "Thank you for caring for my son. I know he's in good hands."

Bridgette reassured her Levi would receive the best of care and wiped away a tear as Eleanor left the room.

Once she was gone, Bridgette sat next to Frost again.

"My mom seems to like you," teased Frost with a grin.

"I like her too," said Bridgette with a matching grin and added, "So… what were we talking about?"

"I think I was saying something about not being very good with words…"

Chapter Forty-Three

The city was just shaking off the remnants of dawn when Bridgette threaded her way along Cambie Street. She wrapped her scarf tighter against the crisp morning air hinting at autumn's approach, each breath forming a fleeting cloud before dissipating into nothingness.

Revolver Cafe emerged ahead, and she was looking forward to seeing Renée Filipucci. It had been a week since they had last caught up, and by their friendship standards, that was an eternity. As she pushed through the front door, the aroma of freshly ground coffee beans greeted her like an unspoken invitation to step out of the morning rush. Bridgette tucked a loose strand of hair behind her ear as she navigated her way to their favorite spot, a cozy table tucked away from the hustle of incoming patrons. Filipucci was already there, her blonde hair falling over most of her face as she typed away furiously on her laptop with her head down.

"Already commanding your digital army?" Bridgette teased as she approached.

Renée, a sub-editor for the Vancouver Sun, looked up, her face relaxing into a smile as she stood. "You know me, can't start the day without a crisis or two."

As they embraced, Renée murmured, "Missed you," her words muffled against Bridgette's shoulder.

Renée's hug lingered just a second longer than necessary, a testament to their days apart. As they separated, Bridgette caught sight of the slight crease between Renée's brows—a worry line that spoke volumes.

"Everything okay?" Bridgette questioned, her gaze probing gently for the truth beneath the surface.

Renée murmured, "I'm fine. A lot going on at work is all."

As they settled into their seats, Bridgette said, "Have you ordered?"

Filipucci nodded. "I figured you hadn't had your morning coffee yet, so I ordered you a flat white."

Bridgette usually limited herself to one coffee a day before switching to peppermint tea and said, "Perfect. Thank you."

"Feels like it's been ages," said Bridgette.

"It has. Seven days, actually."

"Sorry."

"You've got a lot going on right now. Any time you make news in our paper, you're swamped." Renée studied Bridgette's face briefly and added, "It looks like your bruising has gone down?"

"Almost back to normal. If I go heavy on the makeup, I don't think anyone notices anymore."

"I can't believe an airbag can do that. It's normally the bad guys that leave you beaten up."

Bridgette laughed. "Just an airbag this time."

"My paper has been keeping tabs on Kurt Mallory. It

looks like he's going to be charged with the Halloran murders as well?"

"It's no secret," said Bridgette with a nod. "I think the chief has a team going to the hospital today to formally lay charges."

"Well, my paper will be there, so your boss will likely wind up on tomorrow's front page."

"Better him than me," said Bridgette with a wink.

The conversation paused for a moment while the server delivered their coffees.

When they were alone again, Renée asked, "So, how's Levi?" as she sipped her coffee.

"He's got another operation scheduled for next week, and if that all goes well, he'll go to a rehab ward shortly after."

"Well, that's good news."

"He's a bit over the hospital environment. The rehab ward has more of a homely feel, so…"

Renée put down her coffee and said, "So what's the deal with you and Levi? Last time we talked, you said you had feelings, but you were a bit confused. Have you made any progress?"

Bridgette sighed. "I knew this was going to come up."

"I'm just looking out for you, BC. Who better to be asking than me?"

"We had a long talk the other day, just after his mom left. It was… I'm not sure how to put it."

"Answer me this then. Are you more than friends?"

There was a lot that Bridgette wanted to share with her best friend. She knew she was in love for the first time in her life. But Levi would be the first person she would share those words with when the time was right. She pulled the sleeve down slightly on her left forearm to hide a bandage.

Although she wasn't a massive fan of tattoos, she had a small concentric ring tattooed on her left forearm that, up until a few days ago, contained the words *Family*, *Friendship*, *Faith*, and *Peace*. These words marked points in her personal journey to wholeness. Three days ago, she had the word *Love* added because this was something she had now experienced for the first time.

It was too soon to make this known to anyone but Levi. So she smiled and simply said, "Yes, we're more than friends. But starting a relationship with someone who will be in hospital for the foreseeable future is kind of weird. Date nights at present are watching movies on his laptop in his hospital room."

Renée's face spread into a huge smile, "Well, that's all I needed to know."

"We're just taking it day by day for now until he gets out of hospital. But right now, I'm very happy." Bridgette frowned and added, "This changes nothing between you and me. We'll still do our gym sessions together and go out for dinner with the girls."

"And I'll still drive you crazy with all my text messages," said Renée with a laugh.

"Some things are destined never to change," said Bridgette with a wry smile.

"I'm happy for you, BC. You give it all in your job, and you make a difference. But it does come at a cost. I see you battle the demons and no one deserves this more than you do."

"Thanks. Now we have to turn our attention to finding the right guy for you."

"Well, you found yourself a great guy," said Renée with a laugh. "So I can be your next project!"

Chapter Forty-Four

The knock felt strangely formal as Bridgette rapped on the door to Delray's office. It had been seven days since she last stood here, physically drained by the shootout at EasyPark. But it seemed a lot longer to Bridgette. Despite the tension between work and recovery—a fine line she was still learning to walk—the week off had reinvigorated her passion for the job. Within that week, some semblance of stability had found its way into her personal life. Even from the confines of his hospital bed, Frost's steady presence was grounding her. Their relationship was a small beacon of certainty in the sea of uncertainty that was her life. Her most pressing question lingered, ready to be voiced when Delray gave her the opportunity. *When could she return to work?*

As if on cue, her boss looked up and said. "Well, well, look who's back," his voice carrying a familiar tone of authority tempered with a touch of warmth reserved for those who earned his respect.

"Hi, Chief," said Bridgette, as she stepped inside.

Delray's gaze lingered before he said, "Looks like the bruising has gone down."

Bridgette managed a wry smile. "The marvels of make-up," she quipped as she sat down in a chair opposite his desk.

"Seriously though, how are you feeling?"

"I'm mending. My nose doesn't hurt anymore, and I'm back working out in the gym."

"That's good to hear," Delray said, his eyes scanning the physician's notes in front of him. "I see you've been to the psychologist, and you've been given the all-clear to return to work."

Bridgette allowed herself a small smile. "You almost look surprised."

Delray removed his glasses. "You can't blame me for being a little cautious." He raised his index finger. "First, your partner is almost killed in a hit and run." His middle finger joined the first, "And then you're knocked unconscious, tied up, and abducted in your own car. And we all know you wouldn't be here now if you hadn't escaped." His ring finger ascended, "And then you get involved in a shootout in an EasyPark, and the media turns you into a hero."

"I guess I've been busy," she joked.

She watched Delray process her jest, his gaze probing, searching for cracks in her armor. Bridgette met his gaze head-on, determined to silence any lingering doubt.

"If the Doc thinks you're okay to come back, then who am I to question her judgment."

Delray leaned back in his chair and added. "I'm assigning you to work with Watson and Holbrook."

"Okay. Sounds great."

"You remember that drowning victim? Levi was actually helping them with the case…"

Bridgette nodded. "The guy they found in the river who had chlorine water in his lungs?"

"That's the case. They're not making much headway, and Watson is happy to have you on his team."

"When do I start?"

"How about now?"

"Now works for me, although there are a couple of things I want to talk to you about first, if that's okay?"

"Shoot."

"Would taking a couple of hours off this afternoon be okay? I promise I'll make the time up, it's just that—"

Delray's eyebrow arched upward like the crescendo of a conductor's baton. "A couple of hours off on your first day back? You'll need a good—"

Bridgette interjected. "It's Remmy Chilton. I saw him yesterday, and he's being released from prison today. I thought I'd go meet him and take him to see his mother's grave, then drop him at the bus stop."

Delray frowned. "He's leaving Vancouver?"

"Too many bad memories, I guess."

"Well," he began, his voice carrying a tone of concession, "I think that's the least we can do for him. And don't worry about clocking off. VPD can cover the time."

"Thanks, Chief."

Delray arched an eyebrow. "What else did you want to talk about?"

Bridgette had two more things on her agenda. She wanted to finish positively and said, "Firstly, I want to talk to you about Levi… or rather Levi and me…"

Delray clasped his hands together. "I think I know where this is going, but tell me anyway."

Bridgette took a deep breath, steeling herself for the next part of the conversation. She had never been good at sharing her feelings, and it was doubly hard with her boss. As she spoke, her words came out disjointed. She flushed with embarrassment as she told Delray that she and Frost had started seeing one another and that their relationship had progressed beyond 'just friends.'

Delray listened, his expression unreadable, yet his eyes betrayed a glint of admiration for the officer who stood before him, unbowed despite the situation's awkwardness.

When she finished, he leaned forward and said, "Thank you for leveling with me, Bridgette. You've always operated with the highest level of integrity, and this again proves that."

Delray scratched his chin. "Firstly, this isn't the first time I've seen this at the VPD." He rested his elbows on his cluttered desk. Bridgette noted the way his brow creased with concern rather than censure. "So... don't feel guilty. It sometimes happens in workplaces like this."

Her throat constricted further as if his words had physically tightened around it. *How could she not feel guilty?*

She shifted in her seat as Delray added, "I got a medical report from Levi's doctor yesterday," he continued, his tone softening. "He's gone to rehab now?"

The question hung in the air, expectant, and Bridgette managed, "That's correct," her voice steady despite the tremor that threatened to betray her composure.

Delray drummed his fingers on his desk, a soft, rhythmic beat that echoed in the quiet office. "The doctor said his recovery could take six months and maybe longer."

"That's my understanding too."

"Right now," he began, his tone level, "All I want you to do is send me an email acknowledging the relationship. I'll write back and say I've received it. I think that's all we need to do for now."

Bridgette frowned. "Sorry, Chief, I'm a little confused. I thought—"

Delray held up a hand, a gesture that halted her words as effectively as it did the turbulent thoughts churning in her brain. "I don't need to do anything right now because it will be six months or more before Levi returns. When we get closer to that date, and assuming the relationship continues, we'll need to sit down and work things out." His tone was matter-of-fact, but his eyes carried an undercurrent of empathy.

"Okay…"

"The bottom line is, we can't have partners in the same team in VPD. It's a conflict of interest, which I'm sure you're aware of." Delray leaned back in his chair. "But we've got time. No need to decide anything right now."

Bridgette nodded as her gaze settled on the wood grain on Delray's desk—a silent witness to the moment's gravity.

"Bottom line, Bridgette, I enjoy having you both on my team. Levi… giving him a fresh start and seeing him take it and run with it has been very rewarding for me personally."

He leaned forward slightly, as if to turn his desk from a barrier to a bridge. "And having you on the team, well…" Delray continued, his tone shifting to something softer. "You're in a class of your own." He frowned and quickly added, "But that's not to be repeated outside these four walls."

Bridgette looked up and half-smiled. "Thanks, Chief." Her voice came out steady, betraying none of her inner turmoil inside. "I appreciate your confidence."

After a few moments of silence, while they collected

their thoughts, Delray said, "Now... I don't mean to pry, but do you think it serious?"

"I'm hoping so," she said, her response not much more than a whisper.

Delray drummed his fingers on the desk again. "Let's meet again in three months, the three of us—even if it's at the hospital." He folded his hands on top of the scattered paperwork, the lines on his face deepening. "In the meantime, you and Levi have a lot to talk about. One of you will need to leave the team... and I want you two to figure out between you who that's going to be."

Delray's words hung between them, laden with the gravity of change.

"Thanks, Chief. I appreciate your understanding."

"Nothing stays the same forever, Bridgette." His mouth curved upwards, lines creasing at the corners of his eyes as if he shared a private joke with the universe itself. "Sometimes that's a good thing, and sometimes not so good."

"Yeah..."

Delray raised an eyebrow. "Are we good?"

The corner of her mouth twitched as it hinted at a smile. "I think I'd rather have root canal than go through that again."

Delray managed a smile. "Well, for what it's worth, Levi's a great guy. Now... what else did you want to talk about?"

"It's about Levi again, actually the investigation of who was behind the hit-and-run. I think I might have a lead for you."

Delray's eyes widened. "You've been investigating Levi's hit-and-run as well? "

"Not really. In some of my downtime at the hospital, when Levi was sleeping, I got to thinking, who would want to do this to him. I went back through all the basic motives for murder and thought about which is the best fit for what happened to Levi."

"Okay, and what did you come up with?"

"I can't see greed being an angle—he's not overly flush with money from what I can tell. And then I thought about power. Levi is a detective, hardly a position of power, so I dismissed that one as well. Sex or lust? He doesn't strike me as the kind of guy who leaves himself vulnerable in that area. He's never been in a love-triangle that I know of and his ex-wife is very happy in her new relationship."

"I agree."

"So then I thought about the revenge angle."

"And you think that's the motive?"

Bridgette nodded. "A couple of nights before he was hit by the car, we had dinner. He opened up about his life while he was undercover. I have to admit it was a real eye-opener for me. I had no idea how… dark that world was that he operated in."

Delray grimaced. "Yeah, it can be pretty bad.."

"I remember Levi saying to me that sometimes he formed genuine friendships with drug dealers, and then he felt bad when he finally had to arrest them. He told me instances of some drug dealers being more upset about being betrayed than being busted for drugs."

"I guess that's right," said Delray as he raised his eyebrows. "Criminals, are still people after all."

"It got me thinking; maybe someone from his past had an axe to grind. And the more I thought about it, the more I thought it was worthwhile exploring. Anyway, Levi and I were talking about it, but no one immediately came to mind. I did ask him why he was in Gastown where the incident occurred. He hardly ever goes there, and I wondered if he could have been meeting someone."

"But he has no memory of it."

"Right."

"That's an angle we're still exploring," said Delray. "We checked his phone records, and there was one number that he called about half an hour before he got hit by the car. He also called it two days earlier. We've tried to trace it, but it's a burner phone, and they're almost impossible to track down."

"I looked at Levi's phone and saw that number too. I asked him about it, but he has no memory of it."

Delray pushed his glasses slightly up the bridge of his nose and added, "I know the detectives checked CCTV footage and interviewed witnesses. But nobody remembers seeing him with anyone, so it was all a bit of a dead end."

"I decided to try a different approach. I thought, who is most likely to have it in for Levi."

"Probably someone he put behind bars," mused Delray.

"Exactly. So I got Margot to pull a list of everyone he had ever arrested who was released from prison in the last three months."

"And what did you find?"

"Only five people, all men, were released. I went through the list pretty quickly. One of them now has Parkinson's and is confined to a wheelchair, so I thought it was unlikely to be him. The second guy has moved back to the east coast. Margot checked with his parole officer, and he's been reporting weekly and working in the family business."

"So, it's not likely to be him."

"The third guy went straight into a hospital facility. He somehow took an overdose of drugs inside and is barely alive. So I discounted him as well."

"That leaves two."

Bridgette nodded. "These were the two I focused on. The first guy, Levi busted during his last arrest when he worked in Undercover. He wasn't involved in building up the case against him; he was just there as an extra badge for the arrest."

"So, if this guy's got a beef against the police, it probably won't be against Levi."

"That's what I figured."

"Which leaves suspect number five."

"This guy is a lot more interesting. He's thirty-five and has a string of convictions stretching back to when he was sixteen that include two cases of assault and one of attempted murder.

"He sounds like a piece of work."

"Margot checked with his parole officer; he's broken parole conditions before and has a history of wanting to settle old scores."

Delray chewed on the end of a pen. "So, he fits the profile. Did Levi have much to do with him?"

"Yes," said Bridgette with a nod. "He was a low-level buyer that Levi got to know quite well while undercover."

"Okay, this is getting interesting."

"His name is Mark Capper. I got Margot to pull his phone records. You'll never guess what I found…"

Delray's mouth fell open a little. "I can't guess, so don't keep me hanging."

"The day Levi was run down, Capper called the burner number on Levi's phone three times in the two days before."

"Wow! Now we're getting somewhere."

"It gets better. The number for the burner phone called Capper about five minutes before Levi was run down."

Delray dropped the pen and leaned forward. "So… it sounds like the guy who owned the burner phone was calling Capper to tell him to get ready. They were in on it together."

"Margot got the cell tower reports back this morning."

"This should be interesting."

"It was. Capper's phone was pinging off towers around Gastown for two hours before the incident. He was definitely in the area."

"It's got to be him. He didn't like what Levi did to him and wanted to get even by running him down."

"I think Levi probably met with the guy who had the burner phone."

"They drew Levi to a spot where it would be easy to run him down," said Delray with a frown."

"Levi always waited about five minutes after a meetup before he left when he was working undercover."

"That would explain the call five minutes before the hit. Burner guy leaves the bar, calls Capper, and tells him Levi will be on the street shortly." Delray shook his head and added, "How sick can you get."

"We don't have solid proof yet, but Capper is due to meet his parole office next Monday."

"We won't wait that long. I'll get a team onto this today. This is all the evidence we need to bring him in."

They were quiet for a moment before Delray broke the silence. "This is great work, Detective."

"I just hope it leads to an arrest and conviction."

"Yeah. No cop likes to live having to look over their shoulder all the time. This will help give Levi some closure."

"I agree."

Delray's face spread into a smile as he held Bridgette's

gaze. "A good detective thinks outside the box. You've done it again, Bridgette, and it's appreciated."

Bridgette felt herself flushing. "Thanks, Chief."

"Anything else?" asked Delray with a raised brow.

"Not for now."

"Well, I've got some calls to make, so you may as well see Watson and get started."

"Thanks, Chief," said Bridgette as she stood up. "I've… appreciated this meeting."

Delray nodded. "Me too."

When she reached the door, Delray said, "Detective…"

Bridgette turned back to face her boss. "I'll leave it to you and Levi to figure out when you want to tell the rest of the team. Until I hear otherwise, I'll just say you and Levi are partners, and he's on leave."

"Thanks, Chief. I appreciate that."

After stepping out of the office, Bridgette took a deep breath, her gaze drifting to the bustling Homicide room as she walked down the hallway. Officers and detectives moved with purpose, absorbed in their worlds of cases and justice.

"Partners," she murmured to herself. The word had never carried so much weight.

Epilogue

The autumn leaves whispered above as Bridgette maintained her respectful distance, the cemetery's solemn silence enveloping them both. Gloria Chilton's headstone, a somber grey slab engraved with delicate care, stood like a sentinel over memories long past. Remmy's silhouette was hunched in contemplation, his form casting a lonely shadow on the manicured grass.

As he stood at her graveside with his head bowed, Bridgette took a moment to reflect on his life. Arrested and charged with murder twice by the VPD weighed heavily on her. She was grateful he hadn't spent years behind bars. Still, it reminded her of the immense power she had as a law enforcement officer.

'Got to be damn certain,' she reaffirmed silently. *'Every time…'*

Chilton's silhouette was stark against the graying sky, a lone figure dwarfed by the expanse of the cemetery. She watched as he knelt and placed the small bouquet up against the headstone—the flowers a splash of color against the solemn stone. In that moment, she saw not the suspect the VPD had painted him out to be but a son grappling with the finality of loss.

As he stood and turned to walk back towards her, Bridgette could see the lines of sorrow etched on his face. "You can stay longer if you want?" she offered.

Remmy shook his head. "I've said my goodbyes—I know she's not really there, so…" His words trailed off, leaving an echo of resignation. Bridgette nodded, acknowledging his decision as they turned and headed for her car.

"Where are you headed, if you don't mind me asking?"

"I'm thinking of staying in Canada this time. Maybe try my luck on the East Coast."

Bridgette nodded, absorbing his words. "Sounds like a plan. Are you going to stick with boats?"

"Yup. That's all I'm good at, so…"

"It's a good skill to have," Bridgette commented. "I'd rather do what you do than be chained to a desk as an accountant or something."

"Yeah, me too," Remmy replied.

The awkward silence returned as they walked. The late afternoon sun cast long shadows across the cemetery, painting the chrome of Bridgette's meticulously maintained Mustang in a warm glow as they approached. Its dark blue paint job seemed to absorb the light, gleaming like a deep ocean under a summer sky.

Remmy's gaze lingered on the car, his brows lifting with admiration and surprise. "That's a sweet ride you have there, Detective. What is it? A '67 or a '68 Mustang?"

Bridgette's lips curled into a smile as she approached her car. "It's a '67," she confirmed, unable to mask the pride in her voice.

"Did you do the restoration?" Remmy asked as he stopped beside the passenger door.

"No." Bridgette shook her head, and for a moment, her mind wandered back to Sanbury—the small town with its tight-knit community and the man whose skilled hands had breathed new life into the steel and leather. She added, "A man who lives in Sanbury restored it," as she unlocked the doors. "It's a long story, but he gave it to me as a gift."

"Wow! That's some gift," he said, voice rich with genuine astonishment.

His words pulled at the corners of Bridgette's mouth, and she smiled, her heart lightening a fraction as she watched Remmy's demeanor shift. "I thought so."

As they settled into the car, Remmy asked, "Do you get to drive it in police chases and stuff?"

"We try to use VPD cars for that," she said, mindful of the VPD car she had written off in the EasyPark days earlier.

"If it was mine, I'd be driving it all the time."

Bridgette turned the ignition and felt the engine roar to life; a beast awakened. As they sat in the cocoon of the car, the outside world seemed to recede as they cruised out of the cemetery.

"Where to?" she asked.

Remmy's gaze lingered on the rear view mirror, watching the cemetery shrink behind them. "You can just drop me at the interstate bus terminal." His voice was flat, almost lost within the thrumming heartbeat of the car.

"Okay, I know where that is."

A silence had descended between them, thick and contemplative, as Remmy's gaze was lost to the passing landscape. His fingers drummed an absent rhythm against his knee. He said, "You know, when you first interviewed me, I thought you were just another bad-ass cop."

Bridgette glanced at Remmy with half a smile. "So what do you think of me now?"

Finally, he turned toward her, his expression softened. "My lawyer said you're tough… but fair."

Bridgette glanced at Remmy. "Your lawyer said that?"

"When the lawyer who got my case first came and saw me, I told him I was innocent, and then I told him about you and our interview." He turned his head slightly towards her, "He said I should be glad you were the investigating cop. At first, I was a little confused…"

"I think I'm a little confused too," Bridgette admitted, the line between her eyebrows deepening as her car sliced through the twilight.

"He said you don't quit until you find the truth."

"Your lawyer seems to have a lot of faith in me," said Bridgette as the city scape blurred past them. "I'm just glad you're free. Nobody should ever wind up in jail for someone else's crime."

"Yeah… tell me about it. I'm glad it's over, and I can start again."

"You're in control now—nobody gets to write the next chapter in your life but you."

Remmy nodded. "I like that."

Bridgette slowed her car and scanned for a park as they approached the bus terminal. The city bustled with people rushing to their destinations. "Parking can be a little tricky here."

Remmy leaned forward and pointed to a vacant spot ahead. "You can just drop me off here, Detective." His voice was calm and confident despite the chaos around them. It was clear that he had been in control all along.

As she pulled into the parking spot, Remmy reached into the back seat and grabbed his backpack. She felt a strange sense of melancholy and hoped he would be alright.

"Thanks again for driving me here," he said as he opened the car door. He held her gaze and added, "And thanks for believing in me. I'm not gonna forget this."

Bridgette felt a lump in her throat as Remmy got out of the car. She liked him and felt a twinge of sadness as she realized it was unlikely that their paths would ever cross again. "Good luck, Remmy. I wish you happiness for the future."

Remmy leaned in and said, "Thanks again, Detective. And the same for you."

She sighed as he closed the door and walk away. Bridgette watched him enter the terminal and murmured, "Let's hope your next chapter's a good one... You deserve it."

Feeling like she needed a lift, Bridgette hit speed dial on her phone, put her car into gear, and pulled out into the traffic. The call was answered on the fourth ring.

Levi's voice reverberated through the car on her hands-free system. "Hey, Bridge. How are you?"

Bridgette smiled. It was nice to hear his voice. "Well, I survived my first day back. And you?"

"Same old, same old. More X-rays, more doctor appointments, and physio. Just another normal day here in rehab."

Bridgette could detect both sarcasm and humor in Frost's voice. She knew without delving any further that it had been a good day. "Hey, I'm on my way to the hospital. You need me to pick you up anything?"

"Well... now that you ask, I'm having cravings..."

Bridgette rolled her eyes and smiled all at once. "Cravings?"

"I haven't had a Hershey Bar in close to three weeks. I think I'm due."

Bridgette shook her head as she changed lanes. "Are you allowed to eat chocolate yet?"

"Nobody said I couldn't."

Bridgette smiled. She was familiar with the tone of Frost's voice when he feigned innocence. "I'm sure it's against the rules, but I'll see what I can do."

"Thanks, Bridge. It'll be our little secret."

"I'll see you in fifteen."

"Looking forward to it."

Bridgette disconnected. As she cruised back through the city, she admonished herself not to look too far ahead. It was early days in their relationship and a lot could go wrong. But she wasn't in the mood for negative thoughts tonight. Using voice commands, she got Spotify to play one of her favorite Harry Styles playlists. As the words to, *'As It Was,'* pumped through her car, she changed into third gear and accelerated. She tried to think of a time in her life when she had been happier and smiled again as her mind drew a blank.

Also by Trevor Douglas

vinci-books.com/finalproposition

One man. Three million dollars. A choice that will change everything.

Exonerated after years in prison, Adam Wells guards a secret: the location of hidden millions. Desperate to save a dying friend, he sees the cash as their only hope. But claiming it risks the wrath of a powerful drug syndicate.

Turn the page for a free preview…

The Final Proposition: Prologue

Seven Years Ago

Joseph Penmen followed the man through the crosshairs of his Remington rifle as he walked across the empty concrete parking lot at the back of the warehouse. The man stopped, leaned against the front of his van, and lit another cigarette —his fourth in less than twenty minutes. Wearing a light gray sports coat over the top of designer jeans, he looked out of place and was becoming increasingly agitated as he waited for the truck to appear.

From his hidden position, high up on the remote rocky hillside, Joseph had a perfect view of the complex below. He stole a quick look at his watch and then cursed under his breath. He had been in position for over an hour and was now becoming worried.

As if verbalizing his thoughts would magically make his brother appear, he whispered, "Come on, Tony, where are you?"

The man he was watching shifted restlessly before

throwing his cigarette to the ground in disgust. He pushed impatiently off the van and called out to his partner who had remained in the vehicle.

Joseph had not been able to get a good look at the other man until now. The man had been waiting patiently in the van, largely hidden in the shadows of the two-story steel and concrete building. He shifted the rifle position slowly to the right until the crosshairs rested on the second man as he opened the van door to get out. He was slim, had short blond hair, and looked considerably younger than his partner. As Joseph observed the two men in conversation, it was clear from the younger man's hand gestures and controlled demeanor that he was the one in charge. Joseph knew this was the man who was the bigger threat to Tony's safety. If things turned ugly, it would be the blond man who gave the orders.

Joseph used the collar of his sleeve to wipe sweat from his forehead while he waited. His brother had, until recently, run a successful pharmaceutical supplies business. He ate in the finest restaurants, lived in a gated estate with water views, and holidayed in Europe every year. Joseph never imagined Tony having money problems until he arrived at a family function driving a secondhand Toyota several months ago. When Joseph asked him about his Porsche, Tony confided he had some cash flow issues and the car *"had to go."*

Joseph had not realized how serious his brother's predicament was until he called three days ago requesting a meeting. Over coffee, Tony confessed he had business debts in excess of two million dollars and that he was on the verge of bankruptcy. "Within days, I'm going to lose everything I've worked for, Joe. I need a favor, can you help me?"

Joseph assumed the favor would be for money, or a place

to live, or both and was completely taken aback when Tony revealed what he wanted.

"I have an opportunity to sell some of my stock for three million dollars. I can pay out the loans and make a new start somewhere else."

Joseph recalled thinking this sounded like a great deal until Tony gave him the details.

"There's one catch, Joe. The sale's not strictly legal. In fact…"

Tony went on to explain that his stock would be on-sold to suppliers who would use it to produce a range of illegal narcotics. The remainder of the conversation had been little more than an argument. As Joseph replayed the conversation over in his mind, he remembered pleading with Tony to take bankruptcy over doing business with drug dealers, fearing his brother would wind up in prison—or dead.

Tony had promised to think it over before he did anything. The phone call Joseph received barely twenty-four hours later confirmed his worst fears. "I'm going ahead with the deal, Joe. It's too good to pass up. I really need that favor?"

Joseph couldn't refuse his brother's request and knew it was going to be complicated when Tony insisted on driving over to Joseph's house to talk in person. Sitting in Tony's car, their relationship had changed forever when Tony reached into the backseat and lifted a blanket to reveal a Remington rifle fitted with a silencer.

"I need you to be my lookout tomorrow, Joe. Just in case things get complicated with the exchange."

As Joseph sat, staring in disbelief at the rifle, Tony played down the risks.

"I'm not anticipating any problems, Joe. We've agreed on the time and place for the exchange—it's at the back of a warehouse complex, and it's closed on Sundays. I just want a little insurance. You won't be close, and hopefully no one will ever know you were even there."

Sitting hidden in the thick brush cover with the crosshairs of the rifle trained on the chest of the blond man, Joseph now thought the whole situation seemed surreal. Two days ago, he had been a law-abiding citizen, happily married with a young son, working a job he loved, and carrying no criminal record. Now he was prepared to protect his brother, with lethal force if necessary, while Tony engaged in an illegal drug sale that could land them both with lengthy prison sentences if they were caught.

As he shifted his position slightly to keep comfortable, he noticed the two men had stopped talking. Joseph looked up from the rifle and saw a small truck driving slowly down the driveway at the left-hand side of the complex. As the truck drove into the loading area at the back, Joseph's stomach tightened. With Tony's arrival, he knew there was no backing out now for either of them.

He watched as Tony performed a neat U-turn in front of the two men and parked his truck so that it faced back toward the driveway. As Tony got out and walked around the back of his truck toward the two men, Joseph bent down and switched on a small receiver that was connected to an earphone he would use to hopefully monitor the conversation.

Tony didn't think he would be checked for a wire but had decided it wasn't worth the risk. Instead, he had attached a microphone and transmitter under the rear bumper of the truck and arranged a monitoring receiver for Joseph. The audio quality was far from ideal, but he hoped it would be sufficient for Joseph to be able to hear what was happening and intervene if necessary.

After placing the earphone in his left ear and spending several seconds adjusting the volume, Joseph was able to faintly hear Tony's footfalls as he walked across the concrete surface toward the men. Satisfied that he had the sound level about right, Joseph shouldered the rifle and resumed his watch of the two drug dealers through the scope.

Tony stopped a few paces short of where the two men stood waiting. As expected, it was the blond man who spoke first. "You're twenty minutes late. I don't like people who make me wait."

"Sorry, there was roadwork, and I had to make a detour."

The younger man pointed to Tony's truck. "You got my merchandise?"

"It's locked in the back. Have you got the three million?"

"I'll decide what the merchandise is worth."

"We had a deal."

Becoming increasingly anxious about his brother's safety, Joseph whispered, "Be careful, Tony."

The blond man took a step toward Tony and pointed a finger at him. "We have a deal when I say we have a deal and not before. Now open the truck."

"I open it *after* I've seen the money."

Joseph struggled to keep the young drug dealer in the crosshairs of his rifle scope as the man quickly advanced on Tony. By the time he had him back in focus, the man had stopped directly in front of his brother and had the barrel of a gun pressed against his forehead.

As the young drug dealer began screaming threats and obscenities at his brother, Joseph clicked off the safety and rested his index finger on the trigger. Doing his best to control his breathing, Joseph gambled on it being a bluff.

He knew Tony had the cargo area fitted with a heavy combination lock to make it difficult for anyone else to access the drugs. As he watched the drug dealer continue to threaten Tony, Joseph had to admire his brother's nerve.

The seconds seemed like minutes for Joseph until he could see a wry smile beginning to spread across the young drug dealer's face. Joseph breathed a sigh of relief as the man removed the gun from Tony's head. As the drug dealer took a step backward, he said, "You've got balls, I'll give you that much."

The drug dealer turned and spoke with his associate, but his voice was too low to be picked up by the microphone. Joseph lifted his head from the scope and watched as the associate turned and walked back to the van. The associate opened the rear door and removed a black attache case. He found it difficult to breathe as he watched the man move back to his boss and prayed it contained the money and that the transaction would be over quickly.

The drug dealer, who had not taken his eyes off Tony, placed the case at Tony's feet.

"I want this over and done with. The longer we stay here, the more likely we are to be discovered—now unlock the truck. You can count while we do the transfer. None of us should be out here any longer than absolutely necessary."

Joseph watched his brother closely. Tony had told him the truck would remain locked until he was sure he was getting his money. Without responding to the drug dealer, Tony bent down and opened the attache case. He pulled out several bundles of cash and quickly thumbed through them.

Straightening up, he said, "Three million, right?"

"Right."

Joseph watched as Tony debated what to do. Finally, he said, "Okay. You check the load, and I'll check the money. I packed this in under fifteen minutes, so it won't take long. Deal?"

The drug dealer looked at his associate and then responded, "Deal."

Tony nodded in agreement and then turned his back on the two men and began to unlock the rear compartment of his truck. Joseph's stomach tightened for a second time in as many minutes as a third man emerged from the rear of the drug dealers' van. As the man walked determinedly toward his two associates, Joseph didn't need his telescopic sight to see the man was carrying a gun. With his back to the men, Tony continued unlocking the van, oblivious to what was happening behind him. As the third man began to raise his gun to the firing position, Joseph knew the deal was a setup and that his brother was about to be executed.

There was no time to contemplate the morals of what he was about to do or how this would change his life. As the man walked the last few steps toward Tony and his two associates parted to let him through, Joseph had seen enough. He sighted on the man through the crosshairs and pulled the trigger.

Time seemed to slow down for Joseph as his rifle exploded and the man with the gun lurched sideways before collapsing to the concrete. The two other drug dealers immediately pulled guns from their jackets, and both began firing blindly in Joseph's general direction. As Joseph ducked for cover, he caught a glimpse of Tony collapsing to the ground at the back of the truck.

Amid the cacophony of gunfire, Joseph tried to lift his head for a second look at Tony, but a bullet ricocheting off a boulder behind his left shoulder convinced him to keep his head down.

While he waited for the gunfire to die down, Joseph heard the unmistakable sound of police sirens in the background. Risking another look, Joseph was shocked to see everything below turning to chaos as police cars pulled up and blocked both exits from the complex. Six police officers wearing helmets and bulletproof vests emerged from their vehicles and began firing at the two drug dealers who returned fire as they were driven back toward their van.

Joseph focused on Tony. Amid the gunfire and the arrival of the police officers, Tony had lain perfectly still. Joseph's concern for his brother heightened as one of the officers bent down and checked Tony's pulse before quickly moving forward to join his fellow officers who had now cornered the drug dealers behind their van. Joseph feared the worst until he saw Tony's head move slightly.

As the gunfight raged, Joseph was stunned to see his brother rise slowly and unsteadily to his feet. All of the officers had moved past Tony toward the drug van, and nobody noticed as he limped toward the body of the drug dealer Joseph had just shot.

Joseph's hopes rose as he saw Tony pick up the attache case and slowly limp toward his truck. Tony was a long way from free, but at least he had a chance. As Joseph contemplated what to do next, he felt something cold and hard being firmly pressed into the back of his neck.

A measured and controlled voice from behind him said, "Drop the rifle and place your hands in the air."

Joseph froze, contemplating if he should turn around and face whoever it was behind him.

In a louder voice, the command was reissued, "This is the police, drop the weapon now!"

Joseph realized that trying to flee would likely get him killed and dropped the rifle.

As he began to raise his hands, the voice behind him said, "Hands behind your back. You're under arrest for aiding and abetting an illegal sale of narcotics and I would presume murder as well, since the man you shot hasn't moved."

A thousand different thoughts rushed through Joseph's mind as he felt the handcuffs being tightened around his wrists. He thought of his wife Hannah and his baby son. He wondered what they were doing right now and how they would cope with the news of what had just happened. His thoughts about how his life had changed forever in just a few moments were interrupted by the sight of Tony struggling into his truck with the attache case and the crackling sound of a two-way radio coming to life behind him.

The voice behind him spoke again, this time with urgency in his voice. "Penmen's getting away. He's in the truck."

Joseph watched as several of the police officers turned and fired on Tony's truck as it drove erratically toward the exit on the left side of the complex. The truck crashed into one of the two police cars that currently blocked his way out, but the truck's momentum kept it moving. The police officers gave chase and continued firing at Tony's truck as it swerved wildly out of the complex and disappeared onto the street.

The voice behind him swore softly and then pushed Joseph forward and down onto the ground. As he began to pat Joseph down, searching for other weapons, he continued, "You better hope we find your brother before they do. If they get to him first, stealing three million from the cartel will be the least of his worries."

The Final Proposition: Chapter One

HARTBOURNE CORRECTIONAL FACILITY

Present Day

Joseph woke to the sound of heavy footsteps outside his cell. He blinked sleep from his eyes and realized he had dozed off again. As his eyes began to bring his small, drab gray cell back into focus, he stared at the cell's heavy steel door and watched it open and his cellmate walk in. In spite of his incarceration, Adam Wells was usually positive, and Joseph had enjoyed the last eleven months they had spent together as cellmates.

After the guards had closed and locked the door, Joseph asked, "How did it go?"

Adam sat down on the concrete floor opposite the lower bunk bed which Joseph lay on and leaned back against the wall.

In an almost disbelieving voice, he replied, "I'm getting out, Joe... There's still a formal court appeal process to go through, but the DNA evidence now proves conclusively it wasn't me. My lawyer comes in tomorrow to explain it in more detail, but barring any red tape, I'll be a free man within six weeks."

Joseph swung his legs out from the bunk and slowly pulled himself up into a sitting position. "I'm really happy for you, Adam. When you first moved in here, I knew almost straight away you were no murderer."

Reaching out to shake Adam's hand, Joseph continued, "Congratulations, my friend, you deserve it."

Adam thanked Joseph for his good wishes, but his smile turned to a frown as he let the handshake linger. Joseph's grip was feeble, and his hand felt like a block of ice. In recent weeks, Adam had noticed that his cellmate spent a lot of time resting or sitting quietly on his own.

Joseph continued, "So, are you making plans yet for what you'll do when you're released?"

Adam barely heard the question. "Joe, I don't mean to pry, but is everything okay? If you don't mind me saying, you look rundown, and if I didn't know better, I'd say you're losing weight?"

Trying to keep the smile on his face, Joseph thought for a moment about how best he should answer the question. He had planned to tell Adam about his condition in the next few days before it became too obvious—but not today. Today was not the day to burden Adam with his problems. As Joseph contemplated what to say, Adam pressed on.

"Joe, I'm not an idiot. What's happening here?"

Throughout Joseph's seven-year detention, almost all of his cellmates had been violent criminals who rightfully belonged behind bars. Joseph had never liked any of them, and most of them he secretly despised. Adam was different. When Adam had been transferred to the facility and allocated to his cell, he had initially been quiet and withdrawn. Joseph was usually good at reading people, and something about this six-foot-three man with dark, wavy hair and a quiet and gentle disposition stood out. Adam Wells was unlike any other inmate he had ever met, and for the first time in his long stay in prison, Joseph believed a fellow inmate's story of innocence.

He soon realized Adam was not only an innocent man but also highly intelligent. Joseph contemplated the question and knew he would need to answer truthfully. Anything less and Adam would know it was a lie.

Holding his cellmate's gaze, Joseph let out a long sigh and then answered in his softly spoken voice.

"I have pancreatic cancer, Adam. It's incurable. I've got two months at best if I'm lucky."

There was more Joseph wanted to say, but Adam looked completely stunned. As his words hung in the air, Joseph decided to wait until Adam had processed what he had said before he continued. Joseph felt slightly guilty as he watched Adam struggling to make sense of what he had just said. The days that you could celebrate something inside the Hartbourne Correctional Facility were rare. This should have been one of them.

"I'm sorry, Adam. Today should be about you, not me."

"Surely the doctors can do something, Joe. Just two months?"

Shaking his head slowly, Joseph responded in a tired and resigned voice. "The survival rate from pancreatic cancer is low…very low. It's insidious. It kills you in just months according to the doctors. Wouldn't matter how much money I had to throw at treatments even if I was a free man. The bottom line is they don't buy you much time."

Adam got to his feet and started slowly pacing up and down in the confined space of the cell. Joseph let him be. It had taken him weeks to finally accept what was happening. He knew Adam would need time as well.

Finally, Adam stopped, sat down on the floor again, and leaned back against the wall. As they sat in silence, Adam studied Joseph, trying to think of something positive or encouraging that he could say. Joseph suddenly looked far older than his forty-seven years and only a sliver of the robust man Adam had first met eleven months earlier.

In a quiet voice, Adam responded, "Joe, I'm really sorry. How long have you known?"

"About three months."

Adam nodded, and they were silent again.

"Does Hannah know?"

Joseph looked away from Adam. Telling his wife, who had remained loyal and faithful throughout his seven years in prison, had been the hardest thing he had ever done in his life. Joseph remembered her initial shock and the silence that followed when he had broken the news to her on her last visit. His eyes started to glisten as he recalled the sad resignation on her face as she realized there was no hope.

"I told her two weeks ago. She's taking it pretty hard. I don't think Michael knows yet."

Adam nodded but said nothing. He knew Michael was Joseph's only son and his pride and joy. Michael had only been two when Joseph was convicted of murder and sent to prison. Adam knew that having to watch his son grow up from behind bars had been the hardest thing of all for Joseph, even harder than his separation from Hannah.

At only nine years of age, Michael was, by all accounts, an intelligent and well-adjusted young boy. Joseph would often talk fondly about the son he loved and was obviously very proud of. Adam could only begin to imagine how hard it would be to tell Michael his father was dying. Both men were quiet again.

After almost ten minutes, Adam broke the silence. "Joe, is there anything I can do for you?"

Joseph held Adam's gaze for a moment before lowering his head to stare at the floor. This was not the time to be asking favors of Adam, but Joseph knew he needed help. As Adam had grown excited in the past week about the real prospect of freedom, Joseph had spent a lot of his time thinking through his problem. He decided it was now or never. With a slight tremble in his voice, he answered.

"There's something else, Adam. Michael is also very sick... He started having small convulsions every now and then about twelve months ago. They didn't last long, but Hannah was concerned. She took Michael to a number of doctors, but they couldn't find anything. Six months ago, the convulsions started getting worse and then turned into full-blown seizures. They can last up to several minutes and leave Michael very weak and frightened."

Joseph paused for a moment. Adam could clearly see this was hard for Joseph and waited patiently.

"The doctors finally diagnosed a brain tumor. It's got some long name which I don't recall, but it's growing and will eventually..."

Joseph paused again and looked at Adam before he continued. "It's only a matter of time before it..."

Seeing the distress on Joseph's face, Adam interrupted. He didn't need to be a doctor to know that a brain tumor would eventually kill Michael.

"Joe, you don't need to explain. Is there anything they can do?"

Joseph stared at the floor again. Adam waited while he composed himself.

"The brain tumor's very deep in his brain, but there's a new treatment that the doctor he's seeing thinks will work. Even though it's still very new, results so far show it's very successful."

Adam replied cautiously, "It sounds positive."

"It's complicated. Hannah flew Michael to see a specialist in Bolton. He's the best in the business by all reports. The surgery is risky for a boy Michael's age."

"But it can be done."

Joseph's voice trailed off as he replied, "Yes, it can be done."

As both men went quiet again, Adam began to think through the dilemma that Joseph was facing. Clearly, Joseph was not going to be around to support his wife and son through this trial. Adam sensed Joseph wanted to say more and quietly sat and waited.

"The other complication is the money… There's no insurance for this sort of surgery. We have to pay the bill ourselves…"

"How much?"

Joseph looked up at Adam. "Close to half a million dollars with all the specialist care he needs in the first six months."

Adam let out a low whistle and grimaced. He knew most of Joseph's money had been paid to lawyers for his unsuccessful defense seven years ago and that Hannah was now working four days a week to make ends meet. They barely had enough money to cover food and rent. Half a million dollars for an operation was way out of the question.

Joseph let out a sigh, lay back down on his bunk, and closed his eyes. Adam knew the conversation must have been very hard for Joseph and very draining in his condition. As Adam went to rise from the floor, Joseph started speaking again.

"I've never told you the full story about what happened seven years ago. It's time I told you… You need to know."

Grab your copy…
vinci-books.com/finalproposition

About the Author

Trevor Douglas is a multi-award winning author and the recipient of the gold medal for best crime fiction novel, and the gold medal for the best overall novel in the 2024 Global Book Awards.

Trevor is married with two adult sons and when he is not writing, enjoys bushwalking, watching AFL and discovering the best coffee shops in Brisbane with his wife.

After a long and successful career as an IT consultant, Trevor now writes full time.